ATLANTIS

SHIP OF THE GODS

- *A Trilogy* -

-BOOK TWO-

GATHERING TRIBUTARIES

Pat Laughy / David Shearer

Patrick Laughy/David Shearer

Dedication

This book is dedicated to the four musketeers:
David, Jonathan, Brendan and Pat

Patrick Laughy/David Shearer

Acknowledgement

Many people helped in the creation of this novel. We offer special thanks to Jonathan and Brendan for their input and perspective and advice during the planning stages and hours of reading, Suzy for her editing and behind the scenes support and Linette for her input and encouragement.

The Atlantis series is a work of fiction. Names, places, characters and incidents are either a product of the authors' imaginations or are used fictitiously.

Patrick Laughy/David Shearer

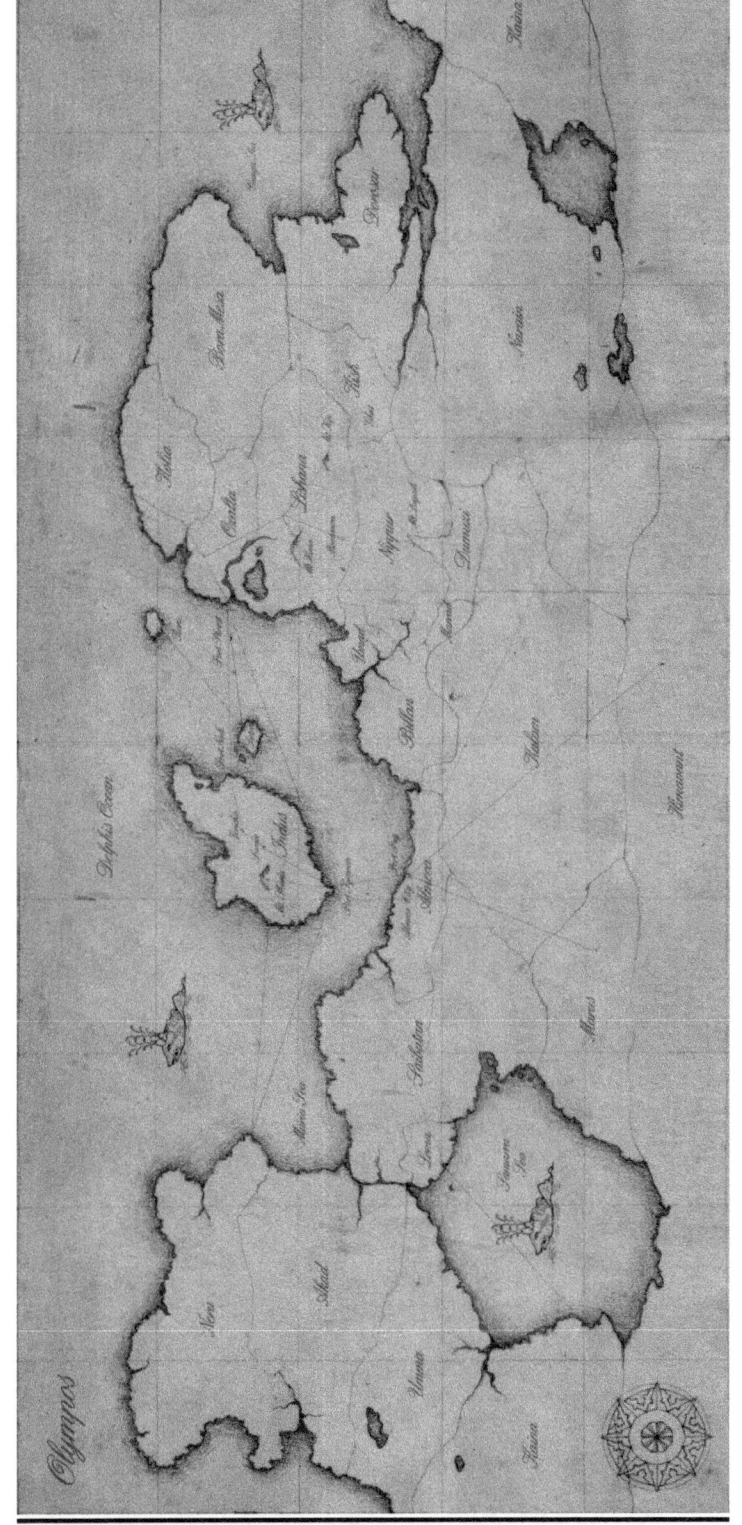

CHAPTER ONE

- Best Laid Plans -

Cleaning up the grizzly aftermath of the Blueface gorilla attack and resulting fire had given Brother Sebastian plenty of time to pray for an epiphany with regard to Gabe's frustrating situation.

He thought of little else as he went about the bull work of helping old Harry put things to rights in the barn.

The monk, a member of the Order of the Golden Ring, had earlier joined the young Neanderthal Gabriel and Venus; a like aged Atlantian female co-traveler and the statuesque daughter of Adon, leader of the team of Atlantians responsible for life within this solar system, on their trip from Sumer to Jericho in the state of Indus.

Having stopped at a way station owned and operated by Sebastian's old friend and ex-partner Harry, and situated just below a mountain pass on the main highway, the travellers had made the fateful decision to spend the night.

In the early morning hours, the isolated station had been attacked by four of the massive Blueface Apes that inhibited the region. Gabriel had been seriously injured during the melee which had resulted in the deaths of three of the animals and the escape of the fourth out through the shattered barn doors and into the bitterly cold night.

The Neanderthal kid was now recuperating inside the single, small, makeshift bedroom offered by Harry's rustic little cabin and was resting under Venus's watchful eyes.

Meanwhile Harry and the monk, after butchering the dead animals, were working to clean up the small barn in the aftermath of the bloody attack. Sebastian had managed to completely drain the fuel tank of Gabriel's bike, Blue, which had been damaged and burned. during the earlier assault by the massive animals. Emptying the tank had made it safe to drag the remnants of the battered vehicle back into the building.

To accomplish the task of moving the heavy machine, which was missing its front wheel; the monk used the still-harnessed horse which Harry had earlier employed to haul the apes' mutilated carcasses outside. He hitched the big animal to the machine and dragged it back through the damaged barn doors. Inside, he propped the bike up against some hay bales against one wall in an area that had escaped the ravages of the brief and quickly doused fire.

That accomplished, he examined the barn's half-door which had been ripped off all but one of its hinges by the determined Bluefaces at the commencement of their attack and after the old station master, who was still industriously cutting slabs of meat from the skinned carcasses, told him where to find the necessary tools; he managed to get it re-hung and was able to make it open and close properly again.

There was little he could do about replacing the supporting beam that had been split in two when the ape threw the bike at it.

When he mentioned it to Harry, the old man told him there was no rush to replace it as the structure was still sound. He advised the monk he would have to find a suitable tree of a size that would afford a replacement beam and indicated he would do that himself later, once the others had continued on their travels.

Sebastian then applied himself to cleaning up the mess inside the barn. He used the horse to manoeuvre the two pieces of the charred beam out in front of the barn and left them near the wood pile for later cutting, then swept up the remaining debris into a pile in the center of the floor and shovelled it into an old wheelbarrow.

When he'd finished that, he used water from snow melted in a bucket set atop the small pot belly stove and a stiff broom to scrub clean both that area and the patch of floor where the dead gorillas had bled out.

He was just finishing up when Harry asked for a hand to carry the butchered meat into the cooling cellar dug into the shale under the foundation at the back of the little cabin, which was located about thirty feet away from the barn.

There was a lot of meat and it took a considerable amount of time to stack it all neatly inside the small rock lined enclosure.

It was just after six in the morning when they finished the job and began to clean themselves up with hot water from additional snow melted in the bucket on top of the stove.

Throughout this process Sebastian continued to concentrate on searching his mind for an option to preclude the need to abort Gabe's trip to his grandmothers' to allow him to receive the gift of invisibility on his upcoming birthday.

He was determined not to betray a confidence but finally and out of utter desperation, he broached the general topic with Harry, not specifying the reason for the urgency, but making it clear to the old man that time was of the essence.

He also strongly inferred it wasn't only Gabriel who was eager for the successful completion of the trip, but that he too, and by implication, the Belief itself had an interest in the trip having a triumphant conclusion.

Sebastian and the old man stood in the centre of the barn by the melted bucket of snow atop the glowing potbelly stove. They worked at cleaning their hands and forearms, removing the traces of material left after the cutting and handling of the meat. Harry's hands dripped warm water as he reached for the strip of burlap sack hanging from a nail on the post behind him and regarding Sebastian closely, used it to slowly dry himself.

"It's that important to you then is it?"

Sebastian accepted the strip of burlap as Harry extended it to him and began to use it on his own hands as he nodded.

After a moments silence, Harry continued.

"I've been pretty hard on the kid, and you know why. When his dad ended up replacing me as your partner I was pretty impressed with his credentials. I figured Hollis Corvin had what it would take to more than fill my shoes. Then when he up and quit after a couple of years; well, frankly, it pissed me off. Not really fair to blame the kid for the actions of his old man of course, but, it's how I felt none the less."

Sebastian bobbed his head in understanding.

"Ya, at first it choked me a mite too, but by then I'd gotten to know him pretty well, and to be honest, I could understand why he was doing it. In the end I wished him well."

Harry arched his eyes knowingly and crossed his arms.

Then, without batting an eye; Harry delivered a miracle.

"Well, waiting for the coach and taking it isn't an option considering how soon you've got to reach where you're headed, and the fact that the coaches only travel during the day. I'll admit horses can't travel as fast as bikes, but I could loan you two temporarily and they'd get you to the next roadhouse where you could leave them for me to pick up later. When you arrived at the roadhouse you could buy two horses there. The coach companies always have extras in case any need a replacement and they'll sell to you for a good price. If you bought a couple of those you could use them to complete the rest of the trip. Be pretty hard riding but if you kept pushing you could still make it. As far as the bike goes, you could leave it here and the kid could pick it up on the way back."

* * * * *

There was a sharp knock at the stateroom door and the Rector of the National Socialist Party of Indus, Koba Eisen shifted his attention from the Ogre sitting across from him to his aid, SS Colonel von Jaeger. He nodded and the officer moved to open the door to admit a dark blue uniformed Navel Captain.

Eisen smiled triumphantly up at the smartly turned out officer.

"Ah Captain, so good of you to join me. A smooth trip so far. What time will we reach Jericho?

"Solar has blessed us with a tailwind my Rector; probably arrive in just over two hours, if it holds."

Eisen nodded with satisfaction.

"Excellent. I asked you here to ensure you were the first to know. Thanks to a recent windfall of gold to the treasury, this

fine ship is no longer on loan but belongs to the party. Your position as Captain is no longer temporary and I wanted to be the first to congratulate you on your new command. Now if you, gentleman will please excuse me, I will try for a little rest before our arrival. I have a busy day ahead."

* * * * *

As daylight began to break through the clouds, the traumatized young, dark-skinned, and strikingly beautiful female Human, Juno, turned her attention toward finding a spot where she could rest and access her options while being in a position to observe the road and yet remain protected from curious eyes.

By sheer determination, she had been able to force the horrific memories of the Troll attack of the night before upon the gypsy wagon train camped at the abandoned mining town, far down into the depths of her mind; but she was still filled with fear and concerned over the likelihood of them pursuing her.

Physically exhausted, aching all over and short of breath, she'd forced herself to keep moving for what she'd guessed to be several hours. Over that period of time, slowly but surely, her anxiety over the possibility of the Trolls catching up with her had begun to ease.

It was becoming unlikely they would have considered it worthwhile to chase her all night and with that realization, she found herself relaxing her pace a little and began to become more aware of her surroundings.

She had been along this roadway a few times before and she knew there were hot springs a short distance off the highway somewhere between the abandoned mining town and the next roadhouse. If memory served, the springs hadn't been very far off the roadway and the trail leading to them was marked by a cairn of rocks situated just off the left side of the highway.

It would be a good place for her to rest and make plans for her next move.

With that in mind, she kept a lookout for the marker as she trudged onward.

* * * * *

Jonah, brother to Venus, only son of Adon the Atlantian leader of the expeditionary team responsible for the development of life within this solar system and on a quest to find and return his wayward little sister to Atlantis, groaned and stretched as best he could within the confines of the lightly padded driver's seat of the halftrack he had borrowed from the Vehicle Storage area aboard Atlantis, to facilitate the trip.

He and his Almie, Sal had transported from Atlantis to a point on the highway between Sumer and Jericho and hidden the vehicle in a small copse of trees on a rise of land above the main roadway where they could keep an eye on it while they waited for their quarry and Jonah, leaving Sal on watch, had wrapped himself in a polar sleeping bag before taking a quick nap.

Atlantians required only a couple hours of sleep a day to feel fully rested and when he awoke, he felt rejuvenated, if cold and stiff.

Sal, his little robot buddy and constant companion, was, as

always, attuned to his master's needs and immediately turned the ignition to start the vehicle and thereby engage the heater.

As Jonah worked his way out of the cramped seat the little Almie picked up the sleeping bag and rolled it up before stowing it neatly in the back of the compact cab of the machine.

Jonah, wiping sleep from his eyes, stretched and looked over at the little robot.

"Can you tell if Venus and Duanna are getting any closer to us?"

Sal shook his head and without vocalizing, silently replied, his words instantly registering in Jonah's mind.

"No, it doesn't work like that. I can only tell you that Duanna is still within communication range."

Jonah nodded and reached up to open the hatch.

"I'm going to stretch my legs and have a look around. See what you can whip up for breakfast pal. I shouldn't be long."

* * * * *

Dawn was breaking over Jericho as the massive airship approached the Party compound six miles south of the city walls.

Colonel Von Jaeger and the Rector were sitting comfortably on the bridge behind the Captain who was standing to the right behind the duty helmsman. The young sailor was concentrating on turning the big ship's wheel slowly to correct course and bring them into line with the immense mooring mast ahead.

Eisen's eyes sparkled as he took in the scene below.

"Look Colonel, see what we have accomplished in a few short months. A completely fenced one-hundred-acre facility, barracks, classrooms, drill field, warehouses bulging with equipment, cafeterias, a massive scientific research facility; even a hospital. It's a small city cut out of virgin forest, our first of many."

As he spoke, the flying machine had been spotted from the ground and there was a sudden burst of activity beneath as the huge doors of the enormous hangar began to slide slowly open.

Uniformed redshirts in large numbers exited from the cavernous interior of the building, racing toward the mooring stations in the centre of the huge grassy field at the far end of the separately fenced aerodrome complex.

The Colonel allowed himself a brief smile.

"Yes my Rector, quite an accomplishment and already five thousand military recruits in training."

* * * * *

Enoch, the son of Marduke, briefly considered reaching his father, the Atlantian charged with advising Olympos on police and military matters, by going through their personal Almies, but thought better of it.

What he had to say to his dad was important. It would be better done face to face so he could see his father's reactions as well as hear them.

He glanced at the clock on the wall. It was shortly before seven and he had nothing important scheduled before his normal working day was to start. He had no way of knowing if his father was up or not, but felt fairly confident that his dad, who was an early riser, would already be at work in Jericho.

Making contact with his father was not something he could put off any longer and he turned to face his personal Almie, Cratus.

"Transport us to father's villa in Jericho."

CHAPTER TWO

- *Intrigue* -

Aabha, a female Ogre holding the rank of Mitra-Varuna within the Belief, the most powerful religion on the planet of Olympos and current Prime Minister of the State of Almeca, had risen early, slightly after the rise of Solar.

It was her intention to be the first to arrive for the morning meeting and she had no difficulty in accomplishing that goal.

Sitting alone in her usual spot to the right of the Devi's chair, at the large conference table, Aabha eagerly awaited the arrival of the other members of the Belief's main governing body.

Her heightened interest in this particular meeting had been stimulated by a decision on the part of the Devi; her aunt, Mitre VII, the God Solar's living representative on this world.

The Devi was showing outward signs of rapidly failing health and on the previous evening had decided to, in furtherance of her plan to have Aabha succeed her as Devi, speak to Mitra-Varuna Cala with regard to treasury monies Cala had promised to make available for a project that was dear to the heart of Mitra-Varuna Paayal.

Cala, considered by the Devi to be Aabha's closest rival for a possible successful election by the conclave to replace the Devi upon her death, was to have been informed by the Devi that she had decided to veto the additional funds for the creation of a teaching sisterhood, which Cala, in her position as Treasury Chair, had promised to Mitra-Varuna Paayal in order to secure her support when the need for such an election arose.

Assuming the Devi had delivered her message the night before as indicated, Cala would have undoubtedly immediately informed Paayal, who held the chair responsible for the rinciples and teachings of the Belief and discussed the situation with her. As there was no way Cala was going to disobey the direct instructions of the Devi, she may well have commiserated with Paayal over the reversal of funds, but she would have been unable to offer little more solace than that. Upon receipt of the news, Paayal would have been devastated and, it was hoped, disappointed and angered enough by the turn of events to drop her support for Cala's bid for the top post and, if things went as planned, choose to back Aabha instead. It was due to this plan that Aabha had reason to be very interested in seeing in what order the other Mitra-Varuna members arrived for the regular meeting and in whose company. The answer to those two happenings could reveal a great deal. For several weeks now Cala and Paayal had been coming to the daily meeting together. Would they arrive together this morning? If they did not, it could well indicate that they'd fallen out over the aborted plan to create the new sisterhood. If Mitra-Varuna Paayal arrived with another member of the council it might indicate that she had dropped Cala but had, overnight, been able to find another ally in her struggle to set up the group. On the other hand, if she arrived on her own that possibility would be unlikely. If Paayal was late in arriving, it might be a good indication that she had spent the evening frantically trying to build support for her plan among several of the others and been unsuccessful. Time would tell.

* * * * *

Harry had declined Venus's offer of the use of her little Almie Duanna to assist in making the morning meal. The old man, strongly distrusting anything mechanical that looked Human, had turned her down cold.

Gabriel, who Venus had decided should remain resting in bed, was propped up against his pillow watching the whole process taking place in the small kitchen of the one-room cabin with some amusement, while Brother Sebastian examined and then re-bandaged the earlier injury to the young Neanderthal's calf.

Sebastian, finished with his re-bandaging, left Gabe to join the others as the old man began to ladle out large dollops of porridge into bowls and place them onto the table.

Gabriel paused for a second and then gingerly swung his feet off the bed and planted them firmly on the floorboards of the cabin.

He kept an eye on Venus as he tentatively raised the rest of his body off the bed, carefully covering himself with the blankets as he rose to his feet.

Suffering a brief period of light-headedness, he had to put one hand back onto the carved wooden bed frame momentarily for support but the feeling passed quickly and he was soon able to stand without bracing himself.

When his vision cleared sufficiently he glanced into the kitchen again.

Venus was sitting at the table with her back to him. Brother Sebastian, who sat in the chair directly across from her on the far side of the table, was observing Gabriel with interest.

The monk parted his lips to speak but Gabriel mouthed the word 'No' while firmly shaking his head from side to side frantically, something he immediately regretted, as the movement caused the earlier wave of dizziness to return.

The monk got the message and when the spell of light-headedness had again passed, Gabriel slowly took the two steps that would allow him to reach the string of blankets on the rope. He used his left hand to quietly draw them together.

The instant they met, he tossed the bedding he'd been clutching in his other hand onto the bed and grabbed for his pants which were draped over the back of the chair Venus had placed by his bedside the night before. He quietly hauled them on and was pleased to note that the bending this manoeuvre necessitated was not accompanied by a further bout of wooziness.

Pants securely belted in place he picked up his shirt and sat down on the bed to put it on.

The creaking of the bed under Gabriel's weight must have tipped off Venus because he had no more than slipped his arms into the shirt when the blankets parted and she was standing in the opening to the little makeshift bedroom with hands on her hips and eyes flashing.

"And what exactly do you think you're doing? You know we can't possibly make it in time now, not with Blue wrecked and you injured. There just isn't enough time to reach your grandmother's before the deadline now if we are forced to travel by coach. You should be staying in that bed and regaining your strength."

She'd taken him completely by surprise and he'd jumped when she'd spoke.

That seemed to please her, which only provided fuel to his growing irritation.

Sebastian, who had been watching the whole process, laughed heartily, serving to piss Gabriel off even more.

His stress level had reached its peak. The death of his mother, the revelation about his father, leaving home on the quest to inherit his father's ability to disappear at whim, leaving behind everyone and everything he knew for the first time - and for what? The trip had been nothing but pain and suffering. He was tired physically and mentally exhausted and he was growing sick of the continued litany of advice he was receiving from others.

He gave the monk a dirty look and then turned the same expression directly on Venus.

He struggled and managed to hold down his anger for a few seconds but it finally overwhelmed him and he lashed out at her.

"What in the evil one's damnation does it look like I'm doing?"

Venus's lower lip began to quiver. Her eyes grew wide and started to mist. Her hands dropped off her hips and fell to her sides as her shoulders slumped and the expression of hurt that filled her face was obvious to everyone in the cabin.

Sebastian spoke, raising his voice in hopes of breaking the building tension.

"Actually I think we can still make it."

Gabriel had difficulty believing his ears.

All eyes were suddenly on the monk, who went on to explain Harry's offer to lend them horses and store Blue.

Sebastian watched with pleasure as Gabe's face, which had been reflecting dark clouds of depression for most of the morning, began to change. As the monk's words began to sink in, Gabe's dour features shifted firstly to an expression of relief and then to one of outright joy.

The possibilities provided by this news raced through his mind.

If Harry provided them with horses, this could still work.

He was feeling pretty good physically. The calf was throbbing less and the swelling on the right side of his face had gone down considerably, due, no doubt at least in part, to the repeated application of cold compresses which Venus had provided throughout the night.

The hurt look on Venus's face had softened slightly as she took in the signs of renewed hope filling Gabriel's features, but when he looked up a her, the distress she'd felt as a result of his recent blast of verbal frustration was still visible and very apparent to him.

It melted Gabe immediately. He swallowed hard as any trace of his earlier anger drained from him to be replaced by a sense of shame. Before he could get out words of apology she had spun around, stomped across to the table and dropped into her chair with her back to him.

Feeling guilty for having taken out his personal frustrations on her, he belatedly tried to make amends.

"I'm sorry I snapped at you; I know you're just concerned about me and I appreciate what you've done, but…"

Venus didn't even bother to turn her head as she cut him off.

"I am not upset, nor am I concerned about you! You are simply acting like a self-centred child. It was just that I didn't want you to foolishly undo what took me all night to accomplish. Had I known you wouldn't have the sense to stay in bed until you had regained your strength I would have gone to sleep instead of staying up half the night to fight your fever."

Sebastian cleared his throat as he bent his arm to pick up the wooden spoon beside his bowl.

"If I didn't know better, I'd think you two had been happily married for several years."

Harry burst out laughing and came very close to dropping the bowl he was filling.

Venus raised her eyes and gave the two of them a scathing look and then, ignoring them completely, began to eat.

* * * * *

Jonah, had been pacing for a good twenty minutes and his Almie, Sal, was well aware of his master's rising impatience. The little robot said nothing, in the full knowledge that the verbal explosion would come soon enough.

He'd no more than finished processing that thought when Jonah swore and raised his hands.

"Shit, where are they? Are they riding on mules or bikes? What can be holding them up? Are they in some kind of trouble? Son of a dog, I've had enough of this! Climb aboard and let's head back south down the highway."

The little Almie had been searching for some time for the right wording to respond to the outburst he'd anticipated. He delivered it now.

"There is no need for us to move. They have to pass this point. We calculated their probable progress very carefully before selecting the co-ordinates best suited for interception. It's to be expected that their advance will have been affected by bad weather and road conditions. It's highly unlikely they've already passed this point. A little patience is required. If Venus was in trouble Duanna would certainly communicate. She knows an Almie is in range. She doesn't know who that Almie is but that would not matter to it her if her mistress was in any danger. She would communicate with me."

It was all true and it made sense but Jonah strongly disliked inactivity and he wasn't going to just sit here all day.

"OK Sal, but if they don't arrive within the next two hours, we hit the road."

* * * * *

Solar had burned off the cloud cover over Jericho by the time Enoch and Cratus appeared on the patio at the rear of his father's villa. It looked like there was a clear but cool day ahead for Jericho and he raised his hand to shield his eyes briefly until they had become accustomed to the brightness.

During the brief transport Enoch had been busily rehearsing what he needed to say to his father and now that he had arrived, he sat down on one of the benches overlooking the city, pausing for a few seconds to gather his thoughts.

He sensed he was going to have only one chance at convincing his father to rethink the situation with Adon. He also knew that once his father made up his mind he rarely, if ever, changed it. Added to those facts was this new, uncharacteristic outlook on life that his dad had recently adopted and which seemed to be more solidly expressing itself daily since his mother's passing.

The proposition that he might be able to change his father's mind was beginning to look rather doubtful to him and suddenly seemed doomed to failure.

He seriously considered dropping the whole idea as futile and transporting back to Atlantis.

But then what? Go to Adon behind his father's back? No, he couldn't do that. He had to at least try to convince his father to drop the whole idea of usurping Adon as leader of the Atlantian team and if he got nowhere, then so be it. He would at least feel justified in telling his father up front how he felt about it and that, under the circumstances, he saw it as his duty to report his opinions to Adon.

His brow furrowed deeply and he pursed his lips.

His stomach churned.

He was convinced he would fail and in all likelihood his father would never forgive him for what he would then have to do.

It was a bitter pill to swallow.

CHAPTER THREE

- *Hard Decisions* -

One of the big doors leading off the hallway into the large conference room opened and two Mitra-Varunas of the Devi's inner circle, Jaboah, accompanied by Eashca bustled inside chatting amicably.

Jaboah, soft spoken and motherly in appearance, held the Belief's Resources Chair. She dropped into place behind Eashca as they crossed the big room, matching the pace set by the rotund, cold tempered, no nonsense holder of the Disciplinary Chair.

At the sight of Aabha their faces brightened and they offered beaming smiles and spoke almost in unison.

"Good morning Aabha."

She looked up from the notes that she had been studying and returned their smiles.

"Jaboah, Eashca, it is a beautiful morning isn't it?"

The two women were still in the process of placing files onto the big table when the door opened and Cala entered the room.

Her withered features served to magnify the deep displeasure registered on her face as her eyes met Aabha's briefly and then shifted to the others.

Jaboah had pulled out her chair and was in the process of sitting down.

"Good morning Cala. You look tired dear; didn't you sleep well?"

Cala's eyes narrowed and her face coloured slightly as she studied Jaboah's features, searching for some hidden meaning. When she found nothing in the motherly woman's expression to support that possibility, she chose to dismiss the comment out of hand and dropped her eyes as she crossed to her chair and pulled it out while managing a short, clipped response.

"I slept very well thank you."

Aabha bent her head downward slightly as she rearranged her papers.

Cala was definitely not in a good mood, and that boded well.

* * * * *

Juno gave a sigh of relief as she spotted the small cairn of rocks on the far side of the roadway.

She recognized it immediately and after checking both north and south for traffic and finding none, hurried across the highway.

Over the past hour or so, scrub brush had steadily given way to a richer diversity of foliage and ahead of her, along the short path leading to the hot springs, she could see several large stands of evergreens, which as she had anticipated, would provide her with cover from any inquisitive eyes that might pass by on the roadway behind her.

She had no trouble finding the trail and her excitement at nearing her goal helped to provide her with a second wind.

The thought of stripping out of her filthy clothes and slipping into the welcoming warmth of the hot spring water filled her with relief. She was very much looking forward to washing away the horror of the night and soaking her aching joints. She could hardly wait to get out of her clothes and take the opportunity to scrub away the muddy slush from the road and the stench of her own vomit.

* * * * *

Enoch took a deep breath and stood up.

He had never, in his entire life, taken a strong position against his father. It was a concept completely alien to him and he was not looking forward to what was coming.

He doubted he would have had the testicular fortitude to even attempt such a thing four months ago. But something had changed in the course of his life over the past three months. He had grown more mature, more confident, since his father had allowed him to take a degree of responsibility in his stead and that responsibility had changed him irrevocably.

He was no longer the uncertain youth he had been.

He filled his lungs with the fresh clean air, crossed to the wall of big glass doors and touched the closest one.

It slipped silently open and with Cratus close behind, he entered the villa.

As the door was whispering closed behind them, Huck, his dad's butler entered the room from the hallway.

"Ah, master Enoch, what a wonderful surprise. We weren't expecting you. I'm sure your father will be pleased to see you; he's in the study having a late breakfast. Shall I announce you?"

Enoch shook his head.

"No, that won't be necessary, but perhaps you could find something for me, I haven't eaten yet today."

The butler nodded and bent slightly from the waist then turned to leave the room.

"I'm sure that can be arranged, I'll see to it straight away."

* * * * *

Gabriel was sitting at the table to Venus's left. With some difficulty in consideration of the size of the cabin, she was managing to avoid looking at him as she ate. The atmosphere in the small kitchen could best be described as chilly. The fact that both Sebastian and the old man found the whole thing amusing was doing nothing to melt Venus's icy persona.

Finally, Brother Sebastian pushed his empty bowl forward and leaned back to stretch. He glanced at the old man and smiled.

"Well that should stick to our ribs for a few hours, Harry."

The old man, in the process of scraping the last of his cereal out of his bowl, nodded and the monk began speaking again, addressing no one in particular.

"I'm afraid Gabriel's bike is the worse for wear after our little set-to with the Bluefaces last night. In view of the fact that Harry has been good enough to offer to store the bike and make us the loan of a couple of horses to get us as far as the next roadhouse where we will be able to purchase two animals to complete the trip, we should head out as soon as Gabriel is well enough to move on."

Gabriel paused, his spoon part way to his mouth.

"I'm ready."

He had spoken very firmly and in a harsher tone than he'd intended and he immediately looked over at Venus to evaluate her reaction. She refused to meet his eyes, intent on ignoring him completely and continuing to eat.

As he continued, Gabriel put a distinct effort into lowering his voice and speaking softly.

"No really, I'm feeling fine; and with having to leave Blue behind and travel by horseback for the rest of the way, well we really don't have any time to lose."

* * * * *

Enoch was idly pushing his food around his plate. He was too wound up to do the meal justice.

His father had finished eating and there was a soft knock at the study door before Huck entered to remove the dishes. When the butler had left the room Marduke leaned back in his chair and looked across his desk at his son.

"So what is it that brings you here?"

Enoch took a deep breath and let his eyes meet his father's.

"It's kind of a bunch of things, Dad. Mostly I'm worried about you, I guess."

Marduke leaned forward and his eyes narrowed slightly as he rested his elbows on the top of the desk, intertwining his fingers and resting his chin on his folded hands.

"Worried about me, in what way?"

Enoch concentrated on his delivery. He'd planned to ease into things and work up to his father's attack on Adon's credibility.

"Well for starters, you're drinking heavily and not getting much sleep. You look like shit, Dad."

Marduke's empty red-rimmed eyes glazed slightly.

"I've been under a lot of pressure lately. Your mother was taken from us before her time. I miss her support... I miss your mother very much."

Enoch nodded, both surprised and encouraged his father had not, as he had done in the recent past, simply dismissed his comments as unfounded. He leaned forward slightly as he continued.

"I know that Dad, but it's been a couple of months now and you're drinking way too much, something you never did when Mom was alive. You're just not yourself. You're doing things you would never have even considered when Mom was here."

Marduke lifted his elbows off the desk and placed his hands, palms down on the surface as he tilted backward into his chair. His eyes had darkened and there was an edge to his voice when he spoke.

"And what kind of things are those exactly?"

Enoch got the message, and as he did he sensed something he'd never felt before when in his father's presence…fear.

He thought very carefully before he responded.

"I don't know exactly, Dad. Your whole outlook on the advisory team's progress with the development of Olympos, questioning Adon's leadership: you're just not thinking the way you used to. It's like you're suddenly being driven by something and I'm not sure I understand why the change came about. I'm not the only one taking notice; others are becoming aware or your divergent activities."

There wasn't even a hint of warmth in Marduke's voice when he responded.

"You are my son Enoch. You will take my place when my time comes and because Adon will have been replaced, you will have to take on the full responsibility for the entire team, not simply assume the responsibility for police and military matters. You are young and just beginning your journey through the early stages of life's discovery within the natural flow. It is because of that fact that I forgive you for what you have just said, because I know you are making judgements on things that you don't yet understand, but don't ever presume to second guess or question my decisions or actions. That's something I will not forgive. Now, I have a very important meeting this morning so I must bring this visit to an end."

* * * * *

Jonah may have agreed to wait another two hours, but he had every intention of being ready to go the instant that specific timeframe had been fulfilled.

After the little Almie had cleaned up the remains of breakfast, he had Sal build a small fire in front of a stump hidden from the road by both the halftrack and the small copse of trees. This accomplished, Sal decided to organize and repack the supplies they had hastily crammed into the limited space inside the cab of the halftrack before using the transporter. It was a relatively cramped area. The little grey robot felt they needed to make the best use of the available space, and he multi-tasked while accomplishing this, drawing on the halftrack's power source to replenish his energy level as he worked.

Jonah was perched on the small stump in front of the fire, binoculars to his eyes, as he kept watch on the roadway below. According to Sal, no traffic had passed during the hours of darkness and as yet nothing had come into sight since the arrival of daylight.

There was no sign of precipitation; the air was cold, crisp and clear.

Visibility was good and when, from their elevated vantage point, Jonah looked southward along the road, he could clearly make out its meandering length for a good mile.

Having finished with the general cleanup within the cab, Sal turned his attention to completing the absorption of the manuals that had come with the vehicle. He hadn't found time to finished analyzing them as thoroughly as he felt obligated to do and it was something he sensed should be remedied while he had some free time.

* * * * *

When Gabriel, in an attempt to break free from the chilly atmosphere in the small cabin, volunteered to help Sebastian get the horses ready to travel, Venus, who had never lifted a domestic finger in her life, surprised everyone including herself, by offering to help Harry clean up the breakfast dishes.

Duanna was absolutely appalled at the very suggestion but a curt look from her mistress forestalled any comment the little Almie might have felt tempted to offer.

Sebastian and Gabriel bundled up and headed out to the barn.

Once inside they paused by what was left of Blue and Gabriel ran his fingers over the blistered paint, punctured tank and mangled front end.

He'd expected some damage but it was far worse than he'd anticipated.

At the sight of the machine his earlier bout of depression returned twofold and his shoulders slumped as he dropped down on his haunches next to Blue.

"Shit, what next!"

CHAPTER FOUR

- On The Move -

Sebastian took his hand away from the bridle he had been reaching for and dropped down to sit on a hay bale beside Gabe.

"Want to talk about it?"

Gabriel, who hadn't intended to speak out loud, glanced over at the monk and took a deep breath and then released it.

"It's just everything I guess. A month ago I was secure in my home life, working steady, enjoying myself and then – wham! First my mom dies, and then I find out that the males in my bloody family have this power. Next I'm racing across the country dragging along some awesome looking but impossible to understand Atlantian chick who, it seems logical to conclude, is simply using me to help her run away from home, which, when you consider who her parent's are, let alone the fact that her older brother dotes on and is very protective of, cannot be a good thing. Not to mention that I'm having to fight, Solar only knows what, crazy beasts to get to some place I've never been, to see a grandmother I've never met and pick up some power that I don't understand and will probably never use. Now my bike, the only thing I've ever owned, is toast and I don't know if I even want to continue on to Jericho. This special ability doesn't even feel real to me any more and after all this suffering and pain, well it just doesn't seem worth it."

Sebastian didn't respond immediately. He let the words hang in the air for several seconds before he replied.

"Look Gabe, your mom's death obviously hit you very hard, but that's normal and you'll get a handle on it over time. From what you've said, it sounds to me like you grew up in a nurturing family and no one can ever take that away from you. It will hold you in good stead for the rest of your life, believe me."

Gabe shifted slightly to look at the monk, and Sebastian nodded his head slowly.

"Once you have a chance to reflect on it you'll find that what I've said is true. In a very few days you've been forced to do a lot of growing up, but that's all part of becoming a man. It would have happened at some point in your life anyway. You may not realize it yet, but from what I know of you, I can tell you unequivocally that you're now on the first of many exciting adventures that will come along over your long life. What you learn and experience on this trip will help you to realign your horizons and broaden and expand your self-determined boundaries. What you observe and experience will give you a much stronger foundation and make you a better man and it will remain with you and serve you forever."

* * * * *

A long silence had passed as the two of them, under Sebastian's supervision, worked at preparing the horses for the trip.

Finally, after carefully weighing the monk's words and still looking decidedly dispirited, Gabe humphed, and turned to look back at the wreckage that had been his pride and joy.

Undeterred, Sebastian continued with his attempt to boost the young Neanderthal's spirits.

"Wisdom doesn't grow on trees Gabe; it's gleaned by accepting something you've been exposed to intimately, deeply within your subconscious. This power your mother wished you to have will act as a bridge to a part of reality that is infinitely unique in your life. Once you see or learn something you can not un-see it. You have no choice but to accept it as an insight into yourself and in so doing you become wiser. Your mother considered the passing of the power to you as your birthright. She strongly desired that you receive it and she was prepared to give up other things, personally important to her, in order to ensure that happen. I think you'll agree with me; that in itself makes the trip necessary. You owe her that much. Between the three of us, we'll see that you make it to Jericho. Trust me when I say that some day you will also be very glad you completed the trip and accepted the power, for it will serve you well throughout your lifetime. When you've finished your quest, you can come back here for Blue and get the bike repaired as good as new."

Gabriel's shoulders lifted slightly.

"Ya, I guess you're right. When I think about it, old Blue was in this bad a shape or worse when I first spotted him. I'll have to get him hauled back to Sumer, but once I get a regular pay packet coming in again, it won't take long to get him back into condition."

Sebastian considered leaving it at that but deep down he knew all the things he'd talked about to that point were only partially responsible for the slump the kid was in. He took a deep breath and chose his words carefully before he picked up the thread.

"And that brings us to the '…dragging along some awesome looking but impossible to understand Atlantian chick who, it seems logical to conclude, is simply using me to help her run away from home, which, when you consider who her parent's are, let alone etc…' part. All I can say about that is you're either a fool or blind if you can't see that she's in lust with you for sure and she may well think she is in love with you."

Gabriel's head snapped around and his mouth dropped open. He was about to speak when the monk stopped him with a raised hand.

"Hang on my son, hear me out. Yes, she's in lust with you, and maybe even the other. But think about it carefully Gabe and you'll realize you're not the only one who's being forced to grow up fast all of a sudden. It's happening to her too. On top of that, at your ages, both of you have a battalion of hormones raging 'the evil one's damnation bent for leather' around in your bodies. Putting aside the obvious scenarios with regard to the parents and the brother, which I agree, in consideration of the fact that they are Atlantians with all the power that inherently expresses, is bad enough; would you want to do something foolish that could screw up both your lives for a chance to satisfy that mutual urge?"

The slouch came out of Gabriel's shoulders.

The words 'you bet I would' flashed to the forefront of his thoughts but as he carefully ran his mind back over everything the monk had said, they faded quickly.

Sebastian was watching Gabe closely; trying to read in the young Neanderthal's features, what, if any, effect his little speech had brought about.

Gabe had snapped out of the slump; that was obvious. But had the talk helped to reduce the kid's overall stress level, or served to elevate it?

Forced to pick from the two, Sebastian decided that some of the stress was gone and it seemed probable that Gabe was busily masticating through the opinions the monk had expressed and doing his best to appraise their worth.

The kid had a good heart and a good mind. He was well built physically and a ruggedly handsome devil for sure. Combat was new to him but what he'd faced, he'd handled well. He was a little too courageous for his own good perhaps, and he had lots of balls in every sense of the word, but the high testosterone levels of youth had a good deal to do with that. For now, that particular trait would not make the reaching of full manhood unscathed an easy task, but in time it would all balance out.

Solar had seen fit to deliver the boy directly into his hands and he could see great potential here, a diamond in the rough. There had only been one previous Neanderthal member of the Order of the Golden Ring in the history of the Belief, and that had unfortunately been short-lived; however, this boy was very much his father's son and had many promising traits.

The Devi had been wise to have him seek out this young man.

* * * * *

Marduke and his Almie, Bellum, appeared on the sidewalk in front of the command building of the National Socialist Party of Indus compound just before 10:00 hours. They were regular visitors and their emergence in a small alcove to one side of the twin glass main doors drew no undue attention.

Marduke entered the building and went directly to the Rector's private offices. When he entered the secretary's outer chamber he was sent through to the inner waiting room where he was greeted by a smiling Colonel von Jaeger.

"Ah Marduke, he is expecting you."

The tall uniformed Ogre let the way to the wide floor to ceiling polished wooden doors at the far end of the room. Black uniformed SS guards armed with an automatic machine-pistol stood on either side of the entrance. As they approached, the two ramrod-erects sentinels slammed their heels together and saluted before moving to grasp the brightly polished brass handles and allow access to the Rector's inner sanctum.

Von Jaeger and Marduke, followed by Bellum, stepped through and the doors closed silently behind them.

It was a very large room.

The walls were finished in a rust-coloured marble and windows ran floor to ceiling along two of the highly polished surfaces.

The Rector sat behind an enormous desk at the far end of the chamber.

He stood and smiled at the sound of the doors closing behind them.

* * * * *

As the meeting progressed Aabha became concerned as to the Devi's condition. The old woman was definitely not herself. She had little colour, couldn't seem to find a comfortable position and made no comment on any of the points raised. Twice she'd drifted off briefly.

Aabha began to push the agenda ahead rapidly and was relieved when Cala, who usually had much to say on whatever topic arose, had been unusually quiet throughout the morning meeting.

Paayal, who had arrived last and immediately seated herself without exchanging greetings with the others, something that was completely out of character for her, was also unusually subdued. Even more out of character, the woman who normally fidgeted when unable to get up and move about for any extended period, demonstrated no sign of that irritating habit this morning.

During the meeting Aabha glanced up several times to find Paayal studying her furtively. Twice she'd offered an encouraging smile across the table toward the other woman but the instant she did, Paayal had promptly averted her eyes down-ward to her note pad.

* * * * * *

Juno carefully studied each of the small groupings of hot springs spaced along the trail as she reached them. She finally settled on a small formation of pools at the very end of the path. The grouping was far from the road and any traffic it might carry and was, in addition, completely sheltered from the winding path itself by a lush growth of thick brush and trees. A fair distance from the highway and hidden from view, she felt it to be the safest choice.

She carefully surveyed the immediate area for some distance around the five small interconnecting pools to satisfy herself that it was unlikely that anyone would be able to approach her without making their presence known. That done, she returned to the larger of the grouping and quickly stripped. Naked, she carried her soiled clothes to the edge of the pool and set them down, then placed her dagger on a nearby rock before slipping into the embracing warmth of the water.

Remaining submerged in the pool, with only her shoulders above the surface, she scrubbed her clothes vigorously before arranging them on the rocks rimming the pool to dry as best they could in the waves of steam that rose off the surface of the water and then eagerly sank down again and closed her eyes.

Her skin began to glow as she gave herself completely to the reviving qualities produced by the hot, gently bubbling spring. Weariness flowed out of her and blissful dreaminess crept in to fill the void.

* * * * *

Harry couldn't be dissuaded from accompanying them up to the pass. He defended his need to do so with the explanation that it was a little tricky going until that point but was smooth sailing, and all down hill, from there.

In truth, the old man was concerned as to Gabriel's ability to manage the large Draft horse, and although he'd provided the young Neanderthal with a gentle creature, he wanted to ensure that Gabe felt confident with the animal before he sent them on their way.

The wind had completely dissipated and although the air was bitterly cold at this elevation, Solar was shining strongly and the crusted snow was sparkling brightly wherever touched by its rays.

Venus took the lead, something Gabriel was not particularly happy about, but Harry had suggested it would make it easier on the horses to have the bike in front of them where they could see it, pointing out that having the noisy machine unseen behind them was likely to make them more skittish.

The road, on a fair incline, was plenty wide enough for the old man to ride beside her and because he was a very competent rider, his horse all but ignored the machine beside him.

Gabriel and Sebastian followed closely behind the others. The monk, a proficient rider who shared the old man's concern as to

Gabriel's horsemanship, kept his eye on him, offering advice now and then, but always in a light-hearted fashion that would not embarrass the young Neanderthal. Gabriel had been the first to admit he was uncomfortable on the animal but self-pride combined with his relative youth, determined that he demonstrate no outward sign of his unease. He rode directly behind Venus, who was still doing a good job of ignoring him. Gabe was unsure of exactly what it was that he had done to warrant such a strong reaction from her; but was definitely regretting both the way he'd handled the decision to get out of bed and of his having taken his frustration out on her when she'd questioned his judgement.

His decision to be the one most capable of deciding when he was well enough to get up and travel had seemed very reasonable to him at the time and, from his perspective, it certainly didn't warrant such an intense response from her. I mean, it was his body after all and who better to make the choice to proceed with the trip?

He was becoming more than a little frustrated over the fact that every attempt he'd made since then to break the ice with her had been either ignored or staunchly rebuffed. Trying to sort the whole mess out in his mind had given him a headache and by this point, it seemed to him that the more time he spent trying to discern what made a woman's mind tick the less he understood them.

CHAPTER FIVE

- *Negotiation* -

Colonel von Jaeger had been dismissed and Bellum was standing at rest at the far end of the room to one side of the big doors.

Eisen's big desk rested on a raised dais, designed to place him above anyone sitting in one of the large overstuffed chairs facing him.

This normally allowed him to look down upon his guests, but as Marduke, who was almost a foot taller than the Rector, approached him Eisen was very much aware that the Atlantian's height negated this advantage.

Eisen found that fact extremely irritating, but his demeanour gave no indication of the fact.

There was no particular sense of trust and certainly no bond of friendship between Marduke and Eisen.

The Atlantian saw Eisen as a megalomaniac brimming with hubris and a means to an end, which was the disruption of law and order on Olympos.

The Rector looked at Marduke as the source of unlimited power and prestige and a very necessary part, for the time being at least, of his plan to place the entire planet under his control.

Their relationship was purely symbiotic.

Neither man was particularly comfortable with the liaison. On the whole, they did not enjoy each other's company and over the two months they had been collaborating, they'd only met a few times, and even then, only when one or the other considered it absolutely necessary.

Over that period of time, the Rector, through his association with Marduke, had been transformed from a minor player in a fringe political party to that of an acknowledged leader who held absolute control over a wildly growing and dominating militaristic, political machine.

He still had difficulty accepting his good fortune, and he was very wary of doing anything that might displease and thereby jeopardize Marduke's support.

The meeting had been called by the Atlantian and below the surface, beneath a carefully presented façade of nonchalance, Eisen was churning with the fear that it might mean Marduke was considering the termination of their agreement.

It was therefore with some trepidation that he initially exchanged small talk with Marduke.

Marduke knew exactly how much the Ogre depended on his cooperation and support, both in advice and material, in his dream to achieve absolute power on the planet. He was also aware of the stress his presence today was causing and was, calmly and with some enjoyment, letting it build to a feverish pitch before speaking specifically about the purpose of the meeting.

Eisen had begun to perspire heavily by the time the Atlantian got to that point.

When he was satisfied the crescendo of that building strain had been reached in the Ogre seated across the desk from him, Marduke changed the topic abruptly.

"Our arrangement may have to change."

Despite a heroic attempt to demonstrate no outward reaction to the Atlantian's words, Eisen was powerless to prevent the colour from draining from his face, a fact that Marduke readily recognized and took the time to savour as he waited for the Rector to respond.

"Change, in what way?"

Marduke's innate dislike for the Ogre sitting across from him allowed him to take pleasure in the unease and concern that he'd perceived on the Rector's features. He might have enjoyed dragging it out even longer, but like it or not, he dared not push too far, he needed this man.

He had staged the session carefully and if he wished to succeed in his task, it was time to let Eisen regain his composure.

"Nothing serious, but it may be necessary to change the timeframe."

Eisen visibly relaxed. He sat back and arranged himself more comfortably in his big leather chair as Marduke continued.

"Our bargain will remain as originally envisioned. I will provide you with an absolute guarantee that within ten years' time you will be the undisputed military dictator of the planet Olympos. In return you will provide me with a military contingent that will enable me to take control of Atlantis by force. The only necessary change in our arrangement will be in the time frame in relation to the need for me to take Atlantis. Circumstances have come to my attention that may require that portion of our bargain to happen in the very near future rather than in a few months. This may become necessary to ensure our plans are not impugned by outside forces. I came to tell you that you must have a substantial force ready to act under my direction from this point forth."

Relieved, Eisen smiled.

"I have several thousands of those drone-like Neanderthals nearing the end of their training now and for officers I would suggest the use of my own SS men. How many men will you require?"

Marduke paused for a second.

"Hmmm, I would think that five hundred well-disciplined men could manage what I need done. I would only need them for a day or two."

Eisen, relieved at the ease in which Marduke's request could be met, smiled broadly.

"I will have such a group structured and organized before the day is out."

* * * * *

Sal was up top in the gun turret of the halftrack.

In order for him to be able to see out through the viewing port in the protective flange of the turret, the little Almie had been forced to use one of the polar sleeping bags as a sort of booster seat. He had partially unfolded one of the bags and was using it to provide the additional padding required to raise his body high enough up off the seat to enable him an unobstructed line of view.

They had been travelling south on the road for close to an hour.

Sal's eyes, searching for any sign of traffic on the road ahead never left the twisting ribbon of highway which stretched out in front and Jonah, encamped in the enclosed driving compartment below, was therein left free to concentrate his complete attention on keeping the halftrack on the road.

As Jonah's confidence in the operation of the vehicle grew, their speed increased, the machine's engine roaring and the tracks thrashing noisily over the slushy uneven surface of the roadway as they moved.

The mainly flat valley floor provided little available cover to them if they found it necessary to get off the highway; some small patches of low-growing brush among the snow-covered scrub grass and the odd grove of trees in an otherwise rather barren landscape. However, they'd met no oncoming traffic so far and moving at the speed they were now travelling, they felt it unlikely any travelers coming from the north would have the ability to overtake them.

A decidedly unhappy Sal was being shaken like a rag doll and hanging on for dear life while Jonah was hauling ass and loving every second of it.

The weather remained cold but clear and the vehicle was covering ground rapidly.

In his mind, Jonah picked up Sal's message.

"I can see mountains ahead."

He dipped his head slightly so he could peer upward out through the driver's window in the front of the armoured cab and from that angle was able to see far enough ahead to spot the area Sal was indicating; about a mile ahead of them where the valley floor met the base of a mountain range and the road began to climb upward from the bottom.

Even at that distance he could make out the switchbacks sections of the track rising up and into the fresh snowline above.

* * * * *

The minute the Devi left the morning meeting, Cala, without a word to those left in the room, stood and followed in her foot-steps.

Aabha dallied on her side of the big table, needlessly busying herself with arranging and stacking her papers.

Jaboah and Eashca spent a few moments speaking animatedly together, then stood and beamed uniformly warm bright smiles across at her, before gathering their files and heading toward the door.

Paayal, who had begun to fidget the moment the Devi left, was bent over her note pad scribbling, her eyes flickering uneasily between the other two women still seated at the table, from time to time.

It didn't take Aabha long to realize that Paayal desperately wanted to speak to her alone and was waiting for Daka, the Mitra-Varuna who held the Diplomatic Chair, to leave the room.

Sensing the nervous woman's discomfort, she let her gaze meet Paayal's and smiled warmly.

In the normal course of events, Daka would routinely leave immediately after the close of the morning meetings and it was readily apparent to Aabha that the Diplomatic Chair was aware of Paayal's wish to speak with her, and was delaying her own departure in order to purposely lengthen Paayal's clearly displayed unease.

The strained silence in the chamber was becoming painful by the time Daka, seemingly finally satisfied that she had milked the moment for all it was worth, stood and gathered her files.

Before she turned to leave the room, she pointedly let her eyes meet those of both Daka and Aabha's briefly and then allowed a crisp little, knowing smirk to form on her thin lips before she spoke.

"Well then, I'll leave you two to it shall I?"

Paayal turned pale and her eyes flashed with anger as she glared at Daka, but she bit her lip and said nothing.

Aabha simply smiled pleasantly and nodded.

* * * * *

The pass through the centre of the mountains turned out to be spectacular. Venus, who had been unusually quiet on the trip up, was in awe.

She placed her bike on its stand and peered skyward wide-eyed.

Her deep blue eyes sparkled brightly as she craned her neck back to look upward toward the peaks of the sheer, stately cliffs which rose majestically upward from either side of the narrow roadway.

The surface of the rock faces was coated in a deep layer of ice and although clouds masked the very tops of them, the hundreds of feet she could see sparkled dazzlingly as the filtered beams of light struck them.

Everywhere the rays of Solar managed to pierce the surface of the ice itself, the colours of the rainbow glittered back downward toward her in an ever changing kaleidoscope of prism-like reflection.

She crossed to Gabriel who had dismounted and took his hand.

"Oh Gabe, look at it! It's so beautiful!"

Gabe looked upward and smiled. He had to admit it was unique, but more importantly he was relieved and pleased that she appeared to have finally thawed out and was prepared to talk to him.

"Yes, I've never seen anything like it."

He squeezed her hand gently and dropped his gaze to look at her surreptitiously as she continued to move her gaze over the ice-coated rock faces above. She was as pleased as a child given a handful of flake and turned loose in a candy store.

He had never seen her more vibrant and animated.

Brother Sebastian dismounted and joined them, his neck craned backwards as he stared up at the shimmering cliffs.

Harry remained mounted and sat smiling down at them, enjoying their reactions.

"On these clear, cold days it's pretty impressive all right."

They were silent for a few seconds as they took it all in then the old man turned his horse and hopped down.

"I'll leave you here. The way down is not too steep, switchbacks to the bottom and the road is wide. It shouldn't take you long to reach the bottom."

Venus pulled her eyes away from the cliffs to look over at him and as she did, she became conscious of the fact that she had been holding Gabriel's hand.

She flushed slightly as she slipped it free.

Gabriel, who had been watching Venus and not the scenery, shifted his gaze and the two of them turned toward the old man as Sebastian crossed to him and wrapped him in a bear hug.

"Thanks for taking us in Harry. We'll leave the horses at the inn for you. If all goes to plan, I'll drop in for a brief visit on the way back from Jericho."

Gabriel extended his hand and Harry took it and shook it firmly then, Venus gave him a peck on each cheek, which brought a warm glow to the old man's eyes. She gave him a big smile and took his hand in both of hers.

"Thank you for everything; I don't know what we would have done without you."

CHAPTER SIX

- *Hook Taken* -

As the doors closed behind Daka the room resounded with a sharp crack and Aabha looked over at Paayal who had been squeezing both ends of her pencil so hard she'd snapped it in two.

Paayal sat staring at the pieces in surprise, and then sheepishly looked over at Aabha.

"I never know what that woman is thinking; she can drive me to distraction at times!"

Aabha laughed and nodded.

"Yes, Daka misses little and is very hard to read when she wishes to be. She is certainly well suited to the Diplomacy Chair."

Aabha's observations were enough to break the tenseness in the air. Some of the strain left Paayal's shoulders and she seemed to relax for the first time since the meeting had begun. She managed a brief smile

"Yes she is and she is also very aware of everything going on about her. I swear she has eyes in the back of her head. She can be so infuriating sometimes."

Aabha smiled in agreement and Paayal took a deep breath and began to speak.

"Aabha, you may or may not be aware that Cala promised me the funds for the new teaching sisters I've been advocating for some time had been found."

She watched Aabha's face tentatively as she spoke and when she got no reaction, continued.

"Anyway she did, and last night the Devi approached me and told me that she had not sanctioned the use of treasury gold for that purpose and had advised Cala that the funds would not be forthcoming. I spoke with Cala about it later and she expressed surprise at the Devi's decision, but said she couldn't do anything about it. I've been working on this for so long and it's needed so badly. I was wondering if you could speak with the Devi, on my behalf and ask her to reconsider her pronouncement."

Aabha set her pencil down onto her pad and shifted back slightly in her chair. Her brow furrowed and she shook her head.

"I don't think I would have much chance of changing the Devi's mind once it was made up and it would seem in this instance at least that she had clearly indicated her position on the matter."

Paayal's shoulders drooped and she lowered her eyes, and then began to get her files in order to leave. Before she could finish and stand, Aabha continued.

"You know, when you first brought the idea up, I felt sure you were going to have difficulty getting the treasury to come up with sufficient gold to initiate a whole new sisterhood, and because I believe as you do that such an endeavour is badly needed, I gave the matter a great deal of thought. As a result, it occurred to me a few days later that there might be another way to reach the goal you have set."

Paayal's hands froze in position. Her head lifted and she looked hopefully across the table at Aabha who now held her undivided attention as she impatiently waited for her to continue.

"As you know I reside on the top floor and take my meals with the members of the Sisters of Penance and on the day the matter came up I happened to be sitting with Sister Ester and was discussing the whole concept with her. She made what I thought then was a rather strange suggestion. Quite honestly, I was a little taken aback and might well have dismissed her comments out of hand. But when I got to thinking about it later that evening I immediately saw the value of her suggestion and recognized then that it may well be the answer to your dilemma. Then, of course, I'd heard Cala had found the gold for you and having no idea the Devi hadn't been consulted with regard to the funds, thereby sanctioning the financing, I naturally assumed things would proceed as you'd planned."

She let the conversation trail off at that point and turned her attention back to her papers again.

Aabha had cast the line. Now, the question was; would Paayal take the hook?

* * * * *

The therapeutic warmth of the hot springs had delightfully drained all the aches and pains from Juno's body. She was dozing lightly and suffering from a nightmare about the horrific scene with the Trolls on the evening before that now yanked her out of the curative bliss of her restless slumber.

She stiffened and sat upright on the rock she had been using as an underwater seat, raising her upper body out of the water and into the cooler air above the gently rippled surface of the pool.

Her senses immediately came in to play and she craned her head about and listened intently.

The only sound was the soft bubbling of the hot spring. She could see no movement in the thick brush surrounding her.

She took a deep breath and relaxed back down into the water.

She knew she should get out but it felt so good.

Perhaps just a few minutes more.

* * * * *

Hook, line, and sinker!

Curiosity and excitement resonated in Daka's response.

"What was Sister Ester's suggestion?"

Aabha, pretending her mind was elsewhere, paused in organizing her notes and thought carefully before responding.

"Oh let me think a moment, I should be able to recall it."

Eyes closed and brow furrowed in thought, she stood and pushed her chair carefully in under the large, intricately inlaid table.

"She said, 'What a perfect job for our Sisterhood! Who was better qualified, than the most uncorrupted organization in the Belief, to educate and transmit the word of Solar to the uninitiated?"

Aabha opened her eyes and a smile touched the sides of her mouth.

"I pointed out that it would mean the sisters would have to travel to all parts of Olympos and enter into uncivilized areas and bear heavy responsibility. She responded with the observation that all the women making up her order lived a very simple and frugal existence by choice and as such required very little to sustain themselves. Her only concern was that her people might find they were being supervised in the field by those of much higher Belief rank and would therefore be unable to carry out their responsibilities with a free and incorrupt hand."

Paayal was hanging on to Aabha's every word now.

"I brought Ester's idea up with the Devi later that day and she felt it had merit. I remember being surprised at how strongly interested she was in the entire concept. She went so far as to indicate she might be convinced to bestow upon the sisterhood a complete independence in the field, a freedom from direction from those in positions of power within the Belief, outside of the Holy See itself. Complete autonomy if you will; guaranteed by 'Deval Decree' to be free from outside interference in their duties. She went so far as to suggest that should the idea be accepted, the order would have to fall under your direct supervision and answer only to you and the Devi herself. She felt the Sisterhood of Penance would be very well suited for the duties that you require, and in addition, could provide her with unbiased intelligence, something that she considers as clearly currently lacking, about the conditions of the delivery of the Belief throughout Olympos."

Paayal's earlier tragic look of doom had gone through several distinct changes as Aabha spoke; a hint of relief, a touch of hope, and now full blown excitement.

"Oh Aabha, it's a wonderful idea!"

Aabha smiled across at her and nodded slowly.

"Yes and it wouldn't require any up-front financing. It would simply be a more sensible utilization of resources which are already available. Of course there would be costs by way of travelling and preparation of educational materials, but those would be minimal and would easily be recouped through the subsequent tithe of the newly converted. And you would need to have larger offices and additional staff to oversee such a significant operation. I personally think it's a well-founded idea and if I were Devi, I would give it my full support. It really is too bad that the Devi's health is deteriorating so rapidly. She is waiting for the end now and doesn't wish to make any long term decisions that may be unwelcomed by her replacement."

Paayal positioned her palms together, extended her fingers and raised them to her lips.

"It's funny you should mention that. As you know, I've been struggling to decide upon whom I should support for Devi come the election. I fear that time is growing very near and I must commit myself if I wish to assist in guaranteeing a successful bid for the person I choose as best suited to receive the reins of the stewardship of the Belief. Of late, I have been much impressed by your organizational abilities and the ease with which you are able to work with all manner of personalities. After much soul searching, I find myself convinced that person should be you Aabha, and I want you to know now that I will do everything in my power to see you elevated to that office when the time comes."

* * * * *

It was Brother Sebastian who picked up on a flash of reflected light glinting off the halftrack's windshield.

He centered his gaze on the vehicle and watched as it progressed rapidly toward the bottom of the mountain and although he was unsure exactly what it was he was looking at, it was clear to him that it was moving very quickly and kicking up a great cloud of snow and muck behind it as it moved.

He reigned in his horse and pointed downward. Gabriel turned his head in the direction Sebastian had indicated and pulled up his horse as he first registered and then strained to see what was causing the shifting flashes of reflected light.

Venus, who had taken the lead down the seemingly never ending switchbacks, took a few seconds to realize the others had stopped behind her. When she did, she brought her bike to a stop and swivelled her head to follow their line of sight, almost immediately picking out the object on the highway below.

* * * * *

Sal, from his position up on the gun turret, was the first to spot the movement about halfway up the mountain, just above the snow line. He looked down at Jonah through the open hatch and pointed ahead.

Jonah peered out the driver's window port and picked out the three figures working their way down the mountain. Without binoculars, he couldn't identify who or what they were.

He brought the halftrack to a stop and climbed up through the hatch to stand beside Sal and then lifted his glasses and placed the binoculars against his eyes.

The little Almie next to him was using the long range glasses built into the turret and Jonah responded out loud to the message he sent him.

"You're sure it's Venus on my bike with two others on horseback? Gabriel has a bike, why would he be on a horse and who is the third person?"

Aligning his search to the direction Sal was looking, it took him only a few moments to pick out the party of three who had now stopped moving.

Once he had them pinpointed he adjusted the field glasses and answered his own questions.

"Hard to tell that's Venus with her wrapped up in the duster and all, but that's definitely an Almie up behind her; and it's my bike all right. Sure looks like Gabe on the horse directly behind her. I haven't got a clue about the other one. It looks like he's got some kind of club or stick. Do you think he's kidnapped them and has got Gabe on horseback so he can use him as a hostage to keep Venus from getting away?"

Sal shook his head slowly and raised his big eyes. The little Almie was used to Jonah's tendency to jump to conclusions, but that didn't make it any easier for him to suffer them with the patience he knew was expected from him.

"No, it seems like more like a walking stick or perhaps a staff that would be carried by a monk. I see no indication of anything untoward or threatening about this situation. The three of them appear to be quite at ease with each other."

Jonah went on, completely oblivious to Sal's comments.

"I wonder what happened to Gabe's bike. They're looking right at us. I guess they must have seen us. They've got a good vantage point from up there. Well if they are kidnapped that guy with the club is in for a big surprise: this baby will run them down in no time at all. Here, I dug out a pair of goggles for you. You'd better wear them if you're going to stay up here, things are gonna get a little hairy by the looks of the grade on that road ahead."

Sal let out a deep sigh of resignation and accepted the eye protectors without further comment.

* * * * *

Sebastian watched carefully as the vehicle, which had stopped momentarily, began to move toward them again. Obviously whoever it was had spotted them and in a matter of a few seconds had begun moving very rapidly toward the bottom of the mountain.

He turned to Venus and Gabriel.

"Any idea who or what it is? I can't make it out very well, it's too far away."

Both Gabe and Venus shook their heads and Sebastian nodded.

"Well they wouldn't have stopped unless they saw us and now that they have they sure seem to be eager to meet us. At the speed that thing's moving there's no way we can outrun it. I'm getting bad vibes about this. There is no cover here, let's move on down the road a little further and see if we can find a good spot for us to set up some kind of defensive position."

CHAPTER SEVEN

- Reunion -

When Enoch and Persephone asked to consult him, Adon had suggested they join him and Gaia for lunch. The minute they arrived he was acutely aware of their shared anxiety. It was so heavy it shrouded them like a dark cloud.

After exchanging pleasantries, and as he led them to the common dining room at the rear of their apartments where Gaia was supervising their Almies, who had just finished setting the table for four, he reached out mentally and passed to them a flood of warmth, strength and support. The flow of tranquility calmed them, but it wasn't enough to completely eradicate the level of apprehension filling them and the moment they entered the eating area Gaia picked up on what remained of it.

Her gaze met Adon's and she could see the concern reflected in his eyes.

Gaia's eyes fluttered gently as she in turn reached out to them. The second burst of support swept over them and Gaia immediate sensed the partial rebalancing of their mental state.

As their concern faded, the young Atlantians smiled broadly across to her.

It was Enoch who spoke.

"Thank you Uncle Adon, Aunt Gaia, I think we both needed that."

* * * * *

Sebastian selected the top pivot point of the next switchback in the roadway as offering at least some protection. At that point in the highway a small grouping of trees stood along the outside of the hairpin curve. It provided at least some cover in an otherwise barren and snow-swept landscape. They quickly got the bike out of sight at the rear of the tiny grove of stunted pine and secured the horses to individual tree trunks and then Sebastian led the others back to the edge of the roadway.

"Whatever it is, it will have to slow down to take the sharp curve here. If we stay out of sight behind these trees until it starts into the corner, we might have a chance of surprising them from the rear. Venus, you stay hidden behind the foliage with Duanna and let Gabe and I deal with them."

They got into position and within a few minutes the clatter of the halftrack's racing treads filled their ears. It wasn't a sound any of them had heard before and it filled all three with a distinct sense of unease.

Gabriel drew his Gladius as Sebastian pressed the recessed switch at the base of his staff to release the blade.

Peering through the branches, they could see clearly down the roadway to the lower hairpin turn from their position. They sucked in deep breaths as the clanking machine came into view, sliding through the bend and then picking up speed as it climbed determinedly toward them.

The infernal sound built as the vehicle accelerated and a rooster-tail of gravel mud and snow shot out of the back end.

When it was halfway up the slope Sebastian spotted the figure standing in the gun turret and tapped Gabriel on the shoulder as he spoke into his ear.

"At least it's only the one vehicle and I can only see a single figure; can you make out what it is?"

Gabriel strained his eyes and tried to focus on the lurching shape that was swaying wildly and the small occupant seemed to be hanging on for all he or she was worth. As the strange vehicle slewed from side to side, the front wheels threw up a steady stream of mud and slush sending it cascading over and onto the floundering passenger.

He could make out huge eyes but little else and turned his head slightly as he answered the monk.

"I have no idea what it is or how large it is from here but the thing in it has the biggest eyes I've ever seen."

Sebastian dipped his head in agreement.

"Ya and its whole body is a weird dirty brown colour. As soon as the machine starts into the corner we'll spring out behind it and see if we can jump up on the back; sound good to you?"

Gabriel was dubious, but having no better suggestion simply nodded and planted his feet firmly.

* * * * *

The polite thing to do would be to wait until they had finished eating and Enoch and Persephone had every intention of doing that.

It was Adon who, after watching them push food around for an agonizing several minutes, rested his fork on his plate and smiled at them.

"Whatever it is you have to tell us must be very important, perhaps we should discuss it while we eat."

Enoch was embarrassed but obviously relieved.

"I'm sorry Uncle Adon, but you're right. I don't know about Persephone, but I'll have no appetite until I've said what must be said."

Persephone flushed slightly and nodded her head in agreement.

Gaia laid her utensils down and raised her napkin to her mouth.

"We are family here. We have no need to be constricted by custom. Please share your burden with us."

* * * * *

Although he had to continually wipe muck from the surface of his goggles, Sal, by using the scope in the gun turret had been able to follow the party's progress down to the trees and had accordingly informed Jonah the three had entered the small grove and not left it.

As they approached the crest of the switchback, Jonah slowed the halftrack and brought it to a stop about twenty feet from the small grouping of trees.

Sal, covered in a good layering of sludge and debris which had

been thrown up by the wildly twisting front tires as the machine weaved its way up the grade pulled his goggles off to reveal two circular patches of clean white skin starkly contrasting an otherwise dirty brown exterior and hung them on the gun as he shifted to the side of the turret to give Jonah room to open the hatch and climb out the top of the cab.

The instant Jonah's head popped up over the top of the turret, Gabriel and Venus exclaimed in unison.

"Jonah!"

At the sound of his name, Jonah jumped down onto a track and then dropped to the ground. Venus rushed over to him and they hugged warmly.

When they parted he smiled.

"Well how is the big adventure going, little sister, and what happened to Gabe's bike?"

Sebastian released the blade on his staff and he and Gabriel moved out into the open. Jonah looked over at them, coolly assessing them as Venus spoke.

"It's really good to see you! I guess Mom and Dad sent you to bring me back?"

Jonah's features softened and he lowered his voice as he shifted his attention back to his sister, turning his back on the others.

"Not really, that was my idea but Dad kyboshed it! I'm supposed to make sure that you're OK, that's all. So where are you going and why is Gabriel on a horse and how does the good brother fit into the picture?"

Venus glanced back toward the two figures on the road near the trees before answering.

"Gabe has to get to Jericho before he turns twenty. We were attacked by Bluefaces and they smashed Gabe's bike so we had to use horses, and that's Brother Sebastian, our travelling companion and the most unusual man of the cloth I've ever met, but good people for sure. Why?"

Jonah tilted his head toward the halftrack.

"Because in order to travel fast; and not having my bike courtesy of my dear sister ...."

He managed an expression of mock anger then continued.

"...I needed a form of transport that was rugged and fast. So I borrowed one from the vehicle storage facility. It isn't something anyone on the planet has ever seen before and for obvious reasons I really don't want anyone who I can't trust to see it. Both Marduke and Dad would have an absolute shit-fit if they knew what I'd done."

Venus bit her lip but couldn't stop the sly smirk from forming on her lips.

"So now both of us have borrowed a vehicle we shouldn't have."

Jonah laughed.

"Ya, except you've already been forgiven but if word about the one I borrowed gets out, I don't think I'll get off as easily."

Jonah turned and nodded toward the others.

"How about it, can I trust those two?"

Venus turned to follow his gaze. Knowing full well that her brother had taken a great risk in removing a vehicle from the Atlantian garage without authorization, she took the time to properly assess his question before answering.

"You know Gabe; he would never betray a confidence. Brother Sebastian is kind of a quandary; he isn't your average monk for sure, but I believe him to be a wise man and one who knows how to keep a secret and in fact a man who carries many wherever he goes."

Jonah let his eyes meet and hold hers.

"So you think they can be trusted, right?"

Venus nodded and smiled.

"Yes, I do."

"OK. Sis, your judgement is good enough for me."

Jonah raised his eyes and arm in arm he and Venus began to walk toward Gabriel and the monk.

Brother Sebastian relaxed his stance and smiled as they approached. Gabriel was apprehensive as he vainly struggled to get a reading of how the Atlantian was feeling from the blank expression on Jonah's face.

Jonah understood why the young Neanderthal was nervous about how his arrival on the scene was going to play out. The big brother part of the scenario caused him to let the young Neanderthal suffer till the last second.

He walked up to Gabriel and planted his feet firmly and slightly apart and then placed his hands on his hips as he looked up and stared directly into Gabe's anxious eyes.

"So Gabe, it looks like you're down one bike. I hope the trip's been otherwise uneventful, in every way."

His eyes pointedly flicked over at Venus and then back to lock with Gabe's again.

Gabriel got the message and frantically shook his head.

"Nothing happened...I mean, it's been cool, well, not nothing happened, stuff happened; but not the kind of stuff you mean...if that's what you're asking..."

Jonah knew Gabe was not a good liar. He was satisfied his question had been both understood and answered.

"Yes that was what I was asking. Now that's out of the way, it seems like we have a lot of catching up to do. For starters, can someone tell me what the crap a Blueface is?"

Gabriel felt the tension leave his body and Venus laughed and slipped her arm through Jonah's.

"It really is good to see you, big brother."

* * * * *

When Aabha got back to her office she went directly across to the doorway leading to the Devi's study and knocked.

The doorway was opened by a brother belonging to her Personal Protection Unit who stood aside for her to enter.

The Devi was seated behind her ornate desk reading a document and she looked up as Aabha entered the room.

"There you are child. I'm afraid I'm not feeling well enough to review the results of the meeting just now. I have some documents I must read and then I think I will lie down. Perhaps we could go over things this afternoon once I've rested."

Aabha could see that her aunt was pale and very weak. She nodded her agreement.

"Of course, in the meantime I'll go over my notes and isolate any areas which require your direct attention."

Mitra VII raised her shaking right hands with some effort and pointed to a large envelope on the corner of her desk.

"That package is for you Aabha. It is to be opened in the event of my death."

Aabha started to speak as she picked up the thick envelope which had been sealed at the flap in red wax and reflected the imprint of the Devi's official signet ring, but Mitra VII cut her off with a shake of her head.

"Offer no false encouragement Aabha, my time is very near and we both know it."

Her eyes welling up with tears, Aabha nodded and returned to the doorway which the brother held open.

She turned to look back at her aunt briefly then continued on into her office and heard the door close softly behind her.

CHAPTER EIGHT

- Plots Thicken -

The words poured out of Enoch in a flood.

When he was finished speaking he paused for a quick breath and then slumped down into his chair, drained but glad to have it done.

Both Adon and Gaia had remained silent while the young pair spoke. Each was deeply affected by what they'd been told.

Adon was finding is very difficult to believe but he did not doubt that it was true. He knew it was paramount to take immediate action, but his first thought was to consider what this visit had cost both Enoch and Persephone.

He looked from one to the other.

"It took great courage for the two of you to come to us with this. You are outstanding examples of Atlantian youth."

Gaia fortified his comment.

"You have done what had to be done. It was the right thing to do, and now you are to worry about it no further. This problem is no longer your problem, but is shared by all around this table."

* * * * *

Old Harry had no warning.

They had parked their truck out of sight behind a rock outcrop south of the way station and they were waiting for him inside the barn.

Six of them - all in full SS uniform.

He didn't have a chance and they took him the instant he opened the barn door to lead his mount inside.

* * * * *

Gabriel's father was lying on his back, naked and spread-eagled on the bone chillingly cold surface of a metal table in one of the small examination rooms within the scientific research facility of the military compound.

His hands and feet had been shackled to hold him firmly in place. A maze of cables snaked down from the shaved patches dispersed over the surface of his skin where electrodes had been affixed to his twitching body. These were busily ferrying information to a computer.

On the far side of the small room a flickering monitor whirred softly as it recorded the data being drained from him.

This session was the second he'd been forced to endure since he'd been transported to the Rector's compound.

A single, and frowning, white-smocked Human scientist attentively monitored the printout pumping out the top of the printer and two red-shirted Neanderthals, obviously weighed down by the boredom of their assignment, observed lethargically from chairs placed on either side of the small doorway that led into the white, brightly lit, but windowless room.

* * * * *

Juno managed to find some edible berries and after making a meal of them she collected as many as she could find and wrapped them in the bright red scarf she'd been wearing around her neck.

She was feeling much better and although she was still consciously blocking out the intensity of what had happened at the abandoned mining town, her mind was beginning to work toward normal function.

Somewhat rested, blissfully clean and her hunger sated for the moment, she began to work her way down the path between the hot springs and back toward the highway.

* * * * *

Bellum received the message from Adon's Almie and immediately passed it on to his master.

Marduke, who had been in the process of pouring himself a drink, set the half-filled glass down and closed his eyes tightly. He stood immobile for a few seconds and then provided Bellum with his reply.

"What a wonderful surprise, I look forward to your arrival."

Bellum forwarded the response and carefully watched his master, who seemed to be frozen in position. After a couple of minutes, Bellum probed gently and Marduke opened his eyes and let out a heartfelt sigh.

"Well Bellum, it seems I was right to bring my plans forward. Transport us to the Rector's compound immediately."

* * * * *

Aabha was sitting at her desk refining her notes when there was a soft knock. She stood, crossed to the door and opened it.

Daka greeted her with a smile.

"Aabha dear, may I have a quick word?"

Aabha returned her smile and stepped aside to welcome the Mitra-Varuna in.

"Yes Daka, of course."

I won't keep you; I know you are busy. I simply wanted to ask you one question."

Aabha closed the door and turned to give Daka her full attention.

Daka, as she was wont, went right to the point.

"If as I suspect, Paayal offered you her support this morning, whom, would you as Devi, appoint to the office of Diplomacy?"

Aabha's expression never changed.

"Why, you, Daka. No one is your equal in that chair."

Daka nodded and bent to one knee.

Aabha struggled to stifle her surprise and then awkwardly extended her right hands and Daka leaned forward to kiss her ring.

* * * * *

They were gathered together at the rear of the halftrack.

With the help of the two Almies, Gabriel, Brother Sebastian and Jonah manhandled Jonah's bike up into the open back of the vehicle and once they had it in position, Jonah left Sal in charge of tying the machine down and turned to face the others.

"I'm sorry, little sister. I can understand why you would want to head directly to the roadhouse, and Solar knows Sal could certainly use a scrubbing, but I have a bit of a problem with that. Firstly, it would not be a good idea to arrive there in the halftrack and secondly I can't leave it unattended."

He looked directly at Gabe.

"You and Sebastian have to take the two horses to the next roadhouse and drop them off. Venus and I will circumvent the roadhouse by going off-road and overland and then wait for you on the highway just past it. After that's out of the way you have to make it to your grandmother's place within three days, is that right?"

Gabriel nodded his agreement and Jonah continued.

"Well I've had a look at the map and based on the speed this thing can do and driving only at night to lessen the risk of anyone seeing the vehicle we should be able to get there in two days easy. I think we should just go for it and save the bathing for after we get there."

Venus was not pleased with the idea. She wanted a proper bath and a proper bed.

"If it will only take two days and we have three, why can't we stop for just one night at a roadhouse? The others require far more sleep than you and I you know."

Jonah shrugged.

"We can sleep during the daylight hours. What if we have a breakdown or some other emergency? How would you feel if we got Gabe there late?"

Sebastian thought for a second and turned to face Gabriel.

"Gabe, could I have a look at that map of yours for a second please. I seem to remember there were some hot springs surrounded by a heavy growth of evergreens not too far past the next roadhouse. Once we've got the roadhouse out of the way, stopping there for the rest of the day might be a compromise that would satisfy everyone. That is if Jonah is prepared to risk driving that short distance in daylight. If Venus will settle for a bath in the springs, we could safely spend the remainder of the day there and then continue our journey after nightfall."

* * * * *

They forced Harry to undress and hung him from one of the barn ceiling beams with ropes tied to his wrists.

A burly SS man stood stripped to the waist and was methodically flaying the skin and strips of flesh off the old mans back as the

Lieutenant in charge repeatedly demanded information on where Gabe was headed and who his traveling companions were.

Harry, who had little information to give and no intention of revealing what he did know was also aware that they knew Gabe had been at the way station because of the bike sitting in the barn; was doing his best to live with the excruciating pain and provide them with no additional help in locating the young Neanderthal and his travelling partners.

In excruciating pain, he slipped in and out of consciousness, revived each time with dumps of cold snow, and in time he died without providing the men with anything more than a confirmation that Gabe had stopped briefly at the small station.

The six SS men did not bother to cut the old man's bloodied old carcass down or to take the time to release the horses from their stalls.

They simply set fire to both the barn and cabin and then piled into their truck and went on up toward the pass to continue their pursuit.

* * * * *

The two redshirts returned Hollis to the small cell down the hall from the white room where he had been examined and as they were placing him inside he managed to whisper the words.

"A confessor, please bring me a confessor."

The Belief was the most powerful religion in the world and like most Neanderthals, his guards were deeply spiritual. Although they had been strongly warned about the care of this man, neither of them found this request unreasonable in the circumstances.

They looked at each other and the taller responded.

"I'll see if I can get the chaplain to come."

* * * * *

It took Juno a half an hour to find a secure spot from which she could safely watch the roadway without being spotted.

This was the main highway to Jericho and although they were determined by the weather it had scheduled coach runs.

She had some emergency flake in packets sewn into her blouse. It wasn't much, but it would be enough.

Nestled in a small grouping of trees just off the road, she settled down to await whatever form of transportation came into view.

She would have to be very careful whom she chose to approach of course, but she was confident that, in time, someone trustworthy would pass and she would ask for and if necessary, pay for a ride.

* * * * *

Eisen was in his office.

The white-smocked scientist who had been working on Gabriel's father earlier was standing uneasily in front of the Rector's huge desk.

"We call it genetic engineering. We had our first success with it when we engineered a malevolent gene transfer for use on Trolls. To date we've released over one hundred of them and they are causing terror wherever they go. Using the same process, we're working on building up a large array of engineered genetic improvements applicable to the standard genetic makeup for all races and animals on Olympos. Simply by switching genes, substituting the ones in place for those we select, we hope to create a super being. This fellow you brought in is fighting us at every turn. It may be that we will have to open the brain and physically have a look for what we are seeking."

There was a sharp knock at the door and the Colonel stuck his head in.

"Sorry to interrupt my Rector, but I thought you should know.
Marduke has just arrived in the compound and is on his way here."
Eisen nodded and turned to the scientist.

"Do what you have to do, but for Solar's sake, do not kill him and cut open his brain and then have the audacity to come and tell me you failed. If you do, I promise you that I'll see to it that you share his fate. Now get out and don't come back until you've been successful."

CHAPTER NINE

- *Prisoners* -

The Colonel ushered Marduke into the massive room the instant the scientist left it.

Marduke waited until the door was closed behind him before he strode down the highly polished floor to Eisen's desk and spoke.

"I need a few reliable men and one officer to accompany me back to my villa. I want them to take charge of two prisoners and hold them securely here temporarily. As soon as that's been accomplished we need to complete my portion of our bargain. As previously discussed, five hundred men and a few officers will suffice, but it must be done immediately you've secured the prisoners. Can you do it?"

Eisen didn't hesitate.

"Yes, I've already had Colonel von Jaeger organize the force and I will advise him of your need immediately. They'll not be fully trained, but close to it and beggars can't be choosers. I'm sure they'll perform well enough to get the job done."

Marduke nodded and turned to leave, then paused.

"Oh and the prisoners will each have an Almie which must be separated from them and also secured and prevented from communicating. I will leave instructions as to how that may be accomplished"

Eisen looked up in surprise.

"Almies, they are Atlantian then, these prisoners?"

Marduke nodded again.

"Yes, do you have a problem with that?"

The Rector took a second to consider the question and then shook his head.

"No, I suppose not, not if you don't have a problem with it."

* * * * *

After months of failing health, Mitra VII passed away peacefully in her own bed while taking her afternoon nap. She was eighty-two years old.

One half hour later The Holy See officially confirmed the death to those of the Belief who were present in the huge palace square. Those in attendance bowed their heads in respect.

The grieving public across the planet were then informed that the Devi had been in strongly declining health for some time and had refused to enter private hospital facilities, choosing instead to remain in her own apartments where she was tended by her personal doctors and the medical staff of the Holy See.

The arrangement for a conclave of the College of the Mitra-Varuna for the election of a new Devi was immediately initiated.

* * * * *

Jonah was behind the wheel of the halftrack and Venus was riding in the passenger seat beside him.

Sal and Duanna shared the cramped space behind them in the cab and Sebastian and Gabriel were riding up top on the lightly padded fold out seats behind the gun in the turret.

A south-easterly wind had been blowing gently for over an hour and the sky was almost cloudless, allowing the weak winter light, aided by the drop in altitude, to lift the temperature a few degrees above the freezing line.

Jonah had the machine mastered and was making good time. The tracks were tearing up the roadway and a steady stream of debris spewed out from the rear of halftrack as they raced along.

The sound of the churning metal bands was almost deafening for Gabriel and Sebastian riding up top, loud enough that they were unable to carry on a conversation.

* * * * *

Juno heard the machine approaching.

The road curved just before the trail that led to the hot springs and she stuck her head out from behind the tree she had been sitting against and watched as it slid around the bend and headed toward her.

She shifted slightly, minimizing her exposure to the roadway, as she watched the halftrack approach.

She did a double take as it grew closer. She had never seen anything like it before.

Although it was certainly intriguing, its general military appearance frightened her and she did not see it as a good prospect for a ride.

As the machine grew closer she picked out the two figures up top and was studying them carefully when the vehicle approached the side road leading to the hot springs and began to slow.

She watched as Sebastian banged on the top of the hatch cover with his staff. The halftrack was no more than forty feet from her as it pulled up and stopped at the turnoff.

Juno's mouth dropped open as the monk bent and opened the cover and spoke to those inside.

She couldn't believe her eyes. Standing up behind the bending brother was a big Neanderthal who looked an awful lot like Gabe.

A wave of relief flowed through her.

Could it really be him?

Sebastian stood again, blocking her view, as the front wheels of the vehicle turned onto the trail leading to the springs and the machine began to move its way down the path, quickly pulling away from her and disappearing into the trees.

* * * * *

Hollis Corvin was awakened by the sound of jingling keys.

He stirred on the thin mattress of the rough cot in his small make-shift cell and closed his eyes against the glare as the single naked overhead light bulb flared into brightness.

Squinting against the dazzle, he raised his upper body and swung his manacled legs off the bed and turned his head to face the door as it opened.

As the rotund female Ogre entered the room he instantly recognized the dark blue cassock broadly trimmed in scarlet and adorned with the ornate chain of woven gold suspending the jewel-encrusted svastika with four dots denoting a Mitra-Varuna of the Belief.

It was with a certain satisfaction, and a sense of relief that Hollis also noted that he had been previously introduced to this particular Ogre.

Although it had been many years before, he picked up on the brief flash of recognition in the old Ogre's eyes, and then the door was closed and locked behind them.

* * * * *

Adon, Gaia and their Almies were surrounded by Redshirts armed with automatic weapons the instant they finished transporting to the patio at the rear of Marduke's Jericho villa.

Supervised by a black-uniformed SS Lieutenant, four of the men immediately covered their little grey robots' large heads with metallic shrouds. These provided them eye holes but prevented them from communicating.

The remainder placed the two Atlantians into restraints.

Adon looked toward the villa and could see Marduke standing behind one of the large windows watching them.

Their eyes met and he shook his head sadly from side to side in a reflection of his dismay and sorrow.

Marduke found it difficult to meet his old friend's gaze.

Instead he turned his back to them and walked away.

* * * * *

Aabha stood staring blankly out the open window of her small room.

She wiped away the last of her tears and closed her eyes as she filled her lungs with the flower-scented air and held the freshness briefly before releasing it and then, with renewed determination she turned and crossed to her desk.

She lifted the big envelope, weighing it. It felt much heavier to her now than it had when she'd originally picked it up from the corner of Mitra VII's desk.

She studied it for several minutes while she willed her sense of loss into her subconscious and then she sat and reached for her letter opener and used it to break the glob of red sealing wax that contained the impression of the late Devi's personal signet ring on the flap.

* * * * *

In much the same way as Juno had done earlier, Jonah continued slowly down the narrow pathway as it led between groups of steaming pools.

He was looking to find the least public grouping and he continued to move until they had reached the end of the trail and the final assemblage of hot springs which was surrounded by a tall, thick stand of evergreens.

* * * * *

Juno moved to the edge of the roadway and looked both ways carefully before she crossed to the other side and then hurried along the pathway leading to the hot springs.

She could no longer see the machine but concentrated on the sound of the clanking tracks ahead and did her best to pace herself to its steady progress.

The brief sighting earlier was still fresh in her mind, and although she was still half convinced that the Neanderthal in the back of the vehicle could have been Gabriel, she was far from certain.

* * * * *

Hollis and the Mitra-Varuna stared at each other in silence as the sound of rattling keys marked the guard's progress as he walked away down the hallway.

Without speaking, Hollis raised his cuffed hands to his shirt and opened the top three buttons to reveal the ring that hung around his neck from a simple leather cord.

He held it out and the Mitra-Varuna immediately dropped to one knee and bent forward to kiss the crest topping the thick golden circle.

Hollis squeezed the two sides firmly and the top of the ring which held the raised svastika and four points sprung open to reveal a perfect replica of the Devi Mitra VII's personal crest.

It denoted him as holding the Belief rank of Verendus and as a member of the select 'Holy Order of the Golden Ring'. This was the Devi order of chivalry that was only presented to those who had provided outstanding service to the Belief.

An appointment to the order was life-long. It meant that at all times the bearer stood in the Devi's stead, with all the powers of the Devi herself and that the holder had been absolved of all sin and could commit no future sin within the eyes of the Belief. The order was so exclusive that its membership was never allowed to exceed that which could be counted on the twenty digits comprising a Devi's hands

* * * * *.

After sitting quietly in prayer for some time, Aabha neatly emptied the contents of the envelope out onto the scarred surface of her small desk and set the envelope aside.

Lifting the top sheet from the considerable pile of documents she felt her eyes begin to mist again as she recognized the wavering hand of her aunt's script. Without reading, she set the sheet down beside the others and slowly fanned the remainder of the papers.

It was all written in her own hand. Likely no one else had seen or even been aware of the contents of the envelope.

For the love of Solar, when had she found the time and where had she found the strength?

She laid them down and poured a cup of tea to provide her with a little time to clear her vision, and then she picked up that top page and began to read.

* * * * *

Back on Atlantis, Marduke, accompanied by Bellum, had gone straight to Adon's apartments and accessed the computer terminal.

He went directly to the Advisory Council manpower list and sent out a request for an emergency meeting of the council to be held an hour later in the conference room.

He did so using an 'Immediate Priority' designation and sent it under Adon's name, knowing full well that the message would be automatically transmitted instantaneously to all members of the team by way of their Almies.

CHAPTER TEN

- *Betrayal* -

At Venus's request, Duanna was working on getting a fire lit in preparation for a hot meal.

In view of gathering clouds and the threat of rain, Sal was in the midst of setting up a large square of canvass over the top of the halftrack with the intention of covering the area between the vehicle and the biggest of the pools in that particular grouping which consisted of five bubbling hot springs surrounded by a forest of large evergreens and enclosed by a thick layer of underbrush.

After voicing her intention to bathe, Venus had excused herself to make use of the privacy offered by the pool Juno had used earlier. It, being sheltered from the rest of the grouping by an extra heavy layer of undergrowth, seemed much more attractive under the circumstances...

She placed her change of clothes down on a rock and then stripped quickly and slipped into the deliciously naturally heated water.

Jonah was up in the back of the halftrack adjusting the straps holding his bike in place and Sebastian was sorting out the provisions stored in the back part of the cab of the vehicle, selecting the victuals that would make up their meal.

Gabriel sat lounging in the driver's seat of the machine, flipping through the manual as the monk rummaged about in the stash of supplies behind him.

* * * * *

Juno heard the vehicle come to a stop.

She slowed her pace and carefully worked her way up to the trees and slipped into the dense brush as she made her way toward the small grouping of pools she'd used earlier.

The layout of the site was still clear in her mind and she quietly made her way to the specific pool she had bathed in several hours before.

She arrived in time to observe a nude Venus entering the enveloping warmth of the bubbling spring fed tarn.

Her eyes grew round as saucers and she covered her mouth to stifle a surprised exclamation.

My Solar, it was a young female Atlantian! What a strange band those traveling in the bizarre vehicle were turning out to be.

A monk, an Atlantian, and a Neanderthal that just possibly might be Gabriel!

She couldn't believe her eyes.

She'd rarely seen an Atlantian, never a female and certainly never a naked one.

Unclothed they were quite 'Human' looking, albeit taller and not quite as well rounded, although this one was definitely beautiful.

She watched in utter fascination for a few seconds, waiting for the beating of her heart to settle, and then she quietly worked her way deeper into the covering foliage and toward the clearing located at the far side of the remaining pools in the grouping.

* * * * *

Hollis watched the over-weight Mitra-Varuna carefully as she struggled to her feet and stood looking down at him.

He rolled what he could recall about the woman around in his head and then he added to that information the impression he'd received as she'd paid homage to his title and position.

This Ogre was, after all, the Chaplain of the Rector's troops and as such, it was in Hollis's interest to assess her sense of duty.

Was it foremost for the Belief, or had it been affected by her current placement?

The Ogre, as though reading his thoughts, smiled and shook her head.

"Please do not question my loyalty to the Belief, Brother.

Your mistress is also mine. I was chosen very carefully for the posting I hold and my instructions at the time were from Her Holiness and made very clear. I may be the Nasi Party's military Chaplain, but I act in the interest of her holiness Mitra VII and no other. Your order and your ring make you her representative wherever you travel. Do not doubt that you have my full allegiance.

How may I be of assistance?"

* * * * *

Aabha drew out a fresh pad from the single drawer of her small desk and placed it, with a freshly sharpened pencil, to the right of the stack of documents.

She then poured herself a fresh cup of tea, took a sip and began to read the top page.

Aabha,

As you read this, I know you will be mourning my passing and I ask you to put that aside, at least temporarily and, as quickly as you can. I know the great affection I had for you was sincerely returned but ask that you consider two things.

Firstly, I've had a good long life and honestly have few, if any, regrets. I have lived in a great deal of pain for some time and truthfully welcome my journey from this world to the next.

Please accept my passing as a blessing, as I do, and remember fondly the time we had together, but do not despair over my death.

Secondly, and for both our sakes more importantly, understand that as cold as it must sound to you now, you have no time to waste on grieving, but must immediately harness all your strength to meet the looming challenge.

I want you to honour and make good use of the information contained in this envelope, for I have taken considerable time and effort to provide it for you and I am sure there is material within that will help pave your way to your successful campaign to replace me and help you to steer a clear course to the general benefit of the Belief and all it stands for.

Read it all now. Do not put it off.

Gird your loins my girl and make me proud. Never doubt that I will be looking down with great and attentive interest and wishing you every success.

Love,

Mitra VII

* * * * *

Marduke, trailed by Bellum, entered the vehicle storage area on Atlantis and walked directly to the small office.

The Atlantian engineer responsible for the vehicle and equipment storage area and transporter room was seated at a small desk.

His son was standing beside him at the counter checking some papers.

Their Almies were standing behind them at rest against the wall.

The two Atlantians looked up as he approached.

Marduke exchanged greetings with them and the engineer smiled. "Here for the meeting early I see."

Marduke nodded.

"Yes, Adon asked me to drop down to see you. He wondered if you and your son would be good enough to go down to the conference room and arrange for light refreshments in preparation for the arrival of the others."

It was an unusual request and the Engineering Advisor stood and traded a quizzical look with his son, who was also getting to his feet before he responded.

"Certainly, do you know what it's all about; I can't ever remember an emergency meeting being called before?"

Marduke shook his head.

"No, Adon didn't say."

* * * * *

Completely refreshed, Venus towelled herself dry and slipped into the clean clothes, then piled her long hair on top of her head and wrapped it in the towel.

After clipping the absorbent material firmly into place, she picked up her soiled clothing and started back to join the others.

As she was entering the small clearing where the halftrack was parked Gabriel emerged from the open hatch at the top of the machine and began to stack up the food selected for their meal on the floor of the gun turret as Sebastian handed it up to him.

All of them, involved in their own thoughts, were silently going about their business and it was with some alarm that they reacted to the shrill cry from the undergrowth just behind Venus.

"Yes!!!"

Brother Sebastian poked his head through the hatch and reached for his staff.

Gabriel dropped several containers of food to the floor as he lurched upright and Jonah's right hand clamped firmly on the stock of the machine pistol resting beside him on the back of the vehicle.

Venus dropped her soiled clothing in shock and spun around.

They all looked toward the source of the noise and watched in amazement as Juno broke free of the underbrush and into the clearing behind Venus.

Jonah's eyes widened. A man did not easily forget a woman so beautifully put together. A glance at the dagger tucked behind her belt confirmed his initial reaction.

It was the stunning young gypsy girl from the wagon train.

He opened his mouth to speak and then thought better of it.

It would not be wise to tie himself to the shooting scene on the highway.

There was a touch of hysteria in Juno's voice as she exclaimed.

"I thought it was you Gabe, and boy, am I ever glad to see you!"

Taken completely by surprise, Gabriel took a second to respond.

The best he could do was a shocked.

"Juno?"

* * * * *

The second the engineer and his son left the chamber Marduke and Bellum went to the doorway and Marduke watched as his Almie removed the cap on the locking mechanism.

The little grey robot went about reprogramming it and then they turned and hurried toward the back behind the aisles of stacked and crated equipment.

Within a few moments they were making their way up to the transporter room control tower.

Marduke watched as Bellum opened the software component and entered the co-ordinates they'd agreed upon, then the Almie looked up at his master questioningly and after a quick prayer that all was ready at the Rector's compound, Marduke nodded instructing Bellum to hit the switch.

The huge transport chamber below him went completely black. There was a wisp of brightening light floating in the air above the floor of the transporter platform before the scene before him reached completion.

Suddenly it was filled with armed redshirted troops standing in formation facing three black uniformed SS officers.

Marduke released the breath he had been holding and quickly made his way down to the chamber below where he immediately addressed the SS Colonel in charge who he recognized at the Rector's own aid, Von Jaeger.

Colonel, keep your men here until I return. I will be less than an hour."

* * * * *

Aabha removed her glasses and wiped her eyes before replacing them.

She took up the initial page from the stack of documents and turned it upside down onto the desk beside the pile, then began to read the next.

It consisted of a list of the remaining documents.

Different writing instruments both pencil and quill and ink had been used on the paper making it obvious to Aabha that it had been an ongoing endeavour over a long period of time.

The first item listed was 'Things you need to know now'.

As she read down the lines the topics varied and the final sentence indicated that the majority of the remaining documents consisted of monthly journals covering the important events that had occurred during Mitra VII's term as Devi.

Some of the topics catalogued instantly piqued her curiosity and it was with some hesitation that she didn't try to seek these out first and instead followed her aunt's direction by adding the index page upside down onto the first page to the left of the stack.

She turned her attention to 'Things you need to know now'.

CHAPTER ELEVEN

- *Coup* -

Marduke stood beside Bellum just inside the doorway leading into the circular conference room.

He held a complete list of the names of the members of the advisory council team in his hand and was checking them off as they took their seats.

It was with some relief that he noted the only members not in attendance, besides Adon and Gaia, were Venus and Jonah. He asked Bellum to attempt to contact the young Atlantian's Almies but the little robot had no success and as a result Marduke was satisfied that they must be somewhere on Olympos and out of communication range.

A smile formed on his face as he left the room with Bellum in tow. Once outside he nodded to the Almie, who turned to the locking mechanism, removed the cover and reprogrammed it.

It was almost over and so far it had gone down as smoothly as Neanderthal honeyed tea.

With a little tidying up, Atlantis was his.

He was humming softly to himself as he returned to the equipment storage area and gave Von Jaeger the new entry code to the conference room and relayed his instructions.

He and Bellum then led the force through empty hallways and back to the doorway leading to the conference room where Marduke took time to ensure Von Jaeger understood what had to be done, then arranged to meet him and his prisoners back in the transporter room a half hour later.

* * * * *

Gabriel was somewhat embarrassed by the fact that Juno was clinging to him like a second skin.

She couldn't seem to let go of his hand.

They had finished eating and were sitting around the fire while they brought Juno up to date on their trip to Jericho and Juno, in turn, breathlessly related the horror of the Troll attack on the wagon train the night before.

When she'd finished, Jonah stood and stretched.

"Well, I for one will be glad when we get Gabe to Jericho and Venus and I can get back to civilization and our normal lives."

Sebastian grunted and peered across the fire at him.

"Normal rests in the eyes of the beholder my son, and is as static as the wayward wind."

Jonah scowled at the monk.

"Ya, whatever, it's going to be dark soon, I suggest we guys take advantage of the hot springs to get cleaned up and then we'd better pack up and hit the road."

* * * * *

Aabha made several notes on her pad as she read through the six pages of hand written material.

Finished, she picked them up and squared them before turned them upside down to add to the growing pile beside the remaining unread stack.

Dusk had settled over the bay and she got up and crossed to the window. She left it open for fresh air but pulled the curtain closed and lit a candle before returning to her desk to begin reviewing what she had written.

Having been the Devi's secretary, as well as her confidant and companion, Aabha had been aware of most things that had come before the Devi; however, the things contained in the envelope had related to other matters, meetings and incidents that she had not been privy to at the time.

Of the several points she had considered worth noting, one stood out.

It consisted of a single sentence indicating that a month previously Mitra VII had initiated an investigation, by way of a Brother of the Order of the Golden Ring, into the financial handling of certain monies from the treasury in which some question had been raised with reference to Cala, the chair of that office, in what might have been a questionable and inappropriate set of transactions.

The name of the brother involved in carrying out the investigation was not indicated but the date of the meeting between he and the Devi had been provided and she decided it might be worthwhile to select the journal for that particular month from those within the remaining documents to see if further information on the investigation could be readily retrieved.

While making her notes she had underlined the sentence boldly, circled the date and placed a star beside it and her eyes were drawn to that star now.

She began to check the journals and located the one that covered the timeframe including the particular date indicated and worked her way through it until she found the page reflecting the specific day she'd noted.

She quickly found the reference she was looking for.

There was no indication of specifics with regard to what the subject had been but there was a clear reference to an investigation initiated and to which brother of the Order of the Golden Ring it had been assigned.

Brother Eustace.

Aabha was not sure why, but she was intrigued about the situation and felt inwardly driven to pursue it.

She got up slowly and stretched hoping to lessen the pain in her lower back. It did little good, but then she was used to living with the discomfort if she sat for too long and she quickly dismissed it as she moved across the small room and opened her door.

Pulling it closed behind her, she turned to her left and moved down the hall, away from the cafeteria and washrooms toward the sleeping areas. When she reached Sister Ester's door she knocked softly.

She could hear movement inside the room and smiled with the realization that Ester was not out and busy with her duties.

She trusted Ester and would use the sister as a go between to arrange a meeting between her and Brother Eustace as soon as was practicable.

* * * * *

Marduke met the invading force and their encircled prisoners in the transporter room.

After a short exchange with the Colonel, he pushed through the outer ring of Redshirts and shouted for silence.

"Quiet, all of you; give me your attention."

The Atlantians stopped milling about and turned to face him. When they recognized him, they grew silent and he nodded with satisfaction.

"There has been a change in leadership. I have replaced Adon. Each of you now has a decision to make. Individually you will have to decide whether you can support me in a renewed vision of our mission, or not. You have some time to make up your minds. I will be interviewing you over the next few weeks to determine who will make up our new team. In the meantime, you will remain on Olympus. You'll be free to do as you wish until I speak to you. I know you have questions but please be patient, I will get to each of you in turn, in order of seniority and as quickly as I can. Demeter will act as my go-between on Olympos until I find time to see you each in turn."

Several pairs of eyes settle on Demeter and she shifted uncomfortably under their gaze but refused to be cowed.

Enoch moved to the front of the group and started toward his father but a Redshirt intervened to block him.

Concern filled his face as he looked over the uniformed Neanderthal's shoulder.

"Father what have you done?"

Marduke met his son's eyes squarely and he lowered his voice when he replied.

"You had your chance Enoch, you made your choice and now you'll have to wait with the others.

Perhaps in time you will come to see the wisdom of my vision. For both our sakes I sincerely hope so."

He turned on his heel and he and Bellum headed back up into the control tower where they promptly reversed the procedure that had brought the force to Atlantis.

That accomplished, Marduke returned to Adon's apartments and accessed the computer terminal again.

He had Bellum work his way through the system until he had successfully raised the ship's outer shield and once that had been accomplished he let out a deep sigh of satisfaction.

It was done.

The blast shield was virtually impenetrable.

He had control of the computer, meaning only he could lower it if that became necessary.

No one could transport to or from Atlantis from Olympos now, unless he sanctioned it.

* * * * *

Jonah had taken it upon himself to ensure that Sal was properly cleaned and the little Almie endured the process in great embarrassment.

As a result, it was dark by the time the three men and the little Almie had finished bathing.

While they'd been gone, Juno had fidgeted endlessly, impatient to have Gabriel back at her side. Flashes of the horror of the night before filled her mind whenever she didn't have her attention committed elsewhere. Since she had found him she only felt completely safe when she could physically touch him.

She began talking to him non-stop the instant he returned to the campsite.

Gabriel had initially sympathized with her need for support earlier, after she'd related her story about the horror of the Troll attack, and although somewhat worn down by the intensity of her need, he had to admit he was enjoying the beautiful gypsies undivided attention, no matter the reason why.

The depth of her need became even more evident to him when it came time to get back on the road.

It took him several minutes to convince her she would be safer riding inside the cab rather than outside in the open with him and Sebastian.

With the monk's assurance that Gabriel was right, she finally agreed and joined the two Almies behind Jonah and Venus in the rear of the small cab. Despite the cramped space, she settled comfortably on stacked sleeping bags between the two little robots.

The halftrack got under way with Jonah and Venus seated up front, Sebastian and Gabriel, wrapped in their dusters, riding up top and Juno perched in back between Almie bookends.

The threatening clouds had proved a short-lived phenomenon. They had quickly given way to a clear, cold night sky which allowed the three moons to cast a bright bluish light over the passing countryside.

As a result, Jonah could see clearly ahead for over a mile and once under way he kept the halftrack at top speed making the best use of the excellent condition of the roadway.

* * * * *

There was a soft rapping at her door and Aabha got up from her desk and crossed her small chamber to answer it.

A smiling Ester stood outside. She had a folded piece of paper in her hand which she handed Aabha.

"The brother awaits you."

Aabha reached out and took the slip of paper and smiled.

"Thank you Sister Ester."

Ester nodded and with a swift glance down the hallway in both directions to ensure she had been unobserved, she turned and was gone. Aabha closed the door and crossed to her desk where she opened the folded paper and read it and then she blew the candle out and left for her office.

As she crossed the courtyard to the main administration building she found herself regretting that she hadn't worn a cloak.

Silly really, it wasn't that cold, but for some reason she felt a chill.

She knew what it was of course.

It was Eustace.

She'd always been uncomfortable in the presence of the powerfully built Human brother.

It was the eyes mostly, expressionless, like those of a corpse, no matter what the circumstances.

Her aunt, the Devi, who had often used the brother for internal investigations and seemed to trust him implicitly, had always dismissed her unease as foolish, but Aabha had never been what she considered at ease around him.

CHAPTER TWELVE

- A Warning -

Hollis sat back down on the bed as the Mitra-Varuna knocked loudly on the door. A few seconds later they heard approaching footsteps and the jingle of keys. They exchanged glances briefly before the door swung open and a guard looked inside inquisitively.

The Chaplain leaned forward toward the big redshirted Neanderthal and spoke softly.

"He wishes to be confessed my son and I cannot provide for him when he is manacled. Would you remove his restraints please? You may secure the door behind us and I will re-shackle him when we have finished and then summon you."

The guard looked past her to Hollis and started to shake his head.

"We've been told to keep him in restraints at all times."

The Chaplain cut him off, raising her eyebrows questioningly and pointedly staring at the silver svastika with dots that hung from the silver chain around the fellow's neck as she spoke.

"Would you risk eternal damnation my son, for that would be the result of your refusal to allow this man to seek the forgiveness of Solar in his time of need."

The colour drained from the Neanderthal's face, at the slow but determined rate of a clogged sink.

He grunted and brushed past the Mira-Varuna, hauling out his key ring as he crossed to where Gabe's father was sitting.

* * * * *

The administration building was in darkness and Aabha had to use her master key to unlock the main doors to gain entry.

Large windows at the front of the building provided just enough moonlight to dimly illuminate the entranceway, allowing her to see enough to select a candle from the stack near the door.

She took one, lit it and held it up to light her way down the dark, shadow-filled corridor leading to her office. Here she used her keys again and slipped inside, closing the door behind her.

As it shut, the gas lamp over her desk flickered for a split second and then burst into flame filling the room with light.

Aabha snorted in surprise and felt a jolt of fear grip her.

She froze and dropped the candle.

The burning taper didn't make it to the richly carpeted floor.

A darkly clothed figure that had been standing behind the door reached out and caught it in a blur of motion then blew it out and handed it to her.

Aabha, who had raised her right hands to her heart the instant the room was illuminated moved the top arm from her chest and closed her fingers around the candle without thinking as she struggled to force herself to take a breath.

Eustace was shorter than she, but very strongly built and try as she might to ignore it, his presence intimidated her.

She could sense not a trace of sincerity in his voice as he spoke.

"I'm sorry if I frightened you Mitra-Varuna."

* * * * *

They'd brought the halftrack to a stop every couple of hours for bathroom breaks and a chance to stretch their legs but had left the road only briefly on each occasion.

Sal spelled Jonah behind the wheel after one of the pit stops but the Almie wasn't prepared to travel flat out and Jonah soon became impatient with his little friend and ordered a halt so he could reclaim the driver's seat.

Over the thirteen hours of darkness, despite varying road conditions and three occasions when they had been forced to leave the roadway to seek shelter from the inquisitive eyes of oncoming traffic, they'd managed to cover three hundred and sixty miles.

They were only forty miles from Jericho.

* * * * *

After a few moments Aabha, with a very determined effort, managed to shake off most of her initial reaction at finding Eustace waiting in her dark office behind what she was sure had been a locked door.

Her heart stopped racing once she'd composed herself enough to get to the chair behind her desk and settle into it.

She asked the brother to sit and he took one of the two armchairs facing her on the other side of the desk.

As uncomfortable as she was, Aabha had no desire to make the meeting an extended one and she got to the point as soon as Eustace was seated.

"Last month the Devi authorized you to commence an investigation into funds that she had reason to believe may have had been misused by the Treasury Chair."

Eustace held her gaze but offered no response. Aabha was left to conclude that the lack of an answer confirmed the fact and, refusing to be intimidated by the monk, she pushed the issue.

"Have you completed that investigation?'

Eustace's lifeless eyes seemed to be looking through hers, probing into her mind and the growing silence in the room began to irritate Aabha. She raised her voice slightly as she continued.

"Brother Eustace?"

The monk's blank expression did not change when he replied.

"Mitra-Varuna Aabha, I believe you are aware that members of the Order of the Golden Ring are, by Holy law, unable to discuss their duties or assignments with anyone other than the Devi herself. The Devi is dead, and I do not believe that you have been elected to replace her as our new Holy Mother. Am I correct in that assumption?"

Aabha drew on her inner strength and she forced herself to hold the monk's lifeless gaze in a fixed stare despite her intense dislike for the deep pools of coldness registered there.

She reached into her robe and pulled out the folded first page from the documents her aunt had provided to her. Her eyes didn't waver from his as she unfolded it and placed it on the table in front of him.

Determined that he would be the first to break eye contact, she held the stare until the brother dropped his eyes to study the lightly creased sheet.

As he read it she broke the silence.

"Brother Eustace, Mitra-Varuna Cala could well win that election to Holy Mother. Would you have the Belief fall under the control of a traitor?" On the document in front of you Mitre VII clearly states her intention that I be made aware of the outcome of the investigation she assigned to you and although she is no longer with us you are honour-bound to carry out her wishes in this matter. Answer my question!"

Eustace finished reading before raising his eyes to meet hers again, and after a second he nodded.

Moments later Aabha was, with considerable relief, returning back across the courtyard toward the building housing the Sister's of Penance dormitory.

She had steeled herself during the brief meeting, determined not to let Eustace see, from her physical reactions or speech, the depth to which his simple presence affected her.

Going over it in her mind as she walked, she was relatively confident she'd managed to hold her own with him.

However, now that she was alone and had dropped her defences, the lingering effect of spending time with the monk could not be denied.

She felt herself trembling slightly as a result and as soon as she got back to her small cell she immediately made a pot of tea for the warmth and comfort it would provide and while she waited for it to steep, she meditated for a few minutes to help remove her unease and got back to normal, then she sat and began to go over her notes containing the information Eustace had provided her.

The facts revealed had been disquieting to say the least.

She was unsure of exactly what she should, or could do about it and she decided to let it gel in her mind, pushing it into her subconscious temporarily while she turned her attention to the resumption of reading the contents of the envelope left by her aunt.

After several hours and having emptied her third full pot of tea, she leaned back in her chair and removed her glasses letting them drop down between her breasts to the end of their restraining cord as she rubbed her eyes. .

Her second candle of the evening had begun to sputter in the holder, flickering fitfully, its subdued light sending black shadows dancing around her small room and she suddenly found herself very tired.

Moving her fingertips to her temples, she rubbed them absently as she got up and crossed over to her small window and pulled the curtain back.

She had no idea of the time, but the moons were high in the sky and she knew it must be close to midnight.

Filling her lungs with a few deep breaths to give her whirling mind time to quiet a little, she stared upward at the three spheres briefly before letting the curtain drop back into place and returning to her desk where she placed the several pages of new notes she'd made into a neat pile to the right of the remaining stack of unread documents which was now considerably reduced in volume.

She blew out the guttering candle, undressed in the dark and slipped into a light-weight sleeping before making her way to her bed.

* * * * *

The first signs of impending dawn flickered through the early morning sky as the halftrack left the road and clattered across a patch of open ground toward a small lake a few hundred feet off the highway and then made its way along the edge of the water and well into the depths of a thick growth of tall evergreens, pulling up in a tiny clearing which opened onto a small sandy beach.

Here the travelers felt safe in having a fire for warmth and a hot meal before splitting off to their separate endeavours.

Venus, trailed by Duanna headed off toward the lake to freshen up.

Jonah stretched out on sleeping bags in the back of the halftrack and Sal joined him on the vehicle, climbing up onto the warm hood and laying on his back with his little arms cupped behind his head.

Gabriel, Juno and Brother Sebastian who had slept little during the wild ride, took advantage of the availability of sleeping bags and were soon resting peacefully around the fire.

The sky was clear of any sign of cloud cover, allowing the rays of Solar to beam its weak winter warmth down on them causing the temperature to begin climbing slowly.

* * * * *

Despite her late night Aabha woke early. It was six when she joined the Sisters of Penance for their morning meal.

As she entered the dining hall in the steadily moving line, Sister

Ester spotted her and immediately got up from a chair against the wall across from the doorway and walked quickly toward her, demonstrating a haste that was uncharacteristic and thereby immediately drawing Aabha's attention.

When their eyes met Ester beckoned with a finger and slowed her pace.

Aabha didn't respond for a second, hesitant to lose her spot in line, but the serious countenance revealed within the lined features of the elder sister's face bespoke of urgency. Aabha left the queue and crossed the room to where Ester had seated herself at a small two-person table located some distance from the other, larger tables, located in the room.

The concerned expression previously filling the woman's face subsided somewhat as Aabha dropped into the seat across from her.

She kept her voice low as she spoke.

"What is it sister?"

Ester's eyes moved furtively about the room before she answered and when she did her voice was only slightly above a whisper.

"Some information I've received…I hope you do not think me presumptuous, but I've asked Sister Anne to watch for you and she will be bringing you your morning meal."

Aabha frowned quizzically. She opened her mouth to speak but a shake of Ester's head silenced her.

"Please give no indication to anyone of anything untoward. I know you would normally never consider jumping the line and I do regret what I've had to ask you to do but there was no time. I will explain all to you once we can find time to speak privately. I'm sure you have a busy schedule but it is absolutely imperative that we speak together again before you take your lunch later today."

It was in Aabha's nature to question mysterious events and she had to check her instinctive urge.

She knew sister Ester to be a no-nonsense and practical woman who rarely allowed her emotions to cloud her decisions and the concern currently reflected in the woman's features clearly indicated to Aabha that whatever was upsetting the sister had in all probability been weighed extremely carefully before a decision had been reached as to how it should be handled.

Sister Ester was not a woman who made mountains out of mole-hills.

All her instincts told Aabha to question nothing the woman across the table from her had asked of her.

CHAPTER THIRTEEN

- A Trap Is Set -

The travellers gathered around the fire again for a mid day meal and it wasn't until then that Gabriel began to realize that Venus was acting coolly toward him again, something Sebastian had picked up on much earlier in the day.

The monk had been watching Gabe carefully, waiting for the change in Venus to register on him, and when it did, couldn't help smiling as he watched the big Neanderthal's brow furrow in consternation.

As she had for most of the day, Juno was sitting beside Gabe like a little shadow, engaging him in steady conversation as they ate.

She did not seem to notice when Gabriel became silent and looked through the lazily rising sparks drifting upward from the fire to where Venus was sitting studying the Atlantian carefully while she stared blankly down at her plate, listlessly toying with what remained of her food.

What the hell had he done this time?

Nothing he could remember. Solar, she was a moody one! How could anyone ever know where they stood with her?

He shook his head and turned his attention back to Juno, who was still chattering away.

Sebastian rose from his seat on the other side of the flickering flames and carried his bowl and spoon down to the water's edge to wash them.

He could only feel sorry for Gabriel.

The young Neanderthal was very much out of his depth dealing with one female, let alone two. He could be considered lucky of course; they were both, although perhaps for different reasons, pursuing him, after all.

On the other hand, if things continued as they were, Gabriel was in for a rough ride for sure.

Ah, the joys of growing into manhood!

* * * * *

It was almost one in the afternoon by the time Aabha could manage to squeeze in enough time to see Ester alone. They had arranged to meet in her room and Aabha had been so intrigued about what the Sister was going to tell her that most of her morning had swept by in a blur.

She had no more than returned and opened her window to allow in some fresh air when she heard a knock at the door of her small room.

When she opened the door she was surprised to find that Sister Ester was not alone but accompanied by the tall broad shouldered presence of Brother Jacob, the senior monk who headed and supervised the members of the Order of the Golden Ring.

Aabha waved them inside and scanned the hallway in both directions to ensure their visit had gone unnoticed before she stepped inside and closed the door firmly behind her.

Sister Ester, a little flushed, let out a long-held breath before she spoke.

"I know it was risky to bring Brother Jacob here, but we waited until afternoon prayers had begun before we came. I suspect I shall be missed and there will be questions, but this simply could not wait."

* * * * *

The Chaplain was sweating profusely as she paused by the locked cell door and swivelled her head back over her shoulder to make one last check to satisfy herself that the manacles appeared secure before she raised her hand and knocked loudly.

Hollis held himself motionless and looked down at the floor.

As his ears picked up the sound of footsteps he regulated his breathing carefully, his chest barely moving as he filled and emptied his lungs.

If the Neanderthal guard decided to check his shackles, the deception would be instantly exposed and he would have to act immediately. Doing that would mean directly implicating the Mitra-Varuna in his escape, something to be avoided at all costs...

For both their sakes he prayed to Solar that the guard would be content with a visual check from the doorway.

The door swung open and the Mitra-Varuna managed a smile as she met and held the Neanderthals' eyes.

"Solar bless you for what you have done today."

The guard briefly raised his hand to the medallion hanging around his neck and caressed it and then managed a brief nod and craned his neck to look around the woman of the cloth to check that the manacles had been placed back onto the prisoner.

The Mitra-Varuna allowed him to make a split second inspection before she rested her right hands on the guard's left forearm.

"And how long has it been since your last confession my son."

The guard flushed slightly, obviously embarrassed at the question and as the Mitra-Varuna exited the room he used the need to close and lock the door to provide him with the time to construct a plausible reply to the question.

"…Well I haven't had much free time of late Chaplain, but it was my intention to attend services this weekend."

As the key in the lock turned, Hollis let out the breath he had been holding in a rush and threw his head back in relief as he heard their departing footsteps echoing in the hallway.

When he shifted position the cuff on his thick right wrist opened and dropped downward toward the concrete floor.

Heart in his mouth, he lurched forward and caught it before it clattered against the hard surface.

He froze until the sound of thudding boots drifted away into silence and then he let out a soft sigh and carefully opened and removed the manacles from his left hand and around his ankles before placing them onto the bunk behind him.

After so many years of another life it had been a harrowing encounter for him and he paused for a few moments as he forced himself to rest until he got his racing pulse down and was breathing normally.

* * * * *

The colour drained from Aabha's face.

"Poison me! You must be mistaken Sister…yes there is competition and certainly some animosity…but poison, no, I will not believe anyone would even consider such a thing."

The deadpan look on Brother Jacob's face didn't change.

"You would be surprised what the mind is capable of, Mitra-Varuna, and I assure you that it is true. As I am sure you are aware, the Order of the Golden Ring does not concern itself with matters not of immediate and direct concern to the Devi. However, before her death, Mitra VII ordered me to seek intelligence regarding the possibility of a plot against you and although, up until recently, I had been unable to find any indication of any threat of that nature, early this morning I received information indicating it was indeed in the works. The Devi also commanded that if she should die before my investigation was completed I was to immediately pass my findings on to you. You understand that I may show no bias toward the upcoming election; it is absolutely forbidden for my brotherhood to become in any way involved in that process. However, as I was commanded by the Devi in the event of her death to pass the results of this investigation on to you personally, I am under obligation to do so."

Aabha sat down heavily on the end of her small bed,

"You are sure brother, this is not speculation, and you have evidence and proof."

"I am sure of the intent Mitra-Varuna. I have it from the horse's mouth as it were. I will have proof before this day is out, but in order to ensure that proof does not include your death, I will need you and Sister Ester to take part in a little charade once the Sisterhood of Penance have completed their devotions and gather to sit down to lunch."

* * * * *

In the company of Sister Ester, Aabha joined the line of Sisters of Penance outside the small cafeteria doorway.

Several sisters approached them as they waited, wondering why Ester had missed devotion and commiserated with her when she explained that she had felt unwell and therefore unable to attend.

Doing their best to follow Brother Jacob's instructions to the letter, they exchanged small-talk, laughing quietly from time to time and Aabha pointedly avoided paying undue attention to those serving as those ahead of her in line picked up their bowls of broth and pieces of heavy black bread.

However, she could not resist a quick study of the young novice ladling out their meagre portions of soup but did, as she normally would, smile and thank both her and the matronly sister who was slicing and stacking the bread, before she and Ester left the serving tables.

It was during this brief evaluation that she came to the conclusion that there was good cause to believe Brother Jacob's earlier words, and it was then that she realized she could probably provide Jacob with a motive for such an attempt on her life.

The novice was new and although those serving were normally found perspiring somewhat due to the heat from the stoves, the young Human was sweating very heavily and seemed unable to meet Aabha's eyes.

When she and Ester reached the small table they sat and the sister, acting as if it were the most natural thing in the world, surreptitiously slipped a tight fitting lidded porcelain carafe out from under the folds of her robe and placed it on the table. She opened it, setting the lid to one side and then carefully poured the entire contents of Aabha's bowl into the container before retrieving the lid and closing the carafe securely and then returning it from whence it had come.

Aabha then set her empty bowl aside and she and Sister Ester shared the contents of the remaining bowl. When they'd finished eating they left the room and went directly to Aabha's office to meet Brother Jacob who was patiently awaiting their arrival.

He took the container from Ester and smiled.

"All went smoothly then."

Aabha nodded.

"What will you do now, have it tested for poison?"

The monk shook his head and a smile touched the corners of his lips.

"No, I don't think that will become necessary. I will bring the novice in for questioning and she will confess her part in this plot and subsequently implicate the person or persons responsible. At that point I will place those responsible under Palace arrest and immediately bring them before a triumvirate of Mitra-Varuna under the leadership of Mitra-Varuna Eashca for judgement. The individual I suspect to be the main instigator holds a high position in the belief and it would be unseemly to allow the matter to become public. All things considered, I would think demotion from her present position to that of novice and exile to some distant, lowly and obscure convent might be punishment enough and if that is what the triumvirate so decrees, I will carry it or whatever other punishment they may deem necessary out. Would you care to participate on the tribunal as one of the three selected Mitra-Varuna Aabha?"

Aabha shook her head firmly.

"No, as this plot was directed against me, I don't think that would be a good choice. Let this triumvirate be seen to be completely unbiased in its judgement."

Brother Jacob nodded.

"In my humble opinion, you make a wise choice."

Aabha let her eyes meet his.

"I believe I may know what motivated this plan Brother, but because I might just be wrong, I will not cloud your investigation with information that cannot be confirmed. I will however, suggest that you may wish to speak with Brother Eustace of your order and ask him to share with you the confidential conversation he and I had last evening. If I am right in my assumption you will want to tread warily with the brother however, as I would logically suspect that it might well be as a result of him warning the party responsible for the matter and was done as a result of the interest I expressed in a certain misuse of funds that may have taken place a short time ago. I will say no more on the matter now, but if and when you get a suspect you believe to be responsible for my planned assassination please inform me immediately and if it turns out to be the person I suspect, I will be able to provide you with the motive, in which case you will need to speak again with Brother Eustace about the entire matter. After all, only two living persons were aware of the incident: me, and Eustace, and if the guilty party learned of my interest in it, I can assure it was not from me."

The monk's brows arched and she caught a glint in his eye.

"In view of the fact that Brother Eustace is a very competent and effective member of his order and is considered by many who know him well, to be a very dangerous man, coupled with the fact that the Devi, and only the Devi, may remove or appoint a member of the Order of the Golden Ring, it might perhaps be sensible to let that part of the investigation await the election of a new Holy Mother."

Aabha nodded in agreement.

"That would probably be for the best, Brother."

CHAPTER FOURTEEN

- Escape -

The sky was purpling into dusk as Jonah joined the others around the fire.

His senses instantly picked up the tension in the air

He couldn't put his finger on the cause and after looking around the circle from face to face to no effect, he gave up trying to nail it down.

He cleared his throat to get everyone's attention.

"We can get back on the road shortly; I thought we should probably have a talk about what happens once we reach Jericho. It isn't going to take us long to get there: about an hour or so I would think. Venus tells me you have a map showing where your grandmother lives, Gabe. Could you show it to us?"

Gabe nodded and they all got up and drifted over toward him as he pulled the oft folded paper out of his pocket and crossed over to the halftrack to spread it out on the hood.

When they'd all gathered around, he pointed to the 'x' marked just off the highway.

"She's on a small farm here, about five miles this side of Jericho. I've never been there myself, so I can't tell you much about the place."

Jonah pursed his lips and spoke to no one in particular.

"I wonder if she has some kind of outbuilding where we could store the halftrack out of sight."

Gabriel shrugged and looked over at him.

"I imagine so, probably a small barn or something of that sort. I know she has a few animals."

The furrow in Jonah's brow faded.

"Sounds good; I don't expect that Venus and I will stay longer than necessary for you to do what you have to do in any case."

He lifted his head to look at his sister. There was more than a hint of reproach in her eyes as she met his gaze.

"Well we can hardly leave Gabe at his grandmother's, can we? His bike is sitting at old Harry's and we have to pick it up and take it back to Sumer anyway, so he can ride back with us."

Jonah snorted derisively.

"How did we become responsible for getting Gabe back to Sumer? Maybe Gabe doesn't even want to go back. Have I missed something here?"

Gabriel opened his mouth to speak but Venus beat him to the punch. Her eyes locked with Jonah's and became as sharp as flint as she spoke.

"Gabe was good enough to allow me to accompany him on this trip and I'm certainly not going to abandon him until he's safely back home. If you don't want to come with us, I'm sure we can manage on our own."

Gabriel registered her indignant tone and tried to get a word in again, but this was definitely a brother-sister exchange and he didn't get the chance.

Jonah raised his hands in supplication and shook his head slowly.

"Easy little sister, no prob, we take Gabe back to Sumer with his bike and then we go home; fair enough?"

Venus smiled with satisfaction and nodded, but she had no intention of leaving it there. She looked over at Sebastian.

"Will you need us to drop you off closer to Jericho, Brother, before we go to Gabe's grandmothers?"

Sebastian weighed her question for a few seconds, considering how much he was prepared to reveal to them before answering.

"I am not headed for Jericho itself; I'm meeting with a Mitra-Varuna, a Chaplain. She serves at a military base which is also on the outskirts of Jericho. From what Gabe has told us I believe that the base is located quite close to Gabe's grandmother's farm and if so I can make my way from there on my own. But thank you for asking."

Juno had been standing a little apart from the others, listening to the conversation with what Gabriel immediately recognized as a hint of a hangdog expression on her face.

He immediately reached out and slipped his arm around her waist and gently drew her closer into the group.

"What about you Juno? What are your plans?"

She was near tears. Her eyes glistening with moisture, she did her best to smile. He felt a shiver move through her as she spoke.

"To be honest, I'm not really sure. The only family I have left now is my aunt in Sumer. I stayed with her while I attended school. I suppose I'll go on into Jericho and find some work until I can get enough flake together to go back there."

Gabriel felt her pain and plaintively looked around at the others. He didn't feel he was in any position to propose that she accompany him, Venus and Jonah on their return trip to Sumer in the hopes that one of the Atlantians would step in and make that very suggestion.

Based on Jonah's attitude to date he was looking more to Venus for support than her brother. Surprisingly she had looked away and was staring off toward the lake.

She appeared not to have heard. There was a painful silence and as it expanded Gabe felt Juno tense up.

Finally, Jonah took a deep breath and let it out in a rush.

"The more the merrier I suppose. You might just as well come on back with us."

Both surprised and relieved at this unexpected suggestion coming from Jonah, Gabriel gave Juno's waist a reassuring squeeze and smiled down at her.

"What a wonderful idea!"

Sebastian, who'd been following the interchange carefully, took note of Venus's reaction.

She was still facing away from the rest of the group and apparently studying the lake. After Jonah's comment she had begun to chew at her bottom lip and although she made no comment, her eyes rolled upward to reflect obvious annoyance.

Taking her reaction in, the monk was glad he wouldn't be travelling with them on the trip back. He was of course taking into account that Juno was still suffering new-found grief which was temporarily clouding her feelings for Gabe somewhat, but that would begin to ease soon enough; and unless he missed his guess, sparks were going to fly between the two females when they began to compete for Gabriel's future affections.

From his observations of the two, he expected all aspects of that competition to harden well before they completed the return trip to Sumer.

While they had been talking, Solar had slipped below the horizon. Jonah looked up into the sky at the three moons which were just coming into their own and handed the map back to Gabe.

It was going to be another near cloudless night and the light given off from the trio of bright orbs in the sky was already leaving long shadows extending outward from the base of the massive evergreens surrounding the small campsite.

He waited until Gabriel had folded the paper and slipped it back into his pocket before jumping up onto one of the tracks and climbing into the vehicle.

"Hop aboard everyone. As long as we don't run into too much traffic we should be at Grandma's in about an hour."

* * * * *

Patiently waiting for the arrival of his evening meal, Hollis was preparing himself, breathing shallowly in a regular pattern.

When he heard the sound of a single pair of heavy boots approaching he filled his lungs and moved to the side of the doorframe and leaned back against the wall.

At the sound of the key entering the lock he closed his eyes, forced himself to concentrate his will and then promptly faded from sight.

When the door opened and before the guard realized the room was empty, Hollis reached out with one hand and with his thumb and forefinger, locked on to a pressure point at the back of the Redshirt's neck.

It took only seconds and then with his free hand he caught the food bowl as it slipped free of the Neanderthal's hand and followed the guard's inert form as it slumped to the floor, easing the fall before placing the bowl gently onto the cement while pushing out with his right foot to kick the door closed.

Despite his rustiness and previous solemn determination not to use his gift ever again, he'd felt a surge of pure delight trickle its way through his body as he'd dematerialized and the buzz still filled him as he stood and crossed to the small cot to retrieve the manacles.

Forbidden or not, it felt good to be back in the saddle again.

He used the shackles on the guard and laid the Redshirt face down on the cot. The man appeared to be breathing, but shallowly.

A look of concern contorted Hollis's features. He knew he was definitely out of practice and hoped he hadn't killed the man. He felt for and found a pulse and held his fingers there for a few seconds.

A sense of relief filled him and his features relaxed a little.

Thank Solar, the guard was still alive!

As he rose back to his feet he let the spell go and immediately returned to visibility.

He judged he would need to rest now for at least fifteen minutes before he made his break for freedom. That should allow him the time to replenish his strength to the point that he would be able to slip back into invisibility again and remain in that condition just long enough to cover the distance to the hangar.

Earlier, when they had arrived at the base he had mentally timed the walk when they'd brought him in restraints from the airship to the building.

It had been a short walk, no more than ten minutes.

If all went well, he should be able to accomplish the return trip back to the hangar while in a state of invisibility safely before he'd be obliged to return to visibility and forced to rest again.

It would be cutting it close and it would mean that he would be left with no choice but to have to sleep for several hours after the escape was completed, but he was fairly confident he could do it.

His only concern now was how long it took the guard's partner to come looking for him.

Solar willing, it would be longer than fifteen minutes.

* * * * *

Jonah tried to engage his sister in light banter as the halftrack roared down the otherwise vacant highway, but he didn't have much luck.

He was receiving more grunts and nods than verbal responses.

After awhile he simply gave up.

He had no idea what was eating his sister's ass but he knew only too well that she was quite capable of becoming moody for the dumbest of reasons, especially since Gabe had come into her life.

He decided to ignore her and turned his full attention to his driving.

They were making good time and a half hour into the run he sent Sal up top to ask Gabe to keep his eyes peeled for the farm and to let him know when he spotted it.

* * * * *

After a ten-minute rest the strain of waiting became too much and Hollis made the decision to make his move. He placed his ear against the door and listened intently.

Nothing; not a sound; all was quiet.

He closed his eyes, concentrated all his effort and slipped into invisibility, then eased the door open, stepped into the hallway and did a quick check left and right.

Empty. He could hear muted voices to the right

A bit of luck, he knew the entrance they had brought him through was to his left.

He gently pulled the door closed and began to move rapidly down the hallway in the opposite direction.

A door opened just ahead of him and he slowed his pace as he sucked in a deep breath.

He didn't stop moving but he was careful to make no noise as a Human, wearing a white smock and reading information from a clipboard walked purposely toward him down the centre of the hallway.

Hollis hugged the wall on his left and continued to move. Time determined he didn't have the luxury of standing still and the scientist seemed completely absorbed in what he was reading in any event.

Hollis watched him out of the corner of his eye as they came abreast of each other and saw no indication that the man was aware of him. However, as he passed him, the scientist lowered the clipboard, paused mid step, and looked around inquisitively.

Hollis kept moving, knowing that in his current state his presence lowered the temperature around him several degrees and realized the man had felt the chill as they passed.

From past experience he knew the effect would pass quickly and as the distance between them grew, he picked up his pace slightly. He came to a T in the hallway and he stopped to check around the corner to his left and right before he made the turn to the left. The hallway he entered was empty and it was a relief to recognize the outside door of the building at the far end.

About half way down the corridor he turned to look over his

shoulder to check behind him to ensure he was still alone and then shifted his eyes back to his front and broke into a lope.

When he reached the doorway he peered out through the small window centered in the top and with the benefit of the light provided by a small outside lamp was quickly able to determine there was no one in sight outside the building.

He pushed the door open, oriented himself for a second and then began to run toward the fenced aerodrome compound which was about one hundred feet away and brightly lit.

CHAPTER FIFTEEN

- Treachery Abounds -

The selected triumvirate of Mitra-Varuna judges chaired by Eashca, rounded out with Daka and Jaboah and utilizing Paayal as an alternate, should the need become necessary, met in the conference room at six that evening.

They had been provided with no insight into the facts of the case they were to adjudicate, nor had they been provided with the name of the person or persons accused.

This unusual lack of pertinent information, coupled with the urgency of the call to justice had left them all somewhat uneasy and very definitely curious.

Gathered together in the big room just before six, each was quietly going over the possibilities in her own mind as the double doors to the room opened.

Brother Jacob entered and was immediately followed by Mitre-Varuna Cala and the young novice, each being escorted by a member of the Devi's personal security force.

Shock and disbelief filled the features of the three-woman panel and although not as apparent in her as in the others, it was clear to the administrative staff in the room that even the normally emotionless features of Mitra-Varuna Daka had registered a touch of surprise at seeing Cala enter the chamber under obvious arrest.

Paayal, as alternate, was sitting to one side in a chair against the curtained windows. It was she who demonstrated the most obvious surprise at seeing the restrained, but definitely unbowed, Treasury Chair being brought before them.

She uttered a surprised gasp and dropped the notepad and pencil from her lap the instant Cala came into view.

Eashca, noting the general reaction among her confederates, lifted her gavel and brought it down with a single no-nonsense whack that caused everyone else in the chamber to instinctively flinch.

"I'll have order and silence."

* * * * *

When the hatch opened Jonah felt a blast of fresh cool air swirl into the warm interior of the halftrack's cab.

He took his foot off the throttle letting the machine slow as Gabriel's words reached him.

"I think that's it just up on the right there. Stop when you get to the driveway and I'll have a closer look."

Venus, who had been dozing in the passenger seat, pulled herself upright, rubbed her eyes and leaned forward slightly to look out at the roadway ahead.

Gabriel left the hatch open and moved forward into the turret to rest his hands on the armoured front area of the housing to better stabilize his position atop the gyrating machine.

The vehicle briefly picked up speed again before coming to a stop abreast the small track leading off to the right.

Sebastian joined the young Neanderthal on the other side of the gun.

They both turned their attention to the farmhouse just visible in the distance. It was a small structure, but appeared solidly built and with a lazy stalk of smoke trailing upward from its single chimney, warmly welcoming.

A yard light centred between the little dwelling and what looked like a barn and some smaller outbuildings clearly illuminated the neatly trimmed grass and flowerbeds separating them from the little house.

Gabriel let his mind run through his memories of what his mother and father had told him and it seemed to fit.

"Yes, I'm pretty sure that's it."

Jonah turned the vehicle into the narrow drive, switched off the headlights and then shut the halftrack down. He climbed out of the driver's seat and stuck his head up through the hatch.

"We'll stay here until you make sure. Walk on in and if it's the right place give us a wave, and Gabe, see if there's someplace we can safely park this thing out of sight, it sticks out like a sore thumb."

* * * * *

The main gates leading into the Aerodrome compound were closed but as Hollis approached, he noted that the small man-gate they'd used when they'd brought him out of the compound on his arrival, stood open.

A uniformed Redshirt sentry was posted on either side of it.

Hollis slowed to a walk as he approached and paused for a few seconds about thirty feet away to catch his breath.

A light situated above the man-gate clearly illuminated the area where the two armed guards stood but the field on either side was in relative darkness.

He could make out the hangar in the distance behind, and to the right of the gate, its outline brightly illuminated by a row of floodlights fixed high across the front of the looming building.

He spotted several figures who seemed to be coiling large ropes moving about just outside of the huge main doors of the structure which were closed and, straining his eyes, he was just able to locate the smaller doorway his guards had used when they'd brought him out of the hangar and over to the research building.

That man-door was located on the far right side of the front of the building, a good distance from the men on the left who were busy with the ropes.

His breathing pattern back to normal, he filled his lungs and started walking toward the open gateway leading into the compound.

The two guards were standing at ease, one smoking a pipe and the other humming softly.

Hollis concentrated on the point between them and walked quickly through the opening.

As he passed the two sentries, the Neanderthal redshirt on his left who was smoking clenched his teeth down on his pipe stem, hunched his shoulders and shivered.

"Solar! That wind can suddenly blow cold, like a blast from the bloody ice fields."

Hollis picked up his pace and after walking briskly for about thirty yards, broke into a run and began pelting his way toward the small door situated at the front right side of the massive hangar.

* * * * *

Brother Jacob acted as prosecutor.

No one stood as defence council, in that under Belief law, the members of the triumvirate were obligated to offer the accused an opportunity to act in their own defence, free to directly challenge any evidence that was placed before them.

Once the novice had given her testimony in hushed tones, finally breaking down completely after revealing the details of the hastily arranged plan to poison Aabha, she was removed from the room and Jacob asked to speak with the triumvirate privately before he continued.

A few moments later after a brief discussion between the members of the triumvirate, who had been joined by the alternate, his request was duly granted.

* * * * *

As Gabriel began to walk toward the farmhouse the others climbed out of the halftrack to stretch their legs.

Jonah, followed by Sal, walked around to the back with a view to keeping an eye out for road traffic while the others had moved to stand at the front of the machine in a group watching Gabe's progress down the long driveway toward the little farmhouse.

Jonah, standing with one foot resting up on the track at the back of the vehicle was staring off in the direction of the metropolis.

The undersides of the dark, thick clouds covering Jericho were brightly under-lit and reflecting the many lights burning below and looked very much like a glittering jewelled crown resting above the massive city.

Sal's unspoken message brought him out of his appreciative trance.

"We are within communication range. There is a message to all personal Almies. An emergency meeting of the council was called for earlier today."

Jonah turned to face him just as Venus and Duanna hurried around to join them at the back of the halftrack.

Her eyes met Jonah's and he noted the lines of concern etched into her face before she spoke.

"Did you get it?"

Jonah nodded and turned to Sal.

"Contact One, find out what's going on."

Sal reached out and moments later and in consideration of Venus who was watching Jonah's little grey robot intently, vocalized in his soft monotone.

"The signal is very weak…some sort of jamming device is in play. Marduke has taken Atlantis by force. All other Atlantians have been banished to Jericho and Marduke had raised Atlantis's outer blast shield."

Jonah couldn't believe his ears. He shook his head slowly.

"Mother of Solar! We knew he was meddling in things he shouldn't, but this?"

Venus opened her mouth to speak but he cut her off.

"Sal, get what additional information you can from One. Find out where my father is. We'll have to join him at once."

Sal nodded absently, obviously having anticipated the request and studiously concentrating on the information he was already receiving.

* * * * *

Cala, sitting under guard at the far end of the ornate table, was unable to hear the conversation between the monk and the Mitra-Varuna seated at the other end of the room.

The exchange was brief and when they'd finished speaking Jacob turned and addressed her.

"Mira-Varuna Cala you are accused before this body of conspiring to commit murder; do you deny this charge?"

As she had throughout the trial, Cala kept her face clear of expression.

"I most certainly do! The charge is absolutely ridiculous; the girl is demented or lying."

With a flourish, Brother Jacob carefully removed the container from under his robe and rested it on the table for all to see, then turned to the Guard at the door and beckoned him forward.

"Take the broth sealed in this container to the nearest cafeteria and have it heated in a bowl. Be sure that you do not spill even one drop during the warming process, and when you are done, bring it back here to this room."

He paused for effect and then continued, addressing all in the room as he picked up the container and held it high.

"This vessel holds the broth presented to Mitra-Varuna Aabha earlier today for her mid day meal by the very novice you accuse of lying. It contains the broth that she swears she poisoned at your direction. When the soup has been returned to this room I will be offering you the opportunity to simplify these proceedings and prove your innocence or guilt by consuming it in its entirety, which if the novice's testimony was true, and without antidote, will bring about a very painful and agonizing death within two hours. At my request, the triumvirate are prepared to remain in session for that period of time. No one will leave this room until the specified time has run its course."

The mask of calm, virtue and purity Cala had managed to maintain throughout the ordeal to this point cracked and she turned white.

* * * * *

Hollis slowed to a walk and regulated his breathing before approaching the doorway leading into the hangar.

As at the open gate, there were Redshirt sentries on each side of this closed portal and because it was closed, he was unsure of exactly how to approach it.

He was beginning to tire and knew he didn't have time to arrange some form of distraction.

Making his decision, he filled his lungs and moved between the two guards and up to the door. After a short prayer to Solar, he reached for the handle and began to turn it.

To his surprise the handle did not refuse to turn a complete revolution and a surge of relief tilled him as the door popped open. He pushed it just far enough to allow him the space to slip inside then, holding his breath, quickly moved about twenty feet along the back of the massive sliding door next to it before flattening himself against the suspended giant.

The surprised guard who stepped through the opening seconds behind him was holding his machine pistol waist high, his head swivelling rapidly from side to side as he checked the immediate interior of the building for intruders.

He looked around briefly, at one point staring directly at Hollis's invisible form and seeing no one, turned to face his partner who was standing gun raised, framed in the doorway by the bright lights behind him.

"Just blew open with that blast of cold wind I guess; must not have been closed properly."

The two of them went back outside and Hollis heard the door close solidly behind them. He let out the breath he had been holding deep within his lungs and, breathing normally, began to move again.

The Chaplain had suggested he seek sanctuary in a small, rarely used storage room located in the far corner of the hangar.

With little energy left and a determined effort, he moved forward deeper into the yawning interior of the structure on unsteady legs and began to traverse the building beneath the looming bulk of the massive airship.

CHAPTER SIXTEEN

- Driving Lesson -

The halftrack had been stowed safely out of sight in the barn.

Gabriel's grandmother was overjoyed at their arrival.

The lively old woman took their number in stride, welcoming all and going so far as to praise her grandson's foresight in bringing Sebastian along.

"Oh what an intelligent young man you are grandson; you have even brought a man of the cloth; however, did you know we would need one?"

Gabriel frowned quizzically at the comment and opened his mouth to respond but thought better of it.

Having been ushered inside, they were now all crammed into the welcoming warmth of the small farmhouse kitchen. Jonah, Venus and their Almies were standing near the stove at the far end of the room. They were speaking in hushed tones.

Juno, Sebastian, Gabe and his grandmother were seated around the small table.

Gabriel's grandmother, determined they would have fresh rolls to accompany the steaming honey-sweetened tea everyone was now drinking with relish, continued to carry on a conversation while she bustled about popping in and out of her chair like a yoyo, mixing, rolling and shoving trays in and out of the big oven.

A large pot-full of a hastily prepared soup had just begun to simmer on top of the stove. The wonderful aroma it produced was wafting through the room and rapidly making liars out of those who had earlier expressed the view that there was no need to go to the trouble of preparing food. Water for bathing was heating in the big boiler on the side of the huge old freshly-stoked stove and the sleeping arrangements had already been organized.

Venus and Juno were to share the spare bedroom and the men would bunk in the barn.

Every time she found a moment to sit briefly for a sip of tea, her brightly sparkling eyes would mist slightly and then dance with delight as she looked lovingly across the little table at her grandson.

Brother Sebastian remained out of the conversation unless he was asked a direct question. He had not missed the concern registered on the Atlantian's faces earlier when they had been parked at the juncture of the highway and the long driveway and was wondering what had led to their anxiety. It soon became apparent to him that, at least for the present, that brother and sister were not going to share whatever it was that had changed their mood with the rest of them and upon hearing of the sleeping arrangements, he found himself also wishing he could be a fly on the wall of the spare bedroom during the night to be in a position to overhear the conversations of the competing duo for Gabes affections, Juno and Venus, would be sharing.

Due to their mutual interest in Gabriel, it would be pithy without doubt and, alone, with only each other for company, he was certain sparks were bound to fly.

After enjoying that thought for a split second, he turned his attention back to Jonah and Venus who had just put their heads together and were speaking animatedly to each other in low tones.

He immediately concentrated on reading their lips, an undertaking at which he was extremely proficient.

* * * * *

The room was stacked almost to the ceiling with spare supplies for the airship.

Hollis used the last of his energy to climb his way up a pile of folded linens and bedding and then rolled across the top of them until he rested against the back wall of the little room.

His head was beginning to pound.

He released the concentration required to maintain his invisibility with a heartfelt sigh of relief and instantly materialized before dropping into a deep sleep.

* * * * *

After her full confession encompassing both the misdirection of funds and her resulting attempt to remove Aabha permanently once the Mitra-Varuna had stumbled across the impropriety and expressed interest in further perusing the results of that investigation, Cala stoically penned a letter of resignation citing personal and health reasons for her decision.

She was then remanded into the custody of Brother Jacob who was directed to see that the, now demoted to novice member of the Belief, was placed into a selected small convent whose main task was the care of lepers in a forbidding jungle area of the developing world thousands of miles away from any semblance of civilization.

Aabha who was advised of the verdict a short time late immediately, in her capacity as Prime Minister, appointed Jaboah to the Treasury Chair in addition to her other duties.

It was to be a temporary appointment and would hold only until the new Devi had been selected.

The decision as to whether or not the appointment would be made permanent would then rest with the new Holy Mother.

Jaboah managed to accept the additional responsibility humbly, but only achieved the containment of her inner delight at the turn of events with a great deal of difficulty.

When initially advised of the decision she'd fairly beamed with affection for Aabha.

Aabha, although not completely over the shock of accepting the fact that such a thing had happened, was not so overcome as to be unable to appreciate that, as a result, her main competition for the position of Devi had suddenly evaporated.

* * * * *.

Marduke paced slowly back and forth behind his Almie who was seated in front of the computer access keyboard in what had previously been Adon's quarters on Atlantis.

It was taking some time and he was growing impatient but he did not interrupt the little grey robot who was rapidly keying in information.

After what seemed like hours to Marduke, Bellum removed his tiny hands from the keyboard and leaned back in the chair.

His unspoken communication reached Marduke before his master could speak.

"It is done. All departments have been notified. My worker

brothers and sisters are now responding only to my direct instructions. As you directed, I have made no changes. They will continue on with their current projects until notified otherwise."

A smile tugged at one corner of his mouth as Marduke rubbed his hands together in satisfaction.

* * * * *

Their Almies remained against the wall next to the big kitchen stove as Jonah, closely followed by Venus; crossed the room to join the others around the table.

Once he and his sister were seated, Jonah waited until there was a lull in the conversation before speaking.

"There has been a change of plans for Venus and me. Our father has asked us to join him in Jericho. We'll be transporting directly and Venus suggested we bring you up to speed on the halftrack before we leave in case you need to use the machine. There has been a bit of an emergency and I'm not sure how it will affect our future plans, but we'll be back in the morning to let you know. If you can spare a few minutes now, I'll send Sal out to show you how the mechanical beast operates which would then allow you to use it to transport Sebastian wherever he needs to go to finish his business. I would ask though, that you take care to keep the vehicle hidden from inquisitive eyes and ensure that you get it back here safely."

* * * * *

Gabriel sat perched in the driver's seat his hands clutching the steering wheel. He was chortling with delight.

Sebastian, riding in the passenger seat beside him, was hollering punctuated warnings of impending disaster between recurring bursts of hearty and uncontrolled laughter.

Decidedly displeased with their childish behaviour, Sal was standing behind them, feet spread and braced, with an arm on the back of each of their seats to steady himself as they shot through yet another sharp corner, tracks chewing up the turf of the untilled field and sending large clumps of it hurtling out in a cascading stream behind the vehicle.

Gabriel was oblivious to the little grey robot's repeated deep sighs of disapproval.

He was in his element and the normally restrained monk sitting in the seat beside him, grinned from ear to ear and was definitely enjoying the boisterous ride.

To suggest that Sal was distinctly unhappy with his students would have been a gross understatement.

The little Almie simply wanted the entire training episode over and done with as quickly as possible.

A pair of damn fools with no sense of propriety and not even a passing understanding of proper decorum, and one of them a man of the cloth, for Solar's sake!

A young mortal, male thing he supposed, in that the two of them were not actually behaving much differently from his own master when it came down to supposed adults expressing childish behaviour when at the controls of the vehicle.

Needless to say, his shoulders sagged with relief as they lurched back into the barn and Gabe shut the vehicle down. It now remained for Sal to teach them how to operate the gun and he intended to go over that part of their instruction without delay.

In view of their total lack of sober study so far, the little Almie had haughtily decreed to both in no uncertain terms that there would be no actual live-firing of the weapon!

* * * * *

The Atlantian' dispossessed had taken up residence on two full floors of Jericho's best hostelry.

Their appearance en masse had caused Jericho's rumour mills to shift into high gear but Adon had instructed them to go out of their way to do nothing to add fuel to the resulting gossip.

Upon arriving at the hotel lobby, Jonah and Venus were promptly taken to their father and mother's suite, and once the porter had left them, the family embraced warmly.

Greetings having been properly exchanged, Adon looked at his children and his features changed to reflect the seriousness of his tone.

"If you haven't already done so, please have your Almies refuse any communication from Bellum."

Jonah nodded.

"We've already done that Father."

With a one-handed gesture, Gaia directed them to the buffet of food laid out on a side table.

"I thought you might be hungry. We waited for you; let's eat before we talk."

* * * * *

Re-allocation of the evening's sleeping arrangements was the centre of discussion in the small kitchen as Gabriel, his grandmother, Sebastian and Juno dug into large steaming bowls of savoury soup accompanied by a stack of oven-fresh rolls slathered with rapidly melting lumps of newly churned butter.

After a short discussion it was decided.

Juno was to have the spare room.

Once he and Sebastian had completed and returned to the farmhouse from dealing with whatever business the monk had, Gabe and the brother would draw straws for the settee and a sleeping bag on the parlour floor.

After laying out dessert bowls heaped with apple crisp still steaming from the oven, Gabriel's grandmother excused herself temporarily after explaining she had certain arrangements to make for the 'passing' ceremony that would take place at noon on the following day.

Before leaving the room she ruffled Gabe's thick mop of hair with one hand and gave him a quick kiss on the forehead, bringing a hint of colour to his cheeks.

CHAPTER SEVENTEEN

- Secrets Revealed -

Their Almies began to clear the table and Adon suggested they retire to the adjoining sitting room for tea and discussion. When they had seated themselves Adon took a moment to marshal his thoughts and then cleared his throat.

"One advises me that he has provided you with all the information we have and answered all of your questions. Is there anything more you wish to ask me?"

He looked from Jonah to Venus and they both shook their heads.

Adon nodded then paused. Gaia, who was sitting beside him on the luxuriously upholstered loveseat, reached over and took his hand in hers, giving it a gentle squeeze.

"You must tell them Adon. The situation has changed and they have a right to know."

He turned to her and smiled.

"Yes, my dear, I know."

He looked from her reassuring eyes to Jonah and then Venus and then continued.

"Every member of our team, young and old, knows we have the specific responsibility of creating living worlds within this, our assigned solar system. There is however one secret that is shared by only the Atlantian elders of the team. Historically we are forbidden to reveal it to our younger generations until just before a certain incident approaches. Due to Marduke's actions, we, elders have agreed that our children have a right to know and understand just how serious, for the rest of us, Marduke's seizure of Atlantis is at this time. I am therefore going to share it with you now."

* * * * *

Aabha finally finished reading the last of the documents from the envelope. She removed her glasses and let them dangle from their cord as she stretched before lifting her cup to finish her lukewarm tea.

The journals held a tremendous amount of information, some of which might be of value in her bid for the position of Devi. If she was successful in reaching that goal however, the information contained within the documents would be invaluable to her, as they allowed access to the facts and observations of her predecessor for the entire period of her aunt's stewardship of the Belief.

Her own notes based on the review of the envelope's contents now contained another four pages of timely information that she would need to review in the morning and as things now stood she was fairly confident her election, while not certain, was very likely.

It was improbable on the first ballot and was unlikely on a second as the game had to seen as being played, but based on how things now stood, the third or fourth ballot should be hers.

* * * * *

Gaia had finished her tea by the time Adon paused for questions.

Both Jonah and Venus were sitting bolt upright in their chairs. Their tea sat on the table between them, cold and untouched.

The younger Atlantians were unable to speak for a few seconds as they struggled to assimilate and evaluate the information their father had just shared with them.

Finally, Jonah stood and began to pace slowly around the room. His words came haltingly as his mind shifted through the variables. He was speaking softly, to himself as much as for the benefit of the others.

"So Marduke has raised the shield and we no longer have access to Atlantis, and more importantly, Olympos will destruct in a matter of months."

Adon nodded.

"In each galaxy, approximately every four and one half billion years, a single planet is newly created through a massive burst of molten material given off by Solar. The trajectory of this rapidly cooling matter is always the same and as it's blasted away from Solar, the force of its movement sets up a chain reaction with the three other older planets in its path, forcing them each in turn to move further away from Solar. When this occurs, the resulting increase of distance between each of the planets and Solar affects the strength of influence Solar has over the individual planets. The newly created planet begins to cool and slow as it moves away from Solar and finally comes to a stop where it then begins to orbit its creator, taking over the approximate position where the closest planet had been before the new planet was created. The force of its approach has pushed that planet out of its position and as a result it shifts farther away on the same trajectory where it then replaces the next planet in line and so on. The third planet from Solar ends up in an orbit that lends itself to life. It is the responsibility of the members of the Atlantian race assigned to each solar system to bring that possibility of life to fruition. This is done by the Atlantian planning team operating from an interstellar spacecraft identical to Atlantis. All galaxies have their own planning team and are treated the same."

Jonah paused and glanced at his parents to give them a chance to interject and when they didn't he continued.

"This is how Olympos came to be in our galaxy. It is currently the third planet from Solar. All life on it was set in motion by our forefathers and has been overseen ever since its inception by our ancestors. When a new planet is formed and sets up the chain reaction, the third planet from Solar is pushed away by its replacement and when that happens it becomes unable to sustain life and every living thing on it instantly perishes, while that planet that took its spot quickly changes to become capable of sustaining life and the entire process of Atlantian involvement in that creation begins anew. Our planning teams again create the basis for a life sustaining existence, beginning their work as soon as the mass of this shifted planet has cooled sufficiently to do so. Our job is to ensure it is provided with everything needed to support life and then to see to the work of the seamless initiation of the development of all living things that will inhabit this new world. Approximately six and a half billion years later the whole process repeats itself and always has. The time has come for a new planet to be born and for Olympos to suffer the fate of it predecessors as it is pushed away from Solar and into a future of lifeless oblivion."

Venus, her expression blank, shook her head slowly.

"I understood and accepted that we Atlantians were responsible for guiding life on Olympos, for trying to make it the best world it could be, but this is so much more."

She looked up toward her father.

"What parts are Jonah and I and the other younger Atlantians expected to play in this process?"

It was Gaia who smiled and looked up at her inquiring daughter.

"Well Venus, your father and I won't live forever you know. We have about six thousand years left, and when we pass, the responsibility for continuing the cycle in this galaxy will fall next to your generation. We know that Olympos has approximately two months of life left. There are signs that will tell us exactly when Solar will produce a new planet and when those begin to appear we Atlantians would normally all retire to Atlantis and temporarily move the ship a safe distance away from the shifting planets while we discussed our plans for renewed building once the replacement for Olympus is in position. Marduke's seizure of Atlantis has put that entire process in jeopardy."

Adon let out a sigh as he picked up the thread.

"There is no way of knowing what Marduke intends of course, but I would imagine he plans to offer those members of the team who will accept him as leader the chance to join him aboard Atlantis before Olympos is replaced and thereby continue the team's assignment in this solar system under his leadership, instead of mine. For the sake of simplicity in explaining to you what that entails, let's forget for the moment that any change of leadership has taken place and concentrate on the process itself."

Jonah snorted.

"Right, just pretend it didn't happen."

Adon smiled.

Just for the moment, yes please. You need to understand what needs to be done in order to ensure our mission in this solar system is a success and continues as it has been designed to do. It goes without saying that we must turn our energies to thwarting Marduke's plans and retake the ship as he is obviously mentally unbalanced and not capable of leadership. But, I ask you to put that fact aside for now and simply listen and understand the physical process the team must follow in order to properly continue the mission."

Venus, brow furrowed, looked from her father to her brother.

"Leave it be, Jonah! We will deal with Marduke in due time. Let father explain what would be the normal process for the creation of the new planet so that we will understand what is expected of us when the time comes."

Jonah raised his arms and shrugged, but made no comment and Adon continued.

"Once Olympos has been replaced we will move Atlantis back into a moon position over its replacement and the team will begin the work of creating a brand new world, using everything we've learned in the past to improve on what has gone before. The Elders will provide guidance in the beginning, but the majority of the responsibility for the creation and maintenance of this new world will fall to your generation. In time, that responsibility will pass to your children and so on into until the entire process repeats itself as it has done since the start of time."

Gaia set her cup down and reached for Adon's hand.

"That is what was expected to happen, a simple repetition of what has been going on since the arrival of Atlantis in this particular solar system."

Jonah, who had stopped pacing and was standing with his hands resting on the back of Venus's chair, squared his shoulders.

"There must be something we can do. We have to take Atlantis back and when we do we should do to Marduke what he has done to us. We should exile the bastard to Olympos!"

Venus, her thoughts elsewhere, had not been listening to him. Tears had formed in her eyes and although she had not intended to, she spoke out loud.

"...all our friends...everyone on the planet; how horrible, everyone and everything destroyed...surely it doesn't have to be..."

Gaia's features softened and she got up and crossed to where Venus was sitting, kneeling on the floor in front of her daughter and taking her hands in her own.

"Venus, it is the natural way of the universe. It has been going on since the start of time. I know it's horrific to contemplate and that's why the elders are forbidden to allow their children to know what will become of the planet they have come to think of as their own; at least not until the need to do so is absolute. It has to be a closely held secret and you must never reveal it to anyone on Olympos, or even discuss it outside the Atlantian race. If the populace knew of its fate it would lead to immediate chaos and anarchy."

Adon then responded directly to his son's last statement.

"Once the blast proof shield is in place around Atlantis, nothing can penetrate the surface of the ship. There is no way for us to retake Atlantis while the shield is in place."

Jonah snorted but nodded his understanding and distasteful acceptance.

Adon turned to face Venus.

"Venus, you must not lose sight of the fact we Atlantians are not one of the races residing on this planet. We may have formed all life on Olympos, but we are not part of it. We have a higher priority and duty, and it is not just to this particular planet and its occupants, but to those that will follow it in this solar system. Olympos was, as were all previous life sustaining planets of this solar system, created by our Atlantian team and has a limited lifespan. We do not create the solar systems, our job is to see that a planet that will support life is created within each as the opportunity arises and are restricted to work within the limitations presented to us."

* * * * *

Gabriel's grandmother had taken note of Juno's unease in the company of the others and once Gabe and Sebastian left, the old woman went out of her way to include the taciturn young gypsy girl in her menial activities.

She kept up a steady patter as the two of them went to work cleaning up after the meal, doing her best to draw the young woman out of her shell.

They were in the midst of washing dishes when Juno burst into tears.

The old woman put the bowl she was holding back down into the soapy water, dried her hands on her apron, and then enveloped Juno in her arms.

"What is it child? Come sit at the table near the stove. You're shaking like a leaf. I'll put on a fresh pot of tea and you can tell me all about it. There, there, now, you go ahead and cry child, let it all out."

* * * * *

Heavy cloud-cover served to obstruct any light that would have normally been provided by the three moons, and the thickly forested area they were passing through now that they'd turned off the main highway and entered the track leading to the military base was as dark and confined as a mineshaft.

Torn between speeding up to reduce the chance of meeting any oncoming traffic before they reached their goal and slowing to help keep the vehicle to the center of the narrow track, Gabriel chose the second when, at Brother Sebastian's suggestion, he shut off the halftrack's lights shortly after they'd left the highway to follow the gravel roadway leading toward the base through the tall trees.

They'd met no traffic so far and both were straining their eyes through the split windscreen of the vehicle and into the darkness ahead looking for a sign of the cleared area upon which the base had been constructed. The machine was almost at a crawl when Sebastian finally rested his hand on Gabriel's arm.

"There, up ahead on the left, see it."

Gabriel continued to move forward slowly toward the huge clearing, his eyes following the outline of the road which led up to the main gates, which were a good two miles ahead of them.

He stopped the halftrack and looked over at Sebastian.

"What now?"

CHAPTER EIGHTEEN

- *Night Recon* -

They were about twenty feet into the clearing and the monk pointed to the left, over at the tree line, which was a good couple of miles from the fenced and gated compound ahead of them.

"We need to get off the roadway while we do a recon on the place. Skirt along the edge of the trees there and we'll find a spot where we can safely back into them and see if we can make some sense out of the configuration of buildings within the compound behind the security fencing."

In order to minimize the clattering sound of the rolling tracks, which under the circumstances, sounded to Gabriel like rolling thunder, he continued to move at little more than a crawl, hugging the trees at the edge of the cleared area surrounding the fenced and brightly lit complex.

Floodlights on tall, evenly-spaced poles provided pools of overlapping light along the entire perimeter fence line of the compound which sat in the center of the enormous clearing framed by an expansive virgin forest of tall evergreens.

Halfway along the clearing, doing his best to control the halftrack as it lurched slowly over the uneven ground in the pitch black night Gabriel brought the vehicle to a halt and shut it down.

Nestled against the trees, clear of any reflected light emanating from the enclosed compound itself and beyond the circles of illumination provided by the lamps atop the fence line, they huddled together on the passenger seat and peered out the small window in the door to study the well lit compound, in the distance.

They marvelled at the size of it for a few moments and then Sebastian got to his feet and opened the hatch cover and gently let it lock into the open position before he silently led the way up out of the cab.

Faint sounds of muted activity within the complex drifted across the dark open field between them and the fence and they took care to make no noise as the stood up on the top of the gun turret and used the binoculars in turn to inspect the fence line and what they could see of the buildings beyond, then the monk spent some time concentrating his gaze on the main gate and what lay immediately behind it.

When he had finished his inspection he spoke in a soft tone.

"The individual I have to see has a residence inside somewhere. I'm expected and I don't anticipate having any difficulty being admitted inside via the front gate when I present myself. Take me back along the tree line to the road the same way we came in and drop me. I'll walk in from there. You don't need to stick around, Gabe. Thanks for everything; I've enjoyed knowing you and wouldn't have missed it for the world."

He held out his hand.

Gabriel looked at the extended hand for a couple of seconds and then threw back his shoulders, met the monk's eyes and shook his head.

"No way Brother, after all we've been through, you're not getting rid of me that easily. I'll just hang tough until you're finished up here and then we can both head back to the farmhouse and get a good night's sleep. I have a feeling we'll need it."

Deep smile-lines formed in the monk's weathered face and he let his hand drop to his side.

"Are you sure? It's probably not necessary but I will admit I'd feel better knowing you were out here keeping an eye on things."

Gabriel shrugged.

"Since I started this trip nothing seems to have gone according to plan. You just might need a quick exit. Besides, at the moment I've got nothing better to do."

Sebastian's grin broadened and he tilted his head to one side in acknowledgement of his appreciation.

"Thanks Gabe. I appreciate it although I have to say that in view of the way both Venus and Juno have been looking at you lately, there are probably far more interesting things that you could be doing."

Gabe stared at him questioningly and a dismayed Sebastian raised his hands in disbelief and shrugged.

"Forget that for now. I will explain later.

OK, how about you take me back to the road the same way we

came in and drop me off. Then I'll walk in from there, and you can head back over here where you'll have a fairly open view of what's going on inside the complex."

He swivelled his head and raised his hand to indicate the mass of timber behind them.

"You can back into the tree line there and you'll be well out of sight. These built in binoculars on the gun are pretty powerful. They'll allow you to keep an eye on my progress once I get through the gate. With all those lights on inside the compound it's like daylight in there and you should be able to follow my movements. What I have to do won't take very long, no more than an hour and when I'm finished you'll see me come back out the gate, and I'll meet you back at the road at the same spot where you dropped me off".

* * * * *

Once she'd finished crying and had managed to swallow a few sips of tea Juno pushed aside the mental barriers she'd placed around the incident with the Trolls and let it all gush out.

Gabe's grandmother offered loving words of understanding and support to punctuate the outpouring of horror and grief as it spewed forth from the shaking, deeply traumatized young woman.

When Juno finished, the old woman got up and slipped an arm around her.

"Come child, I'll show you to your room and draw a nice hot bubble bath for you. After you take a long soak you can climb into bed and get a decent rest. What you're feeling won't be gone in the morning, but now that you've faced it squarely you'll find it gets a little easier to bear every day and after a good rest, things will look a little brighter I'm sure."

* * * * *

Gabriel stopped the halftrack along the treeline about thirty feet from the roadway leading up to the main gate of the compound.

He and the monk quietly climbed out and made their way up onto the gun platform then Gabriel extended his arm.

"Solar's light protect you brother"

Sebastian took the proffered hand and shook it firmly, then made to release it, but Gabriel held it firmly in his own as his eyes locked with the monk's.

"Look, I don't know what this is all about, but that place doesn't look like a youth camp. Maybe we should have some kind of signal or something you could give me if you need help."

Sebastian's eyes twinkled and he gave a little chuckle.

"You'll be watching me. If I get into any trouble, I'm sure you'll know it, besides I'm an extension of Solar's will and where I go, so goes He."

He clapped a hand on Gabe's shoulder and then as the young Neanderthal released his other hand he dropped down onto one of the tracks and moved quickly toward the roadway.

Gabe watched until the monk reached it and began to make his way confidently toward the big main gates in distance and then he dropped back into the halftrack and turned to creep his way back along the tree line.

He was impatient to get back to the center of the solid wall of evergreens and into position before Sebastian made it to the compound entrance and as a result came close to high centering the machine on stumps twice before he managed to easier himself back into a space between two large trees and shut it off.

Seconds later he was up top in the gun turret.

He had to bend at the waist to keep his eyes pressed against the rubber eyepieces of the fixed telescopic gun viewer. It was an uncomfortable position to maintain and he'd tried to utilize the regular binoculars instead but they hadn't given him anywhere near as clear a picture of the activities within the compound in the distance.

He'd decided to grin and bear it.

He watched Sebastian approach the gate and converse with one of the sentries. The guard appeared to be affable enough and after a short conversation the uniformed Redshirt left the monk standing outside the gate as he disappeared into the small guardhouse on the right hand side.

The guard, a Neanderthal, returned within minutes, spoke briefly with Sebastian and then led the monk into the small building. A short time later Gabriel spotted a figure dressed in the scarlet-trimmed dark blue cassock of a Mitra-Varuna of the Belief approaching the gate under the big lights that burned brightly inside the compound.

There was a second door on the far side of the guard shack which led directly out of the small building and into the compound proper and as the Mitra-Varuna got closer, Sebastian emerged from it and crossed to join the figure in the cassock.

Gabriel was taken by complete surprise as he watched the regally clothed Ogre bend quickly bent from the waist to kiss the monk's extended right hand. The subservient motion was swift and could have been easily missed if he had not been giving the meeting of the two his full attention.

It was a complete reversal of what Gabriel had expected to see when the two figures met. It made no sense and as it had happened so quickly, Gabriel immediately began to question what he thought he'd seen.

He brushed the whole thing from his mind and concentrated on keeping the two figures locked within the viewfinder as they turned and began to walk side by side toward the centre of the compound.

Gabe could see that they were deeply involved in conversation as they moved and then stopped abruptly before turning to face each other.

They spoke briefly again and then Sebastian turned to stare directly in the direction of the halftrack.

Gabe could not make out the expression on the monk's face but he sensed that something was very wrong.

Sebastian stood silently staring in his direction for some time then the monk turned back to face the Mitra-Varuna and spoke again.

Both figures then turned sharply to the left and began to walk rapidly across the main compound toward a secondary enclosure of chain link fencing within the main complex which Gabe could see contained a huge building set against the fence at the far end of a large grass field. The front of the building was made up of what looked like several massive floor to ceiling doors.

Sebastian and the Mitra-Varuna approached the sentries standing guard at a small man-gate which allowed access to this inner compound and then passed through the gateway and began to move hurriedly in the direction of the building itself.

Gabriel watched their purposeful approach toward the right side of the huge structure and observed attentively as the Mitra-Varuna conversed with the two redshirted guards posted on either side of a small doorway and then one of the guards opened the door and the two clerics disappeared inside the strange looking structure.

* * * * *

Hollis opened his eyes and pulled himself into a sitting position on the top of the pile of stacked linen.

For a split second he thought he might have been dreaming, but no, the footsteps echoing inside the massive structure were very clear and much closer to the room now. He rolled over onto his side to face the wall that held the small doorway he'd used to gain entry to the room.

When he heard it begin to open he tensed his muscles, and prepared to fade.

"Hollis…"

He would have recognized that voice anywhere, even after so many years.

"Sebastian?"

There were more footsteps and then the door closed and the room flooded with light.

* * * * *

Jonah's features hardened. His eyes flashed angrily.

"Marduke acted too soon. He should have waited. We have two months Father. Surely that is enough time to find a way to turn the tables on that bloody treacherous maniac."

Adon considered for a second and then nodded.

"Perhaps, but let's hope that possibility doesn't occur to him. At the moment he is under the impression that he holds all the cards. He could, if he wished, permanently remove any real threat to his new found leadership if he sensed any real challenge."

Jonah frowned.

"What do you mean, Father?"

Adon glanced over at Gaia and took a deep breath.

"Once the new planet is born and the others planets begin to move he will have great difficulty in managing Atlantis on his own. He knows that, and as stated earlier, I am sure he intends to welcome any Atlantians that are willing to swear him fidelity back onto the ship before that happens. If, in the meantime, we give him any reason to believe some of us may attempt to interfere with his control of the ship, he could take steps to ensure that didn't happen."

Gaia stiffened.

"Adon, despite everything he has done, Marduke is an Atlantian. He would not..."

Adon cut her off with a raised hand.

"Marduke is not well. His actions have clearly demonstrated that fact. He is no longer the man we knew. It would be foolish of us to continue to think of him in that way. We must bide our time; in all probability we will have only a single opportunity to regain control of Atlantis. Because there will be no second chance, we must plan our move very carefully."

He let his words sink in and then smiled.

"As Jonah pointed out, we have the time to study the problem carefully before we act. Let us rest now. We will speak more on this in the morning."

CHAPTER NINETEEN

- Eyes Opened -

After reliving the horrific Troll attack Juno was left completely exhausted. She gave serious consideration to climbing straight into bed without the bath, but Gabriel's grandmother wouldn't hear of it.

Once she settled into the lavender-scented hot, bubble-filled tub she realized the old woman had been right to insist. The tension of the past day began to evaporate almost immediately and she closed her eyes and luxuriated in it, letting her mind go blank as she welcomed the hot water's curative powers. Eventually she fell asleep and by the time the old woman awakened her and helped her out of the tub the water was beginning to cool.

She felt herself being enveloped in a huge velvety soft towel and stood limp, still half asleep as the old woman dried her and then led her to the bed. She managed to mumble her thanks as she sank into the pillowy softness of the feather mattress and felt the fluffy comforter float down to cover her. Hugging it to her tightly, she snuggled down, feeling completely safe for the first time in what seemed like years.

She dropped immediately into a deep, therapeutic sleep, and Gabriel's grandmother pulled a chair up beside the bed and sat with her until Juno's deep rhythmic breathing filled the room, and then the old woman smiled to herself and tucked in a loose corner of the comforter before crossing the room to turn out the light and softly pull the door of the small bedroom closed behind her.

* * * * *

Sebastian turned to the Mitra-Varuna.

"The less you know of our future plans the better. Perhaps you could gather up those articles we discussed earlier and return to meet us here when you have them. That will give Hollis and I time to talk privately."

The Mitra-Varuna nodded in agreement.

"Yes that would be for the best. It won't take me long; I can probably find the things you need right here in this building."

Sebastian waited until the Ogre was gone then turned and placed his hands on Hollis's shoulders.

"It's so good to see you again my old fenced friend."

He pulled Hollis into a bear hug and was enveloped in turn. When they parted Hollis grinned.

"How did you know they had taken me?"

Sebastian laughed, his eyes glittering.

"I didn't. I came on a mission to see the Mitra-Varuna and she told me one of my brothers was being held and led me to you. I thought you were happily retired. When I was told it was you who had been taken prisoner, I couldn't believe my ears."

Hollis grinned.

"A pleasant surprise I hope, my gregarious comrade. Solar, it's good to lay eyes on you again after these many years! Now we must talk. Tell me of your mission and I will fill you in on what is going on here and my plan for escape."

* * * * *

Gabriel's back was killing him. What was keeping them? He shifted position, bending his knees so he could straighten his torso and still keep his eyes glued to the eyepieces.

Finally, Sebastian and the Mitra-Varuna exited the building! Sebastian had a large duffle bag over one shoulder and after a brief exchange with the guards on the door the two of them began to walk back across the field in the direction of the man gate through which they had earlier entered the smaller compound.

He watched as the duo passed through that gateway and started moving toward the guardhouse situated next to the large, double front gate which allowed access into, and out of, the huge complex.

The two figures moved at a leisurely pace talking animatedly as they approached then entered the inside door of the little guard shack. Moments later Sebastian emerged alone from the outer door of the small building and stepped out under the harsh lights beside the big main gate. He was still carrying the duffle bag, but had shifted it to his other shoulder. Gabriel let out a sigh of relief at the sight and after watching Sebastian start to walk down the roadway toward him from the complex he stepped away from the fixed binoculars and dropped down through the hatch to slip behind the wheel of the halftrack.

He fired it up and left the lights off as he pulled out of the thick stand of trees and then turned sharply to the right. Keeping the machine at just over an idle, he edged his way back along the tree line toward the road.

He found Sebastian at the spot they'd previously arranged and applied the brakes, bringing the machine to a full stop. They briefly exchanged grins through the windshield and then Gabe felt the machine shift slightly as the monk disappeared from sight and hopped up on a tread.

Gabriel shoved the halftrack into neural, climbed out of the driver's seat and slipped between the two front seats and before moving toward the rear of the compartment.

The duffle bag he'd watched the monk carry out of the compound dropped down through the hatch, and Gabriel grabbed it and tossed it toward the back while Sebastian climbed down and pulled the hatch cover closed before latching it securely into place.

The monk didn't speak as he moved between the seat and into the passenger seat and belted himself in. Gabriel moved back behind the wheel and shifted the vehicle into gear and then gave the halftrack some throttle, turned onto the roadway and began to pull away from the brightly lit gate in the distance.

He drove slowly; leaving the running lights off for about a half a mile, until they were well into the tunnel-like depths of the tree-framed track before switching them on and picking up speed.

Sebastian was normally a man of few words and Gabriel was not surprised at his silence. He had questions of course, but didn't want to appear to be prying into matters that did not concern him. On the other hand, the waiting had been frustrating for him and it was with a good deal of difficulty that he managed to accept the silence while they made their way between the tall trees on either side of the camp access road and finally reached the main highway.

As they turned right onto it and began moving in the direction of the farm he turned to glance at Sebastian and opened his mouth to speak.

The monk, who had been quietly staring ahead through the windscreen at the dark and deserted thoroughfare before them, lifted his right hand to point and beat him to the punch.

"Pull off over there by that clump of trees. We need to talk."

Gabriel quickly did as he had been bid.

* * * * *

Aabha was completely exhausted by the time she'd slipped into her shift and stretched out in her small bed. Her head was whirling with all the information she had taken in over the past twenty-four hours and she realized she needed to focus if she expected to manage to sleep. She prayed quietly for several minutes then stretched and let her mind clear.

She was confident that she had done everything that could be done in preparation for her run for the top spot in the Belief. She would now stay out of that fray until the election.

Until that time, she'd keep a low profile and concentrate on performing her current duties well; duties, which as Prime Minister of a Vacant Holy See, were considerable.

Calm and composed, she closed her eyes and slept.

* * * * *

Venus was sitting on the end of her bed.

She and Jonah had been provided with adjoining rooms and the doorway between stood open. Their Almies stood side by side, resting against the far wall and Jonah sat in the only chair the room provided. As the hour was late they were speaking quietly.

"You heard Father, Jonah. He will be taking no action against Marduke until the time is right. Nothing is going to happen immediately. We have two months, after all. Your kind of kneejerk reaction could screw up everything. Father will prepare a carefully thought out plan."

Jonah leaned forward and rested his head in his hands. His voice was muffled as he spoke.

"I also heard Father say that if Marduke felt there was any danger of some of us retaking Atlantis he would take action to prevent it. I don't like the idea of leaving him with that option. I wish we could find some safe haven here on Olympos where we could seek sanctuary until we were ready to strike back at Marduke, some place safe from his influence. If he could mount an armed force to take over Atlantis, he could certainly send a similar force against us here in Jericho. As it is, he could have his minions selectively kill any or all of us any time he wishes.

Venus could see the logic to her brother's line of thinking.

"Is there such a place? I think you have a valid point and you should raise it with Mom and Dad in the morning."

Jonah lifted his head and managed a brief smile. It faded quickly to a frown.

"I will, but that aside, what is it about this bloody Neanderthal of yours anyway?"

A spot of colour touched Venus's cheeks and she stood up and began to pace with her back to him.

"It has nothing to do with Gabe, well not in the way you think at least. He's a friend and I feel an obligation to see this thing through now that I'm part of it, that's all. Once Gabe has received the power and is safely back home."

Jonah let out a mirthless chuckle as he interrupted her.

"You can BS the others if you like, little sister, but please don't patronize me. I know you too well. You've got a thing for this guy as anyone with two eyes can clearly see. Come to that, so has the gypsy. I think you seriously need to revisit your priorities. You know what situation faces us and you heard what Dad had to say. I mean, seriously, how can you even consider continuing on with this silly adventure at a time like this? We, as a race and you as an individual, have a higher calling and responsibility. Your obligation is to the entire galaxy, that's where your energies and thoughts should lie, not with some silly Neanderthal kid's birthday gift."

Venus turned on him, eyes flashing.

"It may be a silly adventure to you but it isn't to Gabe and I'm part of that now. Under the circumstances I see no reason whatsoever why I shouldn't see it through. For Solar's sake Jonah, we're talking a few days here and Dad has made it clear it will be some time before he will be ready to act against Marduke. If you don't want to come with us, then don't. We managed quite well before you arrived on the scene and I'm sure we can cope with the rest of the trip without you!"

Jonah dropped his hands between his knees and stared across at her in exasperated dismay.

"Oh right. You're lucky to be alive, if I hadn't come along when I did..."

There was a soft knock on the door.

Venus rolled her eyes at her brother and stomped across to open it. Her features softened instantly when she did and she stepped back as her mother and father followed by their Almies joined them in the small bed chamber. Gaia took in the situation in a glance and when Adon had closed the door behind him she smiled at both of her children in turn and each felt the warmth of her concern and affection fill them before she spoke.

"We thought you might be having some difficulty sleeping after absorbing all the news and felt we might be able to ease your concerns somewhat."

Both Jonah and Venus began to speak. Adon smiled indulgently and raised his hand to silence them.

"One at a time please; why don't you start, Venus?"

Venus glanced over at Jonah before responding.

"It's nothing really, just a little sibling rivalry. I'm glad you came though; Jonah has raised a good point."

She glanced over at her brother and both Adon and Gaia listened attentively as Jonah related his concern to them regarding the possibility of Marduke using the forces under his control to selectively remove those Atlantians who might endanger his plans, and the resulting need to seek out some safe haven on the planet to provide them with breathing space and time to plan for their return to Atlantis. When he'd finished, Gaia, concern filling her features, turned to Adon, awaiting his response. He cupped his chin in his right hand and began to nod his head slowly.

"I think you're right Jonah. Marduke is not what he once was. It would be foolish of us not to take whatever steps we can to protect our people from danger until we are ready to make our move to retake Atlantis. There is only one place on Olympos where we might seek sanctuary, support and safety - Almeca. If the Devi would take us under her protection, we could be relatively assured that no one would dare to molest us. She is the spiritual head of sixty percent of the occupants of the planet and all the leaders on Olympos curry her favour. Our people would certainly be much safer within the borders of the Holy See than here in Jericho. We would need to find some way to approach her secretly though. Marduke obviously feels relatively safe with us in Jericho and under his thumb. If he got the slightest indication that we were looking to reach the protection of the Devi, he would act to prevent it. Unfortunately for us the Devi has recently passed and a new selection for her replacement has not yet been completed. We would have to wait until that is done and then find some way to make an unobtrusive approach to the new head of the Holy See. In the meantime, we will have to do our best to keep a low profile and not draw Marduke's attention."

Venus nodded and smiled across at Jonah.

"There is no reason then for me to put aside my plan to help Gabe."

Adon shook his head.

"No, not for the moment, it's best that we all carry on as we have been. Let Marduke be lulled into a false sense of security. If there is any change in our circumstances, we can always reach you. I can see no reason for either you or Jonah to remain here in Jericho with us."

CHAPTER TWENTY

- Learning Curve -

Gabriel pulled off the road and impatiently backed the halftrack through the underbrush and deep into the little grove of trees before shutting it down and turning on the interior light.

Sebastian twisted in his seat to face him, took a deep breath, holding it for a couple of seconds then released it before he spoke.

"You remember when I told you that I had some experience with the gift. That at one time I'd worked with someone who had it?

Gabe thought back. His brow furrowed and then he nodded slowly.

"Ya, you said you had learned a lot about it and might be able to help me discover how to use it more effectively, right?"

Sebastian pursed his lips and sat more erectly in the seat as he searched for the best way to answer Gabe's question without complicating the situation even further.

"Well, what I didn't tell you was that my old partner, the one who had the gift, was your father."

Gabriel stared at him with surprise which quickly turned to disbelief. He stabbed a finger into his chest as he spoke.

"My father, but he's been a miner all his life. Did you work in the mines too?"

Sebastian shook his head slowly and searched for the words he wanted. Gabriel waited impatiently for an answer. The silence in the cab became dense and oppressive before Sebastian determined how to respond.

"No, I was never a miner, but before your father met your mother, he and I were partners. Your father is a lifetime member of my brotherhood. By his own request, he took what amounts to a permanent leave of absence, under a Deval dispensation, prior to marrying your mother."

Gabriel stared vacantly at the monk. After a few seconds he spoke, more to give himself a chance to think, than out of idle curiosity.

"And what was with that bloody...sorry brother, Mitra-Varuna bending a knee and kissing your ring when you first met her back at the military compound all about. Who or what are you anyway?"

Sebastian sucked in a lungful and shrugged.

"Well Gabe, I'm not at liberty to tell you everything, but all things considered, I do owe you some answers. It's not my job to explain to you about your father; that's up to him. But I can't help but feel that Solar had something to do with you and I being thrown together, and I believe He has some role for you to play in the bigger picture. That belief seems strengthened by the powerful group of people who have come into your life over the past few days. Not many Neanderthals on Olympos can claim Atlantians for friends."

He let his eyes fix on Gabriel's.

"The brotherhood your father and I belong to is called the Order of the Golden Ring. At last count, there were only eight of us. We hold the Belief rank of Verendus, and are answerable only to the Devi herself. Once appointed to the brotherhood by the reigning Devi we are all members of the order for life. I can not tell you specifically what we do for the Belief, but to give you a general idea I will tell you that upon appointment each Verendus is absolved of all sin, including all sins of the church up to and including that of causing death to another. This visitation of absolution covers any sins that have been committed previous to his appointment to the order as well as any that may occur for the remainder of his life and are granted by way of Deval decree. You saw the Mitra-Varuna kiss my ring because I technically outrank her within the structure of the Belief. A man of Verendus rank within the church stands in the place of the Devi the minute a member of the Belief sees this ring."

He stretched out his hand, sprung the top of his ring open and showed Gabe the Devial insignia nestled inside.

* * * * *

Droplets of early morning dew clung to the tips of the manicured grass growing between the barn and the small farmhouse. These tiny tears of nature caught the first rays of the day's dawn which was just breaking free over the hills in the east and began to sparkle as Venus and Jonah, accompanied by their Almies, appeared in the narrow driveway near the front door of the compact building.

Neither of the two young Atlantians seemed to notice their natural beauty as they began to walk toward the door. That had a great deal to do with their shared preoccupation and heated, ongoing discussion.

Although Adon and Gaia had made it abundantly clear to their two children that they could see no reason for either Jonah or Venus not to finish the business they'd started with regard to the Neanderthal boy, if that was their wish, brother and sister were still at odds with each other over the situation and deeply lost in trying to sway each other to their own point of view.

They dropped the subject abruptly when the door opened, but still angry with each other and absorbed in their own thoughts, paid little attention to the general atmosphere inside as Brother Sebastian, who had answered the front door, led them into the kitchen where the others were in the midst of eagerly devouring a hearty ploughman's breakfast.

Sebastian picked up his empty plate from the table and Gabe's grandmother stood and gave the two Atlantians a beaming smile.

"Ah there you are! Now you just sit yourselves down and we'll get some food into you so you can start the day proper."

Venus opened her lips to demur but the old woman had already begun to fill two plates from the pans left warming on the top of the stove and the young Atlantian thought better of it. Instead she joined Juno and Gabriel at the table.

Sal and Duanna moved over against the wall by the stove and stood at rest, side by side.

Jonah slipped into the empty chair and smiled in acknowledgement as the old woman bustled over and put heaping plates before him and Venus.

Sebastian, who had not missed the chill in the air when he'd opened the door for the two Atlantians, watched the others eat in silence for several minutes and then exchanged brief looks with Gabe's grandmother before he spoke.

"It feels more like a funeral in here than breakfast on a very special day."

Juno who felt much better after sobbing for several hours and managing a good eight hours of sleep, lifted her eyes and looked around her. She could read the tension in their faces and with some hesitancy, found her way out of her shell for the first time since the incident with the Trolls.

"Yes, it does. Everyone looks so serious, even you Gabe and this is your big day!"

Sebastian picked up on the opening, and directed his response toward Venus and Jonah.

"You two look like you just lost your best friend. Want to let us in on what's going on?"

Gabriel, forehead furrowed in concentration, was still mulling over the information the monk had given him about his father's situation on the previous evening. He pushed that aside for the moment and looked up from his plate.

Venus, toying with her food and biting at her lower lip, took in Gabe's blank expression without comment and pointedly turned her attention to her brother.

Under her intent stare, Jonah put his fork down and leaned back slightly in his chair.

"Something has come up that concerns Venus and I; well, all of us in fact."

He looked across at his sister, meeting her eyes and shifting uncomfortably before continuing.

"Unfortunately we aren't at liberty to discuss all of it, but it is a serious enough situation that we're a little overwhelmed at the moment."

Gabriel pushed back his chair and stood up, then lethargically reached for his empty plate and carried it over to the sink. As he let is slide under the surface of the soapy water, he turned back to look at the others, determinedly locking his eyes with Sebastian's before he spoke.

"Well, you're not alone in receiving startling information. Overwhelmed, after last night, that's a sensation I can readily relate to."

He punctuated his comment with a deep sigh.

Sebastian had been quietly observing the others from the sidelines. He couldn't shake the feeling that there must be some sort of higher power acting behind the scenes in order to bring together such an unusual grouping of characters. Were the members of this strange assemblage meant to accomplish some important task or tasks as a unit and if so what exactly? It seemed unlikely. They had no obvious joint purpose, except perhaps to assist Gabriel in his quest to receive his gift. Even that had been a fractured effort, often clouded by other circumstances, and in several instances, more motivated by an individual member of the team's personal situation, than a strong bond of friendship. The quest certainly hadn't begun as a joint effort, but in fact had simply snowballed from involving only Gabe and Venus to engulfing the widely diversified group currently contained within the walls of the small farm kitchen.

Still, Sebastian found himself unable shake the niggling feeling that there was a deeper purpose here. He thoughtfully rubbed his forehead before he spoke.

"Once you and Venus have finished eating I suggest we take a walk and share our thoughts. I for one have some things to say and it sounds as though you guys have some too."

Gabe's grandmother was pleased to see a hint of light enter the general gloom which had been saturating the small room and she smiled broadly, and then spoke to no one in particular.

"Now that sounds like a good idea, a little fresh air and exercise to settle your meals. You, young people head off and enjoy yourselves. I have a few preparations to finalize for Gabe's awakening, so please be back about fifteen minutes before noon."

* * * * *

The last of the clouds had dissipated by the time they began to walk. The resulting unfettered rays of the early winter brightness, weak, but carrying a breath of warmth, served to frame the peace and tranquility of the small farm and despite the individual personal concerns troubling the participants taking part in the walk; the mood had noticeably lightened from that experienced earlier in the farmhouse.

Despite that improvement, all of them were still very definitely absorbed in their own thoughts as they began to stroll through the field.

Juno, the newest member of the group, was, after a night of finally coming to terms with her grief, climbing slowly out of her traumatic fog and was now at least able to take note of the simple beauty of the countryside surrounding her. She trailed the others a little, walking just behind the two Almies, still unsure of her position within the strange little band.

Jonah was unable to stop thinking about Marduke's capture and control of Atlantis and the threat this presented to the Atlantian team as a whole.

His mind shifted from scenario to scenario, searching for a solution to finding a safe haven in the short term and a longer term plan to ensure the eventual regaining of the control of the ship.

He was chomping at the bit to become proactive. If his father had not all but insisted that he accompany his sister back to the farmhouse, he certainly wouldn't be here. He had nothing against Gabe personally. He seemed a nice enough guy, but he quite honestly had no interest whatsoever in holding this Neanderthal oaf's hand during some pagan ritual baptism. Not with everything else that was going on, at any rate.

As he walked, Gabriel kept going over the conversation he'd had with Sebastian the night before.

He was still finding it difficult to accept that his dad had been anything other than a miner, and he was worried sick about his father's current situation. Once they'd pulled into the small grove of trees and Sebastian had related the facts of his father's current state of affairs, Gabriel had wanted to go to him immediately, but Sebastian quickly pointed out that his father had anticipated just such a reaction and had given Sebastian strict instructions not to let that happen.

Gabriel had argued with the monk, but Sebastian had insisted that he and his father had things under control and any action on his part at that time would not only fail but in all probability make the whole scenario worse.

Well that was easy for them to say, but the idea didn't rest easily with Gabe. At least there was apparently a plan of sorts in place to rescue his dad, though Solar only knew how that was going to work out.

Venus had confidence in her father's ability to solve the Marduke situation within the allotted timeframe. She had some concern as to the overall safety of the members of her race in the long term but if they could find a secure place to stay, she had no difficulty in accepting that they had plenty of time to deal with the problem of retaking Atlantis.

Her current thoughts dwelt primarily on her relationship with

Gabe.

As a result of the one-on-one time they had spent in each other's company over the past few days, she felt even more attracted to the handsome Neanderthal boy, and now that she knew they had only a relatively short period of time left together her feelings for him had grown even stronger.

That had become painfully clear to her when sparks of jealousy had filled her the instant Juno had entered the picture.

What was far more upsetting to her however was the fact that in two months Olympos was going to be snuffed out of existence and as a result not only was her future no longer what she had imagined it could be, her world had been turned completely upside down.

She was left feeling depressed and empty inside, having a great deal of difficulty dealing with all its ramifications and was struggling to accept the fact that she could neither change the inevitability of it, nor, and perhaps more importantly, could she share her newfound knowledge with those members of the other races she'd grown up with.

CHAPTER TWENTY-ONE

- *The Gift* -

They had been walking for some time and were halfway across the big pasture that lay directly behind the barn.

The sound of singing birds occasionally drifted across to them from the trees bordering the far side of the grassy field, otherwise all was quiet.

Initially, none of the group had seen fit to disturb the peacefulness of the open countryside by speaking.

Like the others, Sebastian too was lost in his own thoughts and taking advantage of the opportunity it provided to ponder the current situation.

His assignment on the Devi's behalf had been to evaluate this new fascist based political party and provide Her Holiness with his assessment of where it may be headed and what its future development could mean for the Belief.

As an aside, he was also interested in the recruitment of Gabriel if that proved possible.

He had the information he needed to make his report to the Holy See, and was already working toward further evaluation of Gabe for a possible future addition to his order.

He was impatient to get started on his trip to deliver his report to the Devi, something that, under the circumstances, went hand in hand with the rescuing of Hollis and the capturing the airship, which would serve to make short work of an otherwise much longer trip to Almeca.

Pulling that off might well be accomplished more easily once Gabe had received the gift of invisibility and possession of it would also make him a far better choice for the brotherhood. It therefore made sense for him to be patient until that had been accomplished

His ability to lip-read some of what Venus and Jonah had been discussing earlier in the kitchen had provided some interesting material. From what he had managed to pick up it appeared that something had occurred that caused the Atlantians as a whole to become more than a little anxious.

Something had gone very wrong for them, and when one considered that everything happening on Olympos was either directly or indirectly initiated by an Atlantian, a problem of any sort with that faction could well indicate ramifications for the entire planet.

It was therefore something that could have serious consequences for the Belief, and he felt obliged to find out as much as he could about it in order to alert the Devi.

It was amazing to Sebastian how much knowledge and ability the individual members of their small party held.

As he walked along with them, letting his thoughts and priorities coalesce, it was hard not to feel that Solar had destined them to act as a single entity and had some future purpose in mind for them.

That being the case, if Solar had brought them together with that in mind and if there was indeed some future mission or missions for them to accomplish as a group, what was the part he was expected to play within the little band?

Was it a role of guidance and leadership?

He didn't have the answer to that question but decided he would do well to begin to take an unobtrusive leadership role among them whenever the opportunity arose and see if he could find some way to bring about a spirit of coalition.

Yes, if that was indeed Solar's wish he would concentrate on melding them into a single powerful force for good.

The aimlessly strolling group came upon a small brook lazily bubbling its way through the centre of a grassy field.

Solar had just finished burning off what was left of the morning dew. Sebastian spotted the small semi-circle of large rocks resting on the near bank of the stream overlooking the water and the small moss covered wooden bridge that reached across to the far bank. He pointed toward it.

"That looks like a good spot to talk; everyone, grab a rock." Smiles and nods of agreement met his suggestion and soon they were all sitting comfortably.

Surprisingly, it was Juno who spoke first.

Sitting beside Gabriel and directly across from the monk, she slowly ran her eyes over the group and then allowed them to settle on Sebastian.

"I have only known most of you briefly Brother, but as one who is able to foretell and Gabe's friend, I'm unable to hold my tongue. If my words offend any here, please forgive me, but I must tell you it is clear to me that while we each have our own agenda and carry a bag full of secrets, I perceive exceptionally strong indications that we share a common future."

Her words had commanded their full attention, and at that realization, she smiled shyly, as they silently exchanged looks before, in unison, turning back to face her.

Sebastian's eyebrows arched and he ran his tongue over his lips slowly.

"You carry the gypsy ability to foresee, child?"

Juno flushed slightly as she nodded.

"Yes, I'm still young of course and it is not yet fully developed. Now I see only shadows of what will be but my sightings grow progressively clearer with each day."

Sebastian looked around at the rest of the group who were now all closely following the conversation. This additional information provided by the young gypsy was enough to bring him to speak his mind.

"It is a surprise to me my child that you raise this issue now. You see, it has occurred to me that Solar may have destined the formation of our little group, and that it could be his intention that we perform some task necessary for the overall good of Olympos. Can you tell us what you've foreseen?"

Juno's flush deepened and Gabriel took her hand in an offer of support. Venus arched her eyes at the sight of it and delivered a deep sigh before she spoke.

"Are we to be guided by a teller of fortunes now?"

Jonah frowned and gave his sister a sharp look.

"Let the girl speak, Venus. The ability to foresee among certain females is well documented throughout the history of her race and she could well have some insight into the solving of our current rash of difficulties."

Venus eyes flashed and she prepared to respond but Sebastian cut her off abruptly, as he looked back at Juno.

"Go ahead Juno; please tell us what you've seen."

Juno was beginning to seriously regret bringing the topic up in the first place. She did not enjoy being the center of attention. Gabriel gave her hand a gentle squeeze.

"Tell us Juno, please."

She nodded slowly and closed her eyes as she struggled to find the proper words.

"It is in bits and pieces really; small things I've picked up from each of you since we met. I'm not sure what it all means. To be honest, I've never sensed a series of like visions from so many different people before; it has always been a specific concept from a single person. To pick up the same basic image from a diverse group is very unusual for me and it's the only reason I mention it now."

She opened her eyes and offered a timid smile. Sebastian nodded his understanding with a look of encouragement, and she continued.

"It is a single recurring image, and I have seen it in varying degrees of completeness in all of you, and last night I dreamed the same image myself. I was part of it you see. It involves all of us and we are in some sort of flying contraption and we are high over the water. There is no land to be seen and I became aware that we were frantically escaping from some dark force. In my dream we are successful in accomplishing that, although suffering great hardship and later, all of us here continued to work together as a team to accomplish something very important to us all, something to do with one of the moons. That's all I've seen so far and I really have no idea what it all means."

Sebastian's eyes widened. The colour drained out of Gabriel's face. His grip on Juno's hand unconsciously tightened to the point that she let out a soft cry. Realizing he'd hurt her he released his hold and began to apologize profusely.

While this was taking place Jonah exchanged looks with Venus, then the tall Atlantian stood and began to pace aimlessly.

Sebastian lifted his staff off his lap and stood it against the rock behind him then pressed his hands together before raising them to his lips in thought. He glanced across at Gabe and their eyes met briefly before he looked back at the others.

"Well I have no idea what the last part of your vision means, but I can perhaps shed some light on the part about the dark forces and the airship."

Jonah immediately stopped pacing and turned to face him.

"And I may be an Atlantian and not a member of the Belief or any other faith brother, but I do believe in the truth of a 'Foreteller's' vision and I believe I can explain to you what the last part means."

* * * * *

The small parlour at the front of the farmhouse had been transformed by the time they returned from their walk. They found Gabriel's grandmother waiting there, dressed in a simple white shift with an array of small symbols embroidered just below the high neckline.

The blinds on the single window had been pulled and the only light provided within the room was from two large blue candles bracketing a small bowl of water and a highly polished and timeworn rosewood box situated in the middle of a small table which had been cleared of its usual collection of knickknacks and placed in the centre of the room. The two tapers flickered gently, leaving small pools of darkness in the corners of the room.

The table had been covered with a white satin cloth, framed with a similar set of embroidered symbols to those of his grandmother's shift, along its edges. Seen in other surroundings, the setup could have been easily taken as those of a small altar.

A straight-backed wooden chair sat against and in front of the table, facing into the room. A short sackcloth robe with a simple braided horsehair belt lay draped over the back of the chair.

The old woman who was standing behind the table addressed Sebastian as they entered the room.

"Ah there you are brother. Would you be kind enough to bless these articles for us before we begin?"

She lifted the robe and held it out to him and waved a hand to indicate the bowl and box resting on the small table.

Sebastian took the robe from her outstretched hand and she turned to face the others who were standing facing her near the center of the room, between the table and a line of kitchen chairs she'd earlier placed just inside the doorway. There was an expression of solemn reverence on her face which was surrounded by an aura of soft radiance as she allowed a brief smile to form on her lips before she spoke.

"Please take a seat and share in Gabriel's enrichment. The power he is about to receive has been passed down for untold generations. It is a commanding gift and one which could make his future path in life fraught with difficulties, a path which can only be made easier with the support of good friends."

She folded her hands and held them in front of her as they sat and Sebastian gave the robe, bowl and polished box the blessing of Solar before returning them to their original positions.

When he had finished, she indicated her desire for him to take the one vacant chair remaining beside the others with a tilt of her head and then she turned to Gabriel.

"Now my Grandson, please leave us; remove your clothing and put on the robe. Hurry now, the hour is near."

Gabriel did as he was bid and when he returned to the room his grandmother was standing behind the small table with her eyes closed. She was speaking in a soft undertone, chanting in a language as unfamiliar to him as it was to the others who sat silently, observing.

She seemed immediately aware when he re-entered the room and she opened her eyes and beamed with affection as she raised her hand to indicate the ladder-backed wooden chair, standing against the small table and facing into the interior of the room.

Gabriel crossed to it and took pains to ensure that the rough material of the short robe covered him as he sat.

His grandmother moved from behind the small table and came round to stand beside him. She began to intone again, her voice so soft everyone about her strained to hear, not because they could understand her words, but because those strange primeval utterings seemed to command their absolute attention.

His grandmother rested her hands on Gabriel's forehead briefly and then her stroking fingers gently closed his eyes before she opened the small box.

Once the container was open, she dipped the tips of the fingers of her right hand into the small bowl of water then rested them briefly inside the box before slowly anointing his brow with the mixed grey ashes of a hundred ancestors' adhering to her damp fingertips as she chanted in the ancient tongue of her race.

Gabriel's body visibly stiffened and then seemed to go completely fluid.

Those watching found themselves unable to take their eyes from him and both Venus and Juno let out hushed expressions of concern as they stared at his stilled chest and silently beseeched him to breathe.

All track of time was lost to them and when Gabriel suddenly stiffened abruptly, the candles flared and they all tensed and let out their own held breaths as his chest began to rise and fall rhythmically again.

A look of supreme peace and acceptance filled the young Neanderthal's features and in a matter of moments his breathing pattern had returned to normal. His eyelids lifted and flickers of candlelight were eerily reflected from deep within the pools of his eyes.

He saw nothing; then he saw everything, and he knew it was done.

CHAPTER TWENTY-TWO

- *Hope Abounds* -

The team headed out to the small barn, leaving Gabe's grandmother nursing a cup of tea in the small kitchen. The old woman, who seemed alert enough, was obviously drained from the part she had played in the transference.

They had been hesitant to leave her, but she had assured them she would be fine on her own, and would rest for a short while and then was going to begin final preparations for the small birthday celebration for Gabriel she had planned for later in the day.

Once inside the barn Sebastian opened the duffle bag he'd brought from the Rector's compound, and spread the contents over the hood of the halftrack.

Earlier, sitting out in the field in the semicircle of boulders by the stream they had decided, based on the strength of Brother Sebastian's strong feelings and supported by Juno's foretelling, to stick together and prioritize the individual needs of each with the object of working as a team to solve them one at a time and in order of their importance.

Secrets were still being held. That had been admitted by both the monk and the Atlantians. But all information that could be shared with a clear conscience, in relationship to a personal sense of duty, had been.

Gabriel, a strange serenity flowing through him, was perched on a hay bale and struggling to register what the monk was saying, admittedly with only partial success.

The others were standing around the vehicle listening attentively.

"...and the Mitra-Varuna indicated there are warehouses full of strange military vehicles in crates on the base, so if we use the black paint to apply the party's insignia onto the halftrack and wear these uniforms, we should be able to bluff our way into the compound. She believes the halftrack will be accepted as just another one of the advanced vehicles which are being slowly brought into service by the Rector's scientists via the largesse of your rogue Atlantian military advisor."

Jonah nodded and frowned.

"This airship, how will we manage to operate it if we should be successful in seizing it?"

Sebastian smiled and tapped the hood of the halftrack.

"Well, initially, when there were only going to be the two of us, I'd planned to commandeer the crew and force them to fly it for us. As things now stand, if we are able to learn to handle this machine quickly by utilizing Sal's abilities and with our increased number, perhaps it will be possible for us to fly it ourselves. If we can manage that, we can then use it to get us all to Almeca. Once we are under the Devi's personal protection, the Rector and his baboons won't dare to bother us. They're currently too eager to curry favour with the leader of the Belief for their own purposes to risk her displeasure."

Jonah turned to look at Sal and the little Almie replied to the unasked question before it could be posed.

"If there is a manual for the airship, an understanding of its operation could be accomplished very quickly, but I have no idea how many bodies are required to properly man the machine. I don't know if our party would be large enough to reasonably be expected to handle the task."

Jonah turned back to face the others but before he could say anything Sal began to speak again.

"What will happen to the halftrack if we take the airship?"

Jonah was completely taken aback by his little friend's unprompted question. He frowned and looked back at Sal.

"We'll leave it at the aerodrome I suppose. Why do you ask?"

Sal's oversized forehead furrowed. When he responded he did not vocalize as he had been doing, but instead transmitted it silently and for his master's ears only. Jonah's mouth dropped open.

"What!"

Sebastian responded to the excitement in Jonah's voice.

"What is it?"

Jonah's mouth dropped open again and stayed there while he raised his hand to silence the monk and continued to stare at Sal.

"Are you sure Sal?"

The little Almie nodded.

"Vocalize so the others can understand."

Then, in the by now, familiar metallic monotone, the little Almie's voice filled the small barn.

"Something I read in the manual of the halftrack was bothering me and I couldn't remember what it was, so I was just re-reading it. I thought I had seen something about a transponder and so I checked it just now and the manual clearly states that this vehicle, like all vehicles originating from the transporter room of Atlantis, has a pre-set emergency auto-return command system in place. These systems, when activated, will automatically return any piece of equipment, so equipped, to the..."

He glanced self-consciously around at the others in the barn and gave Jonah a questioning look, seeking support before continuing.

"...to Atlantis when activated. I then checked my memory banks to find out if the raised blast shield would prevent that from happening and as far as I can see it's received by the central computer as an override situation and it wouldn't, which means we could use the halftrack from any location on Olympos to circumvent the effect of the blast shield; that is, as long as the ship's sensors do not register a massive explosion occurring at the same time, as that would of course override the override and..."

Jonah smiled broadly and leaped over to encompass the little Almie in a bear hug, lifting the shocked little creature completely off the floor and spinning him around in circles as he finished the thread for Sal.

"...which means we can board Atlantis whenever we want from wherever we want, as long as we hang on to the halftrack!"

Sebastian frowned.

"But if we take the airship, we won't have the halftrack..."

Gabriel snapped out of his reverie to interject.

"Didn't you say the base Chaplain told you they regularly loaded the Rector's armoured car onto the airship when he travels, so he has transport wherever they land? The halftrack can't be that much heavier than an armoured car, can it?"

Jonah put an obviously embarrassed Sal down none too gently and gave the little Almie a questioning look.

"How about it Sal, what do you think?"

Sal inherently disliked being pressed for a decision on something when he didn't have all the facts before him. He let out a sigh.

"I can't be certain of course, not without knowing the mass of each and the lifting capacity of the airship, but it would seem reasonable to conclude there wouldn't be that much difference in weight."

Jonah rubbed his hands in glee and Sal stepped back a few paces in frantic anticipation of another round of hugging. Instead Jonah, a huge grin spitting his face, spun around to face the others.

"That's it then, we'll load the halftrack onto the airship and take it with us. When we've safely delivered Sebastian to Almeca and he's seen the Devi and arranged for the protection of the Atlantians now at risk in Jericho we can, at our leisure, use the halftrack to pay Marduke a little surprise visit. Sal, connect with One; I've got to let Dad know that I'm going to Almeca to see the Devi and that we have found a way to beat the shield and retake Atlantis."

* * * * *

Just over an hour later, Sebastian, who had been mentoring Gabe in initial experiments with his new found power of invisibility, turned when Jonah called and walked over to admire Sal's handiwork.

The black inverted crosses painted on each door of the halftrack weren't perfectly centred and the paint was still damp but once it dried and they added a little dirt, he was sure they would pass muster.

He gave the little Almie a 'thumbs up' and exchanged grins with Jonah.

The sound of distant barked orders broke the silence and the four of them froze for a second and then moved rapidly across the barn to the big barn doors. Gabriel reached them first and carefully pulled one side open a crack to look out. A military truck, clearly outlined by the setting of Solar, was parked in the driveway next to the farmhouse. An officer was standing beside the truck and was watching as the driver dropped the back board and four black-uniformed SS Ogres troops jumped out and moved sharply into a single rank in front of the officer.

Gabe turned to the others and held his finger to his lips.

He watched silently as the figure in charge detailed two men to stay with the truck and then, pulling on black gloves, spun on his heel and led the other three toward the front door of the farmhouse.

The young Neanderthal made a motion to pull the door fully open and Jonah who was standing behind him on his tip toes and peering out at the scene unfolding in front of them covered Gabriel's hand and held the door firmly in place where it was as he leaned close to Gabe's ear and whispered.

"No, let Sal and I handle it, we'll use the halftrack. It'll be over in a few seconds."

Uncertain as to what Jonah had in mind and concerned about his grandmother's safety, Gabe turned and watched uneasily as Jonah and Sal climbed up over one of the tracks and onto the top of the halftrack.

Sal positioned himself behind the gun and Jonah called out softly.

"Venus, you and Juno stand clear. Gabe, you and Sebastian be ready to open both doors wide the instant you hear me start up, and do it fast. I want to take them by surprise in order to be sure to hit them before they reach the house."

Jonah dropped through the open hatch cover into the cab and Sebastian reached for the door that Gabriel wasn't holding braced his feet and gripped it firmly in both hands then nodded to the young Neanderthal.

"I'll open this side as soon as you open yours, and knowing how Jonah drives, I suggest we get them open as quickly as we can and leap clear of the opening the minute we do."

The words were no more than out of his mouth when the halftrack growled to life behind them and Gabriel, followed by Sebastian, flung the barn doors open and dove for cover. Both felt the rush of air as the thundering sound of the racing tracks echoed through the barn and clattered out into the yard.

Jonah had covered over half the distance to the house in a wide arc to the right before there was any reaction from the small party approaching the house. Heads turned at the sound of the approaching vehicle and a couple of weapons began to come up, but before they could reach a firing position Jonah heard the big gun above him open up. Shell casings began to ricochet around the metal confines of the gun turret and the halftrack rocked wildly as the heavy projectiles thumped out of the barrel moving in an arc from right to left and began chewing up the members of stunned black uniformed group before they could get a shot off.

The gun continued hammering away in it's arc across to where the driver and the other black uniformed Ogre, who had been conversing just in front of the vehicle, turned to see what was happening.

A concentrated cluster of fifty calibre bullets dropped them in an instant.

Gabriel, and Sebastian, followed by Juno, Venus and a horrified Duanna raced across toward the halftrack which was pulling up to a lurching stop.

Sal kept his little hands on the big gun's triggers watching for any sign of movement among the heap of bodies. Jonah stuck his head out of the hatch and shouted back toward them.

"Venus, you and Juno go on into the house and stay there until we join you. Gabe, you and the Brother get their weapons and make sure no one is left alive and likely to be around later to tell any tales."

Sebastian hefted his staff and pressed the recessed button at its base. The extending blade at the top caught the last rays of Solar as the monk turned his attention to the bodies and began to approach cautiously.

He called over his shoulder to Gabe as he moved.

"I can look after this Gabe; you're still a little unsteady on your feet. Why don't you go inside and rest?"

That comment was followed by a dismissive grunt as Gabriel, a look of determination clearly etched into his face, dropped into step beside him.

"Not likely Brother; these guys are from the same bunch of bastards that grabbed my dad and it was my grandmother they were coming to see, not yours. This is personal."

He added almost as an afterthought.

"You realize we're going to have to take her with us when we go. I can't leave her here after this."

Sebastian heard the rasping sound of the Gladius slipping free of its sheath as he and Gabriel approached the gruesome scene.

Gabe's grandmother appeared at the doorway and was promptly intercepted by Juno and Venus followed by Duanna who herded her back inside the small farmhouse.

After ensuring all the black uniformed Ogres were dead, the others loaded the bodies into the back of the truck and Jonah drove it around behind the barn where he and Sal began to unload their grizzly cargo while Gabriel and Sebastian began to work at shifting a section of the manure pile with the intent of then digging a shallow grave in the soft, damp soil beneath.

CHAPTER TWENTY-THREE

- Rescue Attempt -

Once the men departed with their grizzly cargo, Venus left Gabe's grandmother in Juno's capable hands and returned to the scene of the shooting with Duanna in tow. She instructed her little Almie to flush down the blood soaked areas on the grass and driveway where the SS men had died, and supervised the cleanup as the robot used buckets of water from the yard pump to wash away the patches of blood.

Out of her sight, Jonah, standing in the back of the truck which was now parked behind the barn, bent to remove the officer's pistol from his holster and added it to the pile of light machine guns he'd already stacked neatly on the tailgate.

He then stood and used one foot to roll the last corpse out of the rear of the vehicle and onto the others which were lying in a haphazard pile on the ground below him.

"Too bad they're all Ogres; we could have used some of their uniforms otherwise."

Gabriel and Sebastian, who were both sweating despite the coolness of the late afternoon, paused and leaned on their shovels as they looked up inquiringly at Jonah, who was standing in the back of the truck.

Jonah dropped down to sit on the tailgate, resting his feet casually on the stack of bodies.

"Well we've got the three redshirt uniforms Sebastian managed to pick up at the base. Gabe's dad will need one once we reach him and the other two will do for getting us into the compound with the halftrack. The driver can wear one and the other can be worn by whoever sits up top in the gun turret. One obviously belonged to a Neanderthal and will fit Gabe and the other will fit me or Sebastian. But since we have the truck, it would be great to take it along; that way we would be able to put Gabe's grandmother, the girls and the Almies out of sight in the back. Otherwise we'll have to try to hide them in the rear of the halftrack cab and there isn't a lot of room there."

He pointed down at the pile of corpses below him.

"I suppose we could just use the best of these, the ones with the least holes in them, just a jacket, shirt and tie on whoever drives the truck. If the halftrack leads the way, the guards will probably not bother checking the truck anyway, and if they do, all they'll see is the top half of the driver as it goes through the gate."

Sebastian nodded.

"Sounds good, just use the upper arm holes of the jacket, and fold the lower ones out of sight."

Sal, who had been absorbing the information provided by the manual he'd found in the glove compartment of the truck, returned it and then hopped down out of the cab and walked back toward them.

When Sebastian saw what the little Almie was carrying, his eyes grew wide and his mouth slumped open. He abruptly released the handle of the shovel he'd been leaning on and strode purposely toward Sal who, surprised by the monk's facial expression, froze mid-step and spit the metallic tainted words out in his usual monotone obviously tainted with a sense of extreme apprehension.

"It was stuffed behind the seat…it looked so much like yours I…"

Sebastian took the ornate staff from the little Almie's outstretched hand and began to examine it carefully. When he spoke his words were soft and tinged with a mixture of fear and anger.

"It's Harry's! Solar knows, I'd recognize it anywhere. He prized it over all his other possessions. He would never have given it up willingly. They would have had to kill him to take it."

His eyes misted and he turned slowly and returned to the rear of the truck; holding the staff tightly in his right hand. He spat on the pile of bodies resting on the ground below the tailgate.

"Solar damn you and all your brethren, to burn in a continuum of eternal torment and agony!"

* * * * *

It had taken Gabriel, diligently supported by the others, a good half hour to convince his grandmother of the necessity to abandon their planned birthday celebrations and of the need for them to leave the farm immediately as well as the requirement for her to come with them when they left.

An additional forty-five minutes was spent in her convincing them of the need to bring the birthday cake with them and to negotiate what other articles she could take with her once she'd hesitatingly agreed to the need for her to abandon the farm.

Four of them working together were finally able to manhandle and shift the hefty old sea chest full of treasures she couldn't possibly do without, and that was the result of these negotiations, plus one birthday cake, up into the back of the truck.

While awaiting the approach of full darkness they had familiarized themselves with the weapons they'd recovered from the Ogre corpses and gone over their plan of attack several times, Sebastian slipping unobtrusively into a leadership role and carefully outlining what part each of them was destined to play.

* * * * *

There was just a trace of daylight left when the two vehicles, halftrack in the lead, pulled out onto the highway and turned in the direction of the military base.

They ran without lights and met no traffic on the highway and continued without illumination when they turned onto the track leading off in the direction of the military base.

Once into the tunnel-like confines that had been cleared for the roadway running between the walls of massive evergreens, they were forced to slow their progress as the machines were swallowed whole by the depths of ink-like dark shadows swirling about them.

When they reached the huge clearing in which the base was centered, they stopped briefly and used the powerful built-in binoculars on the gun platform of the halftrack to confirm that, as the Mitra-Varuna had assumed, the massive airship was now tethered outside the big hangar after having completed its normal after-flight inspection.

A wave of relief swept Gabriel when he saw the open hangar doors on the empty cavernous structure and the big airship standing majestically, fixed in position on the huge mooring mast located within the aerodrome enclosure at the near end of the big inner compound.

Satisfied all was as they had expected, he turned to wave to the truck behind him and then stomped twice on the metal plate below him and the lights of the halftrack came on, closely followed by those of the truck behind, as the two vehicles began to accelerate toward the gate.

Jonah didn't want to give the redshirt guards standing in front of the gate time to do a lot of thinking. He approached the gate at high speed and only began to slow when the sentries on either side of the gate started to stiffen with concern.

Gabriel stood in the turret, his hands casually resting on the handles of the fifty calibre gun. He was in full redshirt attire and despite the fact that his shoulders were clenched in unconscious tension, did his best to look military and bored.

The doorway in the small gatehouse swung open and a short, impeccably uninformed young Human redshirt sergeant bolted out into the roadway in front of the gate and raised his hand.

Brother Sebastian, wearing the oversized black SS officer's tunic, shirt and tie with the lower arm sleeves of the jacket pinned behind his back, was at the wheel of the lumbering truck which was closely tracking the forward progress of the racing halftrack.

The monk's face was knotted with concentration as he worked at keeping the unfamiliar beast under control and hugging, but not ramming, the rear of the halftrack.

The young redshirt sergeant, squinting in an attempt to see more clearly, raised one hand to shield his eyes against the glare of the vehicles headlights which both drivers had set on high beam.

When the halftrack lurched to a stop, the sergeant began to move across in front of the vehicle, obviously intending to speak with the driver. As he rounded the fender, Sebastian took a deep breath and switched on the cab light. Clearly illuminated by the overhead lamp, he shoved open the driver's door of the truck and used the open door to shield his lower body; as he settled the dead SS officer's hat on his head before raising himself slightly up out of the seat.

He was careful to show only enough of the uniform to make the required impression upon those guarding the gate, and silently asked for Solar's blessing and then took a deep breath and barked.

"Open the bloody gates you imbecile! Quickly now, the Rector awaits my report."

Without waiting for a response he dropped back down into the driver's seat and slammed the door as hard as he could while closing off the cab light.

Now that they had reached the gate, the tension for those in the back of the truck was thick enough to cut with a knife. Under the dense canvas cover and unable to see the reactions of the men guarding the gates, those under the tarpaulin could only wait in silence and pray all would go as planned.

Unknown to each other, the occupants of both vehicles jointly held their breath for what seemed like forever, but in reality, the instant Sebastian spat the words out, the sergeant's face had drained of colour, and his decision was made.

He spun on his heel and waved his hands impatiently, shouting at the two sentries framing the gate.

"You heard the SS officer; don't just stand there. Open the damn gates!"

The redshirts jumped to the task and as the double gates swung open the halftrack shot forward and Sebastian shoved the truck into gear and slammed his foot down on the accelerator.

Clearing the gate, the two vehicles drove straight down the broad roadway between the buildings, then made a sharp right turn behind the two story administration offices immediately slipping out of sight of any prying eyes back at the gate that may have been following their progress.

Jonah took the next left and drove directly to the fenced aerodrome compound. Upon reaching it, the scenario they'd used to gain entrance to the base was repeated almost verbatim, although this time without direct reference to the Rector.

As anticipated, now that they were inside the fences of the main compound, uniformed and in marked vehicles no one was interested in questioning them.

They were promptly admitted.

Without hesitation, they drove straight across the grass field toward the big structure, which was unlit and empty, racing in through the dark gaping mouth at the front of the huge hangar and were swiftly enveloped by the depths of the black interior of the seemingly unguarded building.

The running lights of both machines were extinguished even before the vehicles came to a stop and once they had, Juno, armed with an assault rifle, parted the canvas at the back of the truck, dropped the tailgate and leaped out. Jonah, like-armed, stuck his head and shoulders up out of the hatch of the halftrack and kept his eyes peeled while the nimble gypsy, her face grim and determined, took up a defensive position between the vehicles and the huge gaping doors.

Sebastian accompanied by Gabriel, left the vehicles and hurried toward the storeroom at the back of the cavernous structure.

Moments later, a much relieved Gabriel led the way back to the others and he and Sebastian quickly helped his father, now dressed in full redshirt uniform, into the back of the truck and then immediately returned to their separate vehicles.

Juno, who had been watching their progress, slung her machine-pistol over her shoulder and jumped back into the rear of the truck, pulled the tailgate back up and locked it into position before hauling the canvas cover back into place.

The vehicles, lights off, began to move immediately, slipping back through the gaping opening and into the darkness of the field.

Gabriel's attention was glued to the gondola suspended below the gigantic airship in the distance. There seemed to be only a single light burning inside, and that was at the front of the structure which held the large windscreen and side windows used to navigate the massive airship.

He could make out a shadowy lone figure moving about inside what, he was soon to learn, was the bridge area of the craft.

There appeared to be only a single redshirt sentry present on the ground below the massive airship, standing just behind the two large barn doors that filled most of the square rear wall of the huge gondola.

As they got nearer to the airship Gabriel could see that the big doors were standing open and a long ramp stretched out from the bottom of the yawning dimly-lit space and ran down to the surface of the field below it.

Inside the dark interior he could just make out the ghostly outline of a parked vehicle.

CHAPTER TWENTY-FOUR

- Airborne -

At the sound of the two approaching vehicles the guard, who had been staring listlessly into the back of the gondola, turned to watch them approach. He had an assault rifle slung over his shoulder and stifled a yawn with one hand as they pulled up.

Gabriel stepped onto one of the tracks and hopped down.

He walked directly toward the redshirt and stood between the middle aged Neanderthal guard and the vehicles, obstructing the guard's view with his bulk as he engaged him conversation.

Jonah, looking a little strange in a uniform too large for his slim frame, climbed down and began to walk toward them at a leisurely pace, doing his best to take advantage of Gabriel's looming frame to shield himself from the redshirt as he approached them.

As Jonah neared them, Gabriel sucker-punched the surprised sentry in his soft gut and deftly pulled the gun off the man's shoulder as the Neanderthal groaned and collapsed to the grassy surface of the field.

He and Jonah quickly dragged the guard's passive form up the ramp and through the open doors at the rear of the gondola and then Jonah swiftly tied the sentry up with the rope he'd brought for that purpose and gagged him with a strip of cloth and then dumped him unceremoniously into the trunk of the staff car hulking behind them before closing and locking the lid.

Sebastian, who had by this time changed back into his own garb, met them at the top of the ramp and the three of them turned to move deeper into the yawning maw at the back of the gondola.

They made their way through the door separating the large cargo area from the rest of the suspended cigar-shaped structure of the gondola and then hurried forward along a hallway which led into the distance toward the front of the craft past several closed doorways.

They opened each of the doors as they reached it.

Most were sleeping compartments, some very elaborate.

In addition, there were two lounges, a crew's quarters, galley, a locked unit labelled 'armoury' and several storage rooms.

Each was unoccupied.

They finally reached a doorway in the bulkhead at the end of the passageway, and then after deciding it probably led directly into the bridge, they paused long enough to quietly regroup before bursting inside.

They found themselves facing a single occupant; a young uniformed Human helmsman stared at them with mouth hanging open and eyes as large as saucers.

He was unarmed and when Gabriel pointed the pistol at him the startled sailor instantly raised his hands.

Brother Sebastian beamed across at the youth.

"Bless you my son, you have made a very wise decision."

Once the young man had been securely tied up and gagged, Sebastian and Gabriel carried him back to the rear of the gondola and placed him inside the spacious trunk of the staff-car next to the bound and gagged Redshirt.

Jonah followed and as Gabe and the monk were dealing with the helmsman, he went to get the others out of the truck.

He was in the process of leading them back toward the big opening at the rear of the airship as Sebastian, after a short orientation of its interior, managed to fire up the staff car.

The others waited for him to pull the big vehicle out and park it to one side before heading up the ramp to enter the back of the gondola.

Jonah got the others settled inside the larger of the lounges and then, accompanied by Gabe's dad, joined Gabriel and Sebastian back on the field at the bottom of the ramp.

The four of them, accompanied by the two Almies then crossed over to the back of the truck.

Jonah delegated the responsibility of loading their combined luggage into the aircraft to Sal and Duanna while the four men struggled with grandma's heavy trunk, which, after many grunts and expressions of displeasure, they managed to drag out over the tailgate to the rear of the airship and up the long ramp into the vehicle storage compartment at the rear of the gondola.

They plunked it down against the bulkhead next to the door leading into the passageway that ran forward all the way to the bridge, and then Jonah turned to face them.

"I've told Sal and Duanna to absorb the contents of the manual for operating the airship after they get the luggage aboard. Gabe, why don't you and your dad check and make sure the others in the lounge are doing all right while Sebastian and I tackle the loading of the halftrack?"

Gabriel nodded and he and his father disappeared back inside the gondola.

Once they'd gone, Jonah took a quick look into the gaping doorway and shook his head.

"You're going to have to guide me in Brother, and since you've got some pull with Solar, see if you can get his blessing on this manoeuvre; it doesn't look to me like we've got much wriggle room to work with here."

Sebastian nodded and watched as Jonah crossed over to the halftrack which he'd left idling, climbed up onto a track and then dropped down through the hatch into the cab.

The monk watched as the machine backed up a short distance before arcing forward across the rear of the ramp, straightening out and coming to a stop.

Jonah's head popped up through the hatch and he took a quick look backward then disappeared again.

The halftrack pulled forward and slightly to the right then Sebastian watched as the front wheels straightened and the vehicle began to edge slowly backward.

When the tracks contacted the bottom of the ramp and Sebastian was confident that it was centered, he moved out and up into a position where Jonah could see him through the lowered driver's window.

Slowly, following Sebastian's directions, Jonah reversed the big machine up and into the depths of the dark opening.

Jonah had been right.

There wasn't a lot of excess space on the sides but after a few false starts and a stream of curses from the young Atlantian, they managed to get it up the ramp and inside.

* * * * *

Gabriel and Sebastian used the pinpointed light from shielded gas fired lanterns they'd brought with them as they moved carefully around the exterior of the airship.

Labouring in the dark was a double-edged sword; a blessing in that they were unlikely to be observed, but a curse when it came to finding and untying the mooring ropes from their anchors.

They took them one at a time, working carefully, anxious to get aboard and away but recognizing they were protected by the darkness. Both were very aware that a moment's haste now could jeopardize the whole endeavour.

The unfastening operation seemed to take forever to complete.

Finally, they had the job completed and the two of them then moved quickly back into the rear of the gondola.

Just inside the open hatchway Gabriel located the handle that operated the long ramp.

He studied it for a few seconds and then switched the bar from 'open' to 'close' and the two of them watched in admiration as the metal appendage began to retract, almost silently telescoping into itself, up toward them, until it dropped into its stored position beneath the floorboards of the cargo area.

Sebastian shook his head in wonderment as the soft hydraulically whir audible while the ramp was retracting disappeared and it locked into place below the floor. He then stepped forward; reaching up for the two chains that ran from the tops of the two big doors and through pulleys attached to the roof above his head, and pulled both, closing the doors.

He locked them into place, and then he and Gabriel began to work their way around the bulk of the halftrack toward the door leading to the forward portion of the gondola.

With no discernible breeze, the massive airship, despite having been released from its ground anchors and now only held fast by the mooring mast, had shifted only slightly.

While the two of them had been getting the dirigible readied to take to the air, Hollis, now armed with Harry's staff, had remained with the women.

The four of them followed by Duanna spent their time exploring and getting settled.

After familiarizing themselves with what the gondola had on offer, individual staterooms had been chosen and when Gabriel and Sebastian came across them they were lodged cosily in one of the two comfortably heated, though still unlit, lounges.

They were drinking cups of steaming hot tea, courtesy of Juno who had rummaged around in the galley cupboards with one of the shielded lanterns until she'd found the makings to brew a pot.

When they poked their heads into the room briefly before continuing down the hallway to the bridge, Juno provided each of them with a fresh cup and an extra for Jonah who was up front with Sal.

Sebastian and Gabriel found Jonah sitting in one of the large leather Captains chairs behind Sal who was standing on his tip toes at the big wheel, staring blankly out through the immense glass windshield in front of him and beyond into the darkness at the base of the mooring mast.

Jonah looked at the others, who jointly gave him a 'thumbs up' and then he turned toward Sal.

"OK little buddy, the lines are untied, now what?"

The next step was a nail biter for everyone on board but, especially for Sal.

Could they fly the damn thing?

Having been delegated by his master to take control of the helm and prepare to get them airborne, the little Almie had already accepted, with silent displeasure, the humiliation of Jonah perching the captain's spare cap on the top of his big head.

The little robot raised himself to his full height and then handed Sebastian and Gabriel the schematic showing the location of the mooring rope winders and sent them off to bring the dangling lines onboard.

He suggested they start at the rear and work their way forward.

He asked Jonah to join him beside the big wheel and requested his master watch certain gauges and report any changes in their readings to him, if and when they should occur. As soon as Gabriel and Sebastian returned to the bridge, Sal squared his thin shoulders and reached out with his little hand toward the control panel beside him.

He pressed the first green button in a line of three and held it.

Everyone on board felt the gentle shudder reverberate through the airframe which resulted and felt the airship shift slightly. When Sal repeated the process for the remaining two buttons, each produced a similar result.

Satisfied that all three engines were operating, the little Almie shifted his hand to the release lever for the mast cable and pulled it down sharply.

As the big airship broke free from the mast, Sal, very carefully, released ballast water until the ship began to rise slowly.

As it started to lift, Jonah turned his attention away from the gauges to look out the big front window.

He, as did the others, gathered on the bridge, watched in awe as the mast supports began to slip by in the glass and then the masthead itself came into view and slowly disappeared out of sight below the window.

Sal flashed his master an unhappy look and Jonah managed a contrite grin before he pointedly turned his eyes back to the gauges.

When Sal was sure they had gained enough altitude, he engaged the propellers for all three engines.

The ship began to move slowly ahead.

As it did, Jonah saw a needle in one of the gauges he'd been assigned to monitor shift slightly to the right and Sal got him to identify which one then nodded and released a little more ballast water from the bladders located only at the rear of the ship. The little Almie had to repeat this manoeuvre twice more before the airship levelled out front to back and Jonah was able to confirm that the needle in question was pointing straight up again.

Against all the odds, unobserved, they were airborne!

* * * * *

Each member of the team aboard the airship had brought aboard preconceived notions of what flying would be like, and they were all pleasantly surprised to find how smoothly and gracefully the great airship moved through the sky.

While the term airship was fitting in many ways, any expected sensation of rolling with waves and listening to creaking timbers on the part of those aboard was quickly dispelled. When operating, the craft made little noise, the only sound coming from the churning propeller blades pushing them through the air. Even that was only audible from inside the engine compartment which was situated above the gondola at the very rear of the utilitarian but well-framed interior of the outer covering which encapsulated the numerous gas and ballast bags that allowed the lowering and raising of the craft.

CHAPTER TWENTY-FIVE

- Murder Confirmed -

They had been in the air for just over an hour when Jonah, accompanied by Sebastian, left the others in the lounge where they had been attending a brief meeting to work out what came next and returned to the bridge which they found now dimly lit by a soft blue light.

Sal was holding the wheel firmly with both hands, gazing out and downward at the passing landscape below.

Although he'd been far from the lounge during their meeting, the little Almie had been aware, through his ability to share Jonah's thoughts, of a proposed change in their course.

While discussing which route to take to reach Almeca, Sebastian had requested that they divert briefly from their intended path to reach the Holy See, to include a short stop to check on the operator of some sort of roadhouse station run buy an individual he had referred to in their discussions, as 'Harry".

While those involved in the discussion had not been exact as to where this station was situated, they had indicated it was located on the main highway between Jericho and Sumer just south of a mountain pass.

At the time, Sal had referred to maps found in a cupboard to the left of the wheel and as there was only one mountain pass noted on the main highway running between those two points, he was confident he had pinpointed the general location of the station.

As a result, he'd already adjusted his course in that direction, and had also made an estimation of the time it would take to reach that general area based on the speed the craft had been averaging since lift off.

He'd then been able to communicate that information to Jonah from the bridge while the discussion in the lounge was still taking place. He'd also taken that opportunity to express some concern as to what they might expect in the weather conditions at that altitude, but had then balanced his concerns by pointing out that so far they had been moving through cool but clear skies, and if that situation held as they began to rise up over the mountains, he couldn't foresee any major problems in accomplishing the task safely.

As a group, they had agreed to take the chance, weather permitting.

* * * * *

When the big airship began to approach the base of the mountain range Sal released short bursts of ballast water along the full length of the airbag until the big airship slowly began to lift.

Climbing took them up into colder air but the temperature within the gondola itself was thermostatically controlled and seemed to vary little, regardless of the increasing altitude.

The terrain passing below began to change from browns and greens to a blanket of white as the ship continued to rise and sightings of the passing wintery landscape below clearly indicated a drop in temperature overall and an obvious increasing chill in the air outside the artificial comfort zone of the passenger capsule.

Despite how far they were being forced to climb in order to rise above the mountain peaks, there was no sign of precipitation and the clear skies held.

A thermometer affixed to the outside of the huge windscreen at the front of the gondola indicated an external drop in temperature of nearly twenty degrees since they had begun to rise from the valley floor and although they were still climbing slowly they could now see the tops of the snow-capped mountain peaks coming into view and Sal informed them they would be able to level off soon.

The prospect of flying above the mountain peaks drew everyone on board up into the small bridge area, three walls of which held large windows.

They were all silently enjoying the transient landscape as it slipped past below them.

In the cloudless sky, the combined light given off by the three moons high above Olympos clearly illuminated the mountainous terrain slipping by beneath the ship. The illumination provided by the three was intense enough to cause shadows very similar to those that formed in midsummer daylight.

In the un-forested areas ice crystals caught the light, reflecting it in a stunning array of shimmering sparkles as the ship, casting its own ghostly shadow over the snow below, soared overhead.

It was Juno who quietly verbalized the general consensus.

"It's breathtaking, if a little eerie. I've never seen anything quite like it."

Gabriel nodded and smiled.

"Ya, and I'd figured we would have trouble seeing anything down there at night but with this much moonlight finding Harry's place should be a piece of cake. It's almost as bright as day down there."

As they crested the mountaintop Jonah pointed.

"There's the pass! All we have to do now is follow the road on down the other side to the station."

Gabriel took his eyes off the windscreen long enough to look over at Jonah.

"What do we do when we get there; I mean how do we get down?"

Jonah unconsciously turned toward Sal, but his Almie was already providing the answer without speaking.

Jonah heard his little pal out and then paraphrased for the others.

"Sal figures it won't be too much of a problem. Luckily there's very little wind to contend with. We nose the ship into what there is of it and slow the propellers until they hold us stationary then drop down to just above ground level. Once we've done that we'll have to let go mooring lines which we'll need in place to help us hold our position. He figures two from the tail will be enough to do the job for a quick visit. We'll have to tie them off to trees or maybe the buildings, something that can take the stress."

Over the past few days Gabriel had begun to fully appreciate what the little grey robot was capable of and he had no difficulty in accepting the comments at face value.

He turned his attention back to the window and his eyes narrowed as he strained to keep them on the roadway which wound its way downward from the pass just below the top of the mountain.

"We're getting close now, just around that next bend I think. You'd better slow us down Sal."

Sal turned the wheel slightly, working the nose of the massive airship into the gentle breeze and reduced the revolution of the engines considerably.

Sebastian saw it first.

He groaned audibly.

"What in Solar's name...its gone!"

Gabriel picked the site out now. Covered by a thin skiff of fresh snow, the burned out shells of both the barn and the cabin consisted of only skeletal black-charred remains and the slightly raised outline of the stone foundations.

His initial thought was for Blue but the burned out husk of the barn below left little hope there was any chance of the bike being salvageable and his concerns for the machine quickly faded to be immediately replaced by concern for Harry's wellbeing.

Venus stifled a sob.

"But how could both buildings catch fire? They're separated by so much open ground?"

Any optimism that Sebastian had been clutching to fortify the hope that Harry might still be alive was rapidly slipping away.

When he spoke, his voice had a sharp edge, cold and hard.

"Because this was no accident, someone deliberately burned them to the ground. I think I have a good idea who was responsible and looking at this makes me wish I'd been the one on that fifty calibre gun at the farmhouse. Those Fascist bastards! I pray Solar roasts their bodies and all like them for eternity!"

Sal worked the wheel and slowed the engines a little more and the massive airship drifted to a gentle stop. He began to release gas from the inflatable bags in short bursts along the length of the ship allowing the big craft to settle in increments, ever so gently, downward.

As the little robot worked at the controls he passed unspoken instructions to Jonah, who repeated them aloud.

"We need two bodies to go to the back and lower a rope from each side of the tail. Gabe why don't you and your dad do that? You can show him how the winches holding the mooring lines work. Sebastian and I will get into some winter gear and hop out and look for good spots to tie the ropes down as soon as you've released them."

Jonah left the bridge to go the crew quarters where he had seen some heavy jackets and once he'd gone Sebastian added.

"Perhaps the ladies should remain on board. I don't think what we may find down there is going to be something they'll want to see."

Sal brought them slowly downward to within about fifteen feet of the uneven snow-covered ground and was then doing his best to hold the ship steady as Jonah returned with the jackets and passed one to Sebastian.

When the little robot was satisfied with the manoeuvre and confident that he could maintain their position, he nodded and Jonah uncoiled the rope ladder attached to the wall beside the emergency exterior access door-like hatch cover located at the rear of the port side of the bridge compartment.

Sebastian then unlatched and opened the hinged cover plate and they all felt the chilling gust of cold air invade the bridge and sweep into the temperature controlled room in a wintery blast while he and Jonah dropped the rope ladder out over the doorstep and attached the clamps at the top of it to the rings set into the floor.

Once it was anchored in place the two of them climbed down to the ground and began to work their way under the belly of the hovering craft back toward the two trailing mooring lines which were now drifting down from the rear of the big airship.

Juno waited until the two men were on the ground, and then reached out to pull the hatchway cover back into place, at least as far and as tightly as the ropes obstructing the bottom of the opening would allow and held it there against the pressure of the dangling ladder.

As only a small crack along the edges of the cover remained to admit the outside air, she was able to reduce the intensity of the chill slipping into the bridge considerably.

Aided by the bright moonlight, Sebastian was able to get his mooring line securely fastened around the base of a tree in short order and as soon as it was tied in place he began to work his way through the heavily crusted snow in the direction of what remained of the cabin.

Jonah, who had successfully attached his rope around a rock outcropping turned and started to follow the monk toward the cabin, but about forty feet later changed direction as the monk, apparently having spotted something within the burned out barn, turned away from the cabin and headed toward the charred remains of the other building.

Jonah divided his attention between keeping an eye on Sebastian's progress while ensuring the effectiveness of his own footing as he made his way across the crusted uneven surface of the snow.

When he next looked up he was only twenty feet away from the monk and he immediately slowed his pace when he saw Sebastian drop to one knee and place his face in his hands.

Feeling somewhat of an intruder, the tall Atlantian stopped moving completely as he looked just past the crouched figure before him. He swallowed heavily as he recognized the charred remains from which Sebastian was gently brushing clean the thin layer of recently fallen snow.

Hollis, who had been the man who'd stepped into Harry's boots when the old man was put out to pasture, was watching their progress from behind one of the large gondola side windows. When Jonah froze in mid stride, he immediately shifted his gaze to the monk kneeling on the ground and instantly understood what had transpired.

He did not have to be there on the ground beside Sebastian to know exactly what his brother had found in the ruins of the barn.

Acutely aware of the depth of the bond that had formed between Sebastian and the old man when they had been partners, Hollis's heart went out to the monk's kneeling form. As a Brother of the Golden Ring, in name if no longer in fact, Hollis had no difficulty in understanding the intensity and depth of pain, the anguish his old friend must now be experiencing.

When they'd worked together, Sebastian had told him many old war stories relating to his time as Harry's partner. Hollis knew Sebastian would be hurting and he immediately left the bridge and returned minutes later wearing a heavy winter jacket.

Without comment Juno opened the doorway to allow him access to the ladder so he could leave the ship to join Jonah and the monk on the ground.

* * * * *

Below the snow, the soil was frozen but Sebastian insisted on staying long enough to provide Harry with as proper a burial as circumstances would allow.

Hollis, as a member of the brotherhood, was permitted to assist, but Sebastian declined offers of help from the others, explaining to them that the ceremony was something the members of the brotherhood needed to do alone.

Without hesitation, he and Hollis took on the responsibility for the grizzly task. They gently wrapped Sebastian's old friend and partner in a canvas tarp stripped from the woodpile before laying him out in a small trench near the back of the burned out shell that had been the cabin.

Then carefully, hands near frozen and bleeding from numerous small cuts, they stacked rocks to cover it as best they could.

Jonah stood back at a respectable distance and waited until the two men said their final words over the gravesite and turned to join him.

Suddenly conscious for the first time that the breeze was beginning to pick up and what that could mean to the position of the airship, Jonah who was standing just below the ladder, shouted to the two monks to untie the mooring ropes. He then rapidly scrambled up the suspended rope ladder to climb back aboard the airship to help Sal while Hollis and Sebastian raced through the crusted snow to free the mooring ropes before hurriedly making their way back to the dangling ladder.

CHAPTER TWENTY-SIX

- *Progress Interrupted* -

Three hours had passed since the airship slipped away from the charred remains of the station. The big chronometer on the wall to the left of the wheel registered 10:40 hours.

A gloomy pall, well matched to the darkening clouds and first raindrops outside the airship, hung over everyone aboard as Sal silently guided the big airship toward Sumer. Jonah, who was eager to touch base with his father, had urged the over flight of the city. The intention was to get near enough to the small metropolis to allow him to reach a spot where they would be back in range and able to communicate with Jericho by way of their Almies.

Venus and Juno had retired to their own staterooms to get some rest after getting Gabe's grandmother, who they had decided deserved the big stateroom with full bath that had obviously been designed for the party leader, settled into hers.

The men were all perched on captain's chairs under the soft blue light of the bridge.

Each absorbed in his own thoughts, Gabriel and Jonah sat staring out through the big windows into the darkness while Hollis and Sebastian spoke in soft tones, reminiscing about past adventures with Harry.

* * * * *

A usually confident and self assured Colonel von Jaeger stood frozen stiffly at attention.

Beads of sweat covered his forehead as he watched his Rector pacing furiously back and forth on the polished marble floor in front of his massive desk.

Over the past six hours, the SS officer had overseen a series of four firing squads in which, on the orders of the man who was still ranting in front of him, a total of fourteen Redshirts and one scientist, who the Rector casually dismissed as only 'Human' after all, had perished.

In addition, he had, as ordered, replaced all sentries on the gates of the compound with his own black uniformed SS men.

He had seen the leader displeased before, but never this intensely.

By this point, Von Jaeger, in an attempt to avoid his own turn at the now bullet-etched wall behind the firing range at the far end of the compound, found himself reduced to providing only short unctuous responses to the tirade of questions and accusations that bombarded him from the, all but frothing lips, of his purple-faced leader.

The Rector was currently raging about Marduke who had apparently cut off all communication and had been incommunicado ever since his return to Atlantis, effectively severing the relationship which had provided the guidance and material to help bring the party to its present position of prominence.

* * * * *

Having spoken with his father briefly through their Almies, and after watching the lights of Sumer slip by below them, Jonah, joined by Hollis, Sebastian and Gabriel huddled over the small map table at the rear of the bridge to discuss the next leg of their flight.

After a short exchange, Jonah suggested that Sal be brought into the planning, and Gabriel offered to relieve the little Almie at the wheel so that could be accomplished.

Sal had, after firm admonition to touch nothing but the wheel and then to only hold that steady, relinquished the helm to the Neanderthal reluctantly before joining the others at the table to see what course they had selected and ensure that it was the best choice before getting it clearly registered in his mind.

While verifying the choice they'd made, he made calculations and transmitted them simultaneously to Jonah who vocalized them verbatim.

"From here to Port Symoon on the south coast of Indus will take us at least fourteen hours, perhaps more as the wind velocity is increasing and we will be facing a headwind. Once we leave Symoon we'll be passing over the ocean, crossing the Bay of Angels. We'll be over water all the way to Port Pag at Almeca city.

That will take us another twelve hours at least. Sal suggests we shouldn't count on those times as being precise. He's very concerned about the building storm and resulting headwind; the stronger it gets the longer the trip will take."

Sebastian nodded as he slowly ran the fingertips of his right hand through his moustache and beard.

"Yes he has the right of it. I've made the trip several times by ship and the winds can be treacherous over the bay. I suggest each of us taking a turn at staying on the bridge with Sal, on a rotation basis, in case he needs help, while the rest of us try to get some sleep."

Nods of agreement came from all sides.

* * * * *

With the exception of slower progress due to the wind and a general deterioration of the weather conditions, the trip had been uneventful since passing over Sumer and the general disposition of everyone aboard had improved with the passage of time.

Hollis and Gabriel spent a good spell together during which his father provided him with a sanitized and condensed version of his life before he'd met his mother and reached his decision to change careers for the sake of his family to come.

He answered many of Gabe's questions but remained guarded when pressed for specific details of what his work for the Belief had entailed. Under considerable pressure from Gabe the older man had gone so far to acknowledge that he had undertaken many assignments on behalf of the Devi and that his brotherhood was in effect the Belief's 'Wet Team' and that he had done many things he was not proud of during the period in question, but he refused to provide specifics.

For whatever reason, Venus had become very quiet and thoughtful.

Now whenever they shared each others company, whether in a group or alone, Gabriel found her studying him pensively from time to time and she was pleasant enough to be around but the sparks of interest in the physical sense that had crested between them at the way-station seemed to be missing and she appeared to him as not particularly interested in anything more than polite conversation.

He definitely felt a waning of the tentative sexual tension they had begun to share. For her apparently, for what ever reason, that had been overshadowed by other concerns.

While he would have liked to believe this change would be of a temporary nature, perhaps brought about by the fact that Juno, since joining the group, had been very demanding of his time; something that had been exclusively Venus's prerogative up to that point and was now resented by the beautiful Atlantian.

If that was the case, and he was far from sure it was, then it seemed reasonable to hope that this situation would change in that Juno's need for his support had already lessened noticeably as the young gypsy became more secure in her surroundings.

Surely Venus had noted Juno's reduced need to be physically near him continually to function effectively and hopefully that understanding had to reduce any competitive demand for his attention that had resulted between the two women.

He could only hope that Venus could see that Juno was working her way through the horror she had experienced over the troll attack and was needing less reinforcement from him each day in order to feel safe in her surroundings.

Gabriel couldn't deny that, from a purely physical point of view, he was disappointed and somewhat dispirited by this change on Venus's part. Based on the fact that he no longer caught Venus staring daggers at Juno at every opportunity, he felt he had good reason to hope that this was just a temporary setback and that things might revert to a renewed interest in their relationship.

The changing situation with Juno was also a two-sided coin.

While, on a physical level he missed spending the majority of his time with the vivacious beauty, he had to admit that he was relieved mentally to find her becoming less cloying and demanding.

As Juno worked her way through her grief, she had begun to form a close relationship with his grandmother and seemed to be spending much more of her time in the company of the older woman now than she did with him.

Gabriel had strong feelings for both women and saw this as a positive relationship, of benefit to each.

* * * * *

By the time the sparkling lights of the Port of Symoon had slipped by below the airship and the massive craft had begun to move out over the deep blue waters of the Bay of Angels, the group had settled into a routine.

The women had organized and taken responsibility for looking after tea, coffee, meals and entertaining Grandma while the men ate, slept and took turns on the bridge with Sal, who, despite the steadily increasing wind and rain, was now confident enough to allow them to take brief stints at the wheel while he settled into one of the chairs for a break.

At theses times, he did, however, supervise them very carefully.

* * * * *

The first glimmer of dawn made a desperate attempt to work its way through the blackness of the night sky. It revealed a rapidly building wall of ugly clouds, dark, moisture-swollen and threatening.

Sheets of rain had begun to pelt against the huge windscreen at the front of the gondola in increasing ferocity. The progressively strengthening wind coupled with the airships steady, if slower south-easterly progress caused the near solid cloudbanks to whip past the side windows and move rapidly down the sides of the moving ship.

Visibility was low and the temperature registered on the thermometer affixed to the outside of the windscreen had begun to drop alarmingly.

Gabriel was taking his turn on the bridge with Sal. He sat observing the building storm before them from his chair behind the little grey Almie.

Although Sal had not chosen to communicate since Gabe had arrived to take his shift, the young Neanderthal was beginning to sense stress and concern reflected in the diminutive little robot's movements.

These had progressively become more frequent, and of late were often accompanied by a furrowed brow and soft sighs.

The door to the bridge opened and Juno stuck her head in.

"Fresh coffees on Gabe. The others have finished breakfast and Sebastian and your dad are headed up to relieve you. I've left yours warming in…"

Before she could finish the big airship lurched, the bow dropped briefly but sharply before settling back. A rasping buzzer sounded and a small red light over one of the gauges began to flash ominously.

Gabriel turned his head away from the door to look back at Sal who stood ramrod-straight at the helm.

He watched as the little robot turned his attention to the bank of gauges to his right. The Almie's large black eyes swept over them and then he reached out and sharply punched the three buttons controlling the engines.

The loss of forward motion by the ship was not complete but definitely noticeable to all on board.

Gabe got up off his chair and stepped forward.

"What is it? What's wrong?"

There was the sound of pounding feet and then Juno was unceremoniously shoved through the door as the others crowded onto the bridge, their faces reflecting a variety of expressions, everything from mild concern to outright panic.

Jonah looked over at Sal who had turned his attention away from the control panel and back to the wheel.

" What's happened Sal?"

The little robot moved the wheel slightly before inaudibly responding to his master. A quizzical look formed on Jonah's face as he repeated his little friend's words for the benefit of the others.

"At least two of the three propellers have seized. Sal's shut all three engines down in an attempt to stop them from burning out. He doesn't know what caused the problem yet."

* * * * *

It took them forty-five minutes to figure it out.

During that time Sal had been hard pressed to keep the airship facing into the driving rain and wind which was now blowing them backwards at a fair pace.

The little Almie remained calm and systematically gave the others direction, through Jonah, advising as to what steps needed to be taken to get to the root of the problem.

Sebastian, Hollis and Gabriel had all been sent astern on various missions and it was when they returned to the bridge that Sebastian provided the answer.

CHAPTER TWENTY-SEVEN

- Risky Business -

"It's a mooring rope at the back we think. The winch on one of them gave way and the drum has played out all the rope. We figure the stronger winds we've run into of late must have blown the hawser back and upward and it's wrapped itself around a couple of the propeller shafts preventing them from turning freely."

Jonah looked from Sebastian to Sal, who thought for a few seconds before responding to him.

Jonah nodded to himself slowly as the little robot communicated and then turned back to the others who were all waiting anxiously for him to speak.

"He thinks that's quite probable. There are apparently some ship plans in the cabinet over there and they show tie points up on top of the air bag where a safety line can be attached. The emergency harnesses are stored in a locker back in the vehicle compartment, and there is also a small doorway in there, like the one up front here in the bridge, that gives access to a permanently affixed metal ladder which leads up onto the top of the ship."

Jonah paused and frowned deeply.

"That's the good news. The bad news is that Sal says the wind is gusting more forcefully all the time and if the temperature continues going down, the precipitation is likely to turn to freezing rain. In addition, the manual prohibits anyone using the ladder to go up top when the machine is in flight. Even a slight breeze is enough to make its use suicidal and needless to say, the weather we are currently experiencing goes far beyond that. We're losing altitude and if we don't start the engines soon we'll plummet into the drink. It is unlikely that we would survive the impact. We don't have a lot of time to solve..."

Hollis interrupted.

"'Anyone' is not going up there, I am. The problem occurred because I neglected to use the locking mechanism on the winch when we left Harry's and I'll be the one who goes up to fix it. Under the circumstances we certainly can't wait for ideal conditions; it has to be done quickly or we're going down."

The colour drained from Gabriel's face and he opened his mouth to argue but his father cut him off.

"Everyone on this airship risked their lives to rescue me, and I can do no less for all of you now. My fault; my job Gabe; it's not open for discussion."

A powerful gust rocked the airship slightly. Sal groaned and fought the wheel. Jonah moved forward to give him a hand.

"Looks like were in for a rough ride. Sal says we are only about a quarter of the way between Port Symoon and Port Pag and now we're being forced backward by the headwind."

Hollis turned and started for the door leading to the hallway, calling over his shoulder as he pulled it open.

"Gabe we both know you can't take heights. It's very crowded back in that rear compartment; you stay here. I'll need a clear mind for this and I don't want to be worrying about you. Sebastian, bring the plans showing where these tie points are and come with me. I may need a hand getting into the harness contraption, and Sal, I can't communicate with you once I get up there, so when you reach the point where you either need to fire up the engines or hit the water, don't hesitate; start the engines"

Despite Sal's best efforts to hold them steady, the ship was slowly but inexorably losing altitude.

They had dropped down under the cloud cover now and with considerable trepidation, Jonah watched as the churning water below came into view far below.

In the short period of time he'd been helping his little Almie fight for control of the wheel the surface beneath had changed from a flutter of whitecaps to rising swells and then deep troughs had begun to form in the rolling water; and the surface was rising toward them at an alarming rate.

* * * * *

Sebastian adjusted the buckles on the back of the harness, tightening the webbing across Hollis's shoulders and waist over the thick jacket he had slipped on and then used his hands to turn him around so he could check the bindings at the front.

Satisfied, he picked up the coil of light safety rope from the floor and clipped one end of it to a thick steel eyelet affixed to the front of the harness. He pulled firmly to test it and then followed Hollis into the restricted space available between the halftrack and the wall and partway along that cramped space until they located the small doorway indicated in the ships plans.

The two of them exchanged strained looks before Hollis reached for the door handle and opened it, pulling it inward. The intensity of the wind and pelting raindrops was immediately apparent, lifting tendrils of Hollis's hair and splaying them out behind him in damp disarray.

Grasping both sides of the doorframe firmly and squinting in an attempt to see clearly, he arched his upper body out through the opening and looked first left and then right until he spotted the end of the ladder attached to the side of the gondola. It ran upward over the gondola and then out and around the exterior of the bulging airbag, eventually disappearing from sight at about the halfway point.

Hollis had to raise his voice to be heard over the raging wind.

"Solar grant me the strength to reach the ropes and free those propellers."

His eyes met the monk's as he thrust out his hand.

"Look after my boy, Sebastian."

The monk shook his extended hand briefly and then Hollis was gone, swinging out through the door and grasping a rung of the ladder. He didn't hear Sebastian's reply.

"Solar willing, you'll return safely to us, brother."

Hollis clung tightly to the ladder, working his feet out and placing them firmly on the bottom rung, taking time to condition himself to his new surroundings.

In an attempt to clear his vision, he closed and opened his eyes several times. It was to very little effect. When he felt confident to release one hand from the wet surface of the ladder he used it to brush his eyes clear of moisture.

The wind was powerful and gusting unpredictably, the rain hitting him in sheets. He was already soaked to the skin but because the airship was not under its own power and therefore no longer fighting the wind but moving with it, conditions were less severe than he had anticipated.

He was thankful for that.

Hollis turned his head to look downward.

Vertigo enveloped him and he closed his eyes instantly and lifted his head.

He found himself gripping the rung above him so tightly his knuckles had turned white and it was several seconds before his breathing got anywhere close to being normal.

When it did he opened his eyes again and stared climbing upward along the length of the narrowing ladder, and found himself wondering how in Solar's Light he was going to manage to make his way out and around the billowing cigar-shaped airbag above him.

Where he was positioned wasn't too bad. Standing upright on the ladder, most of his weight, including that of his water logged clothing was supported by his feet but once he reached the spot where the airbag arced outward, his body would be angled outward as well and the majority of his mass would have to be supported by his arms and upper body.

His look down at the raging sea below had made it clear to him that failure was not an option and he knew time was running out.

Hollis focused his mind carefully, dismissing the negatives and concentrating on what had to be done and how best to accomplish it.

Then he began to climb, taking one wet slippery rung at a time.

He reached the top of the gondola relatively quickly, and clamped his eyes shut. By feel alone, he began to move higher, working his way out and around the side of the Airbag. As he moved he realized that it wasn't as spherical as it had appeared from below, more oblong in shape.

Be that as it may, climbing upward was going to be difficult. It would take all his strength to accomplish but at least the task now appeared doable.

He hauled himself upward slowly and carefully. It seemed to take forever to complete the arc and reach a point half way up the bag to a position where he could again use his feet to take more of his weight.

Arms and shoulders aching, he paused at that point and took a short rest before he began to climb again. A few minutes later he found himself fully supported by the circumference of the airbag.

Hollis was crawling more than climbing by the time he reached the top.

He spotted the large ring attached to the highest rung on the ladder and used one hand while hanging on with the other to remove the coil of rope which had been attached to the front of the harness. Shaking it free, he clipped the loose end to the ring, and then let the rope play out slowly as he moved off the ladder and onto the top of the airbag on his hands and knees.

Facing backward and keeping low to stay out of the wind as much as he could, he began to make his way toward the opening between the twin smokestacks and the propellers at the rear of the ship.

The surface of the airbag seemed well supported by its metal frame and strong enough to take his weight. It also had some give to it. It was almost like crawling across a huge firm pillow. He was initially concerned that he might damage the outer covering, puncturing or tearing it as he moved but he really had no choice but to proceed; it had to be done and he pushed his unease aside.

Fortunately, the ladder being situated at the rear of the gondola meant that the distance left to cover to reach the props was relatively short.

He moved carefully, feeding out the safety line as he went. He could see the end of the wayward mooring rope now, flapping wildly in the wind.

He paused as he reached the two short, fixed, wing-like stabilizers that extended horizontally from each side of the body at the very back of the craft. He would have to move out onto one of them to reach the shafts of the propellers which he could now see behind them.

The flailing hawser had wound itself around two of them. He placed one knee onto the top of the fixed wing and put some weight on it. It seemed strong enough to hold him.

Pulling his knife from behind his belt and placing it in his teeth, he began to crawl out onto it moving toward the shafts.

* * * * *

The interior of the bridge area was as quiet as a tomb, only the sound of shallow breathing could be heard. All eyes were riveted on the big windscreen at the front of the gondola.

The raindrops hammering the glass surface had begun to morph into small ice pellets and what could be seen of the surface of the ocean below was closing with the airship at an ominous pace.

The shared tension had an almost electrical feel by the time Jonah finally broke the silence.

"Gabe, maybe you could go back and see if you can get some idea how it's going…, and then come back and let us know?"

Worried sick about his dad and happy to be doing something, anything, Gabriel moved quickly toward the door and once it had closed behind him Jonah continued.

"We're running out of time; I thought it might be easier on Gabe if he wasn't here when we're forced to start the engines."

* * * * *

By stretching out flat on his stomach Hollis was just able to reach the area where the rope was wrapped around the base of first shaft, just at the point it entered the body of the airbag.

He grasped the edge of the short, stabilizing wing firmly in one hand, then used his blade to saw at the mangled fibres at the base of the shaft.

It was slow, painstaking work but he was finally able to dig the offending material clear, then he severed the rope and unwrapped what remained from the shaft before releasing it and watching it fall away to the water below.

Replacing the knife between his teeth he then used both hands to work himself over to the other side of the airship and repeat the process on the second rope-bound shaft.

He found the second binding not as tight as the first and was able to use the point of his knife to loosen it. Once he had unwound the remainder of the rope he dropped it clear of the airship.

Using one hand to hold himself in place, he tucked his knife away with the other. That accomplished, he wriggled his way back across the stabilizer to the main airbag then raised himself up onto his hands and knees and began moving back toward the top of the ladder, this time struggling against the full force of the roaring wind.

When he reached it he carefully released the clip of the safety rope from the ring and began to coil it. What would normally have been a simple task was made frustratingly difficult for him by the fact that his fingers were bleeding profusely and stiff from the cold.

His brain grew perturbed with his hands inability to accomplish as simple a task as fastening the coil to the front of the harness. The effort exhausted him and despite the conditions, he found himself forced to rest where he was for a few moments, in an attempt to regain his strength.

Like all Neanderthals, Hollis didn't feel the cold easily, but he was feeling it now.

He was also having increasing difficulty seeing clearly through the incessant wind-driven barrage of stinging ice pellets.

CHAPTER TWENTY-EIGHT

- *High Price to Pay* -

Gabriel found Sebastian in the cramped space between the halftrack and the outer wall of the gondola.

The monk was squinting against the fury of the wind as he kept his eyes moving from side to side trying to watch the portion of the ladder he was able to see as well as keeping tabs on the rear of the airship.

The concern expressed in Gabriel's features as he approached was mirrored by the monk who shook his head solemnly as he raised his voice to be heard over the sound of the raging wind.

"I can't see much of the ladder from here but he hasn't fallen off the back, and I did see a chunk of rope drop, so he's made it as far as the propellers."

Sebastian's eyes brightened as he picked up movement out of the corner of his eye. He'd spotted Hollis's feet slowly drop one after another into view at the top of the ice covered ladder. Elation filled his voice.

"I see him Gabe! He's done it! He's on his way back down. Let them know up front."

A sense of relief filled Gabriel, and the lump in his throat eased somewhat.

He turned and moved quickly to the doorway leading to the gangway, yanked it open and eagerly sprinted forward toward the bridge at the front of the gondola.

* * * * *

Hollis was shivering uncontrollably, the severe cold leaching into his bones. Clinging to the ladder with the last of his strength, he no longer had any feeling in his fingers and it was only by checking them visibly through the heavy blanket of ice pellets that he knew they were still wrapped around the rung above his head.

There was simply nothing left. He'd given everything he had.

The passage of time seemed to slow.

He had the satisfaction of knowing he'd accomplished what he'd set out to do.

His son was on the right path.

He would soon be with his beloved wife.

He was at peace and had no regrets.

Being the man he was, he was incapable of intentionally releasing his hold on the frozen rung of the ladder but knew his impending fall into the raging sea was inevitable.

His pain faded and was replaced with a numbing acceptance.

* * * * *

Sebastian watched in helpless horror as the boots slipped gently off the rung and Hollis's body, trailing the unwinding coil of harness rope behind it, dropped past him toward the churning surface of the ocean now no more than a hundred feet below.

The big airship lurched slightly as the engines were engaged and then, as the propellers began to cut through the air, it began battling its way forward and angling desperately slowly upward against the ferocity of the storm.

Sebastian ignored the increasing velocity of the freezing rain for a few seconds, staring blankly down into the water, then hunching his shoulders, used both hands to force the small doorway closed against the gale and latched it securely.

He turned around slowly and slumped back against it, letting his lungs empty in a burst of frustration, and then, with shoulders stooped and eyes brimming he sighed deeply before forcing himself erect and refilling his lungs.

* * * * *

Sebastian's report of Hollis's loss hit all of them hard.

It was softened somewhat by the fact that it had occurred before the engines had been started and therefore had not been abetted by the forward motion of the airship; and that Hollis had clearly been aware of the danger as much as any of them and it had been his decision to risk paying the ultimate price to save the ship and the others on board.

Sebastian approached Venus and spoke softly for her ears only.

"I think it would be a good idea for you and Juno to spend some quiet time with Gabe and his grandmother. Jonah and I can give Sal any help he might need here."

Venus didn't reply, she simply nodded and moved to stand by Juno.

Moments later Venus and Juno led Gabriel and his grandmother off of the bridge and down the hallway into the larger lounge, joining to comfort them in dealing with their loss.

The others remained on the bridge as moral support for Sal who was frantically dropping ballast water and adding gas to the huge airbags in an attempt to gain attitude and lift back into the clouds and hopefully clear of the full force of the storm.

The big airship came within fifty feet of the angrily thrashing crests of the deep grey water before it began to rise, painfully slowly at first and then with marked determination.

An obviously relieved Sal turned his full attention to the wheel itself and made some minor adjustments until he had the nose of the massive craft aimed directly into the tumultuous wind.

Sebastian unconsciously wiped away the sweat that had formed on his brow and nudged Jonah, who was seated beside him, gently with his elbow.

"What happens now that we're beginning to climb?"

Jonah, taking pains to make sure he wouldn't disturb Sal's concentration, replied softly.

"He's not sure, but he thinks we might be able to avoid the worst of the storm if we climb up above the clouds. It will depend on what altitude we have to reach to get on top of them. If we get too high, we won't have enough oxygen to breathe apparently. He says we've been blown back toward the coast for the last couple of hours and even with the engines running at full power we can't make much headway in this weather. We really don't have any option but to give climbing higher a try."

It had sounded a reasonable and a relatively simple answer to their problem.

It was anything but.

Rising up to the bottom of the cloud bank was stressful but uneventful. The big airship, now under its own power and skilfully manipulated by Sal's adjustments in ballast performed as hoped but while the weather had been bad below the dense clouds, it turned absolutely horrendous once they entered them.

Complete darkness and wildly gusting winds coupled with rumbling thunder gave the little Almie no respite.

He fought the wheel frantically in an attempt to hold a steady course, while sharp flashes of sheet lightening raged around them.

No one spoke.

Everyone in the group who held even the slightest faith in the Belief, prayed softly to Solar for salvation.

For those crammed into the confines of the bridge it seemed never-ending but suddenly the massive airship broke through the top of the cloudbank and into clear skies and bright light.

No wind to speak of, no rain. They could see for miles ahead over the tops of a mask of dark clouds that completely obliterated any sign of the water passing below them.

Sal's taut shoulders immediately went fluid as he relaxed his death grip on the wheel.

Squinting eyes fought to adjust to the brightness and a general sigh of relief filled the bridge as the brilliant light beamed in through the huge windscreen to warm their faces.

After several minutes of silent reflection, Sal's monotone voice filled the small room.

"If these conditions prevail, we should arrive at Port Pag in about fifteen hours."

* * * * *

When bright beams of light replaced the foreboding darkness beyond the large windows of the lounge and flooded into the compact compartment, all four of the occupants looked up in surprise and relief,

In many ways, both Gabriel and his grandmother had unconsciously accepted the horror of the storm as fitting and appropriate in view of the tragic loss of father and son respectively, as had the two young women who were doing their best to comfort them.

However, that did nothing to dampen the general sense of relief brought on by the sudden passing of the appalling weather they'd been forced to endure for what seemed like hours. The tension which had built up in the four of them in respect to the atrocious and steadily worsening climatic conditions confronting the airship rapidly began to abate as the ship rose into the warm blast of a totally unexpected burst of light.

Juno lifted her hand to shade her eyes and shook her head in disbelief.

"Wow, I wonder how Sal managed that. It's like we just popped out of a long dark tunnel and into the light."

She rose from her chair and crossed over to the light switch on the bulkhead beside the door, flicked it down turning the interior pot lights off, then returned to the small oval table and sat back down before picking up her cup and raising it to her lips.

She waited until Gabe's grandmother had sipped the last of her tea, then looked over at the drained old woman and offered a smile.

"Why don't we get you settled into your bed so you can have a little rest now that things have settled down a little Mrs. Corvin?"

The grey head bobbed up and down slowly and Juno stood and took her elbow, helping the old woman to her feet. Gabe, who had barely spoken since his father's passing, sat head down; shoulders stooped seemingly unaware of those around him and unconcerned as to the abrupt turn in the weather.

He took no notice as Juno and his grandmother left the room.

Venus who was sitting across from him finished her tea. She wanted to ease his suffering, but was unsure of what she could do, hesitant to break into his private grief.

Gabe spoke, his voice barely audible.

"Everything was happening so fast. I never really got a chance to talk to him. I thought I knew him, but the stuff Sebastian told me, it left so many questions to ask and I never got the opportunity to talk to him about all of it."

Venus got up and moved around to the other side of the table, rested her hands on his broad shoulders and began to massage the taut muscles between his shoulder blades gently.

"I didn't know your father for long Gabe, but the man I saw was caring, strong, unselfish and brave. His love for you was obvious, and I don't think anyone could have wished for a better father."

Gabe lifted his head and tilted it back to look up at her.

"Yes you're right. I just wish I'd had the time to tell him how much he meant to me before I lost him."

Venus met his eyes and held them.

"I think he knew that Gabe, now how about we get you to bed for a little rest too. Jonah and Sebastian don't want you standing any more shifts with Sal until you've had time to allow yourself to grieve and remember your dad. Sleep will help that process."

Gabriel rolled his shoulders moving them slowly under her probing fingers.

"Mmmm, that feels good. Yes, I am tired, I feel completely drained. Maybe a shower and some sack time would be a good idea."

Venus stepped back as he stood.

Duanna, who had been at rest against the wall near the small galley sink, opened her eyes and made to join her but Venus shook her head and the little Almie frowned but stayed put.

Venus opened the door leading into the hallway and then closed it behind them and walked with Gabe toward the stateroom he'd been using since they'd boarded the airship.

The young Neanderthal, detached from his surrounding, shuffled along slowly, every step lifeless, as his thoughts shifted listlessly about in his head. Venus felt her heart go out to him and she gave him a big hug when they reached the door, then opened it for him before she stepped back and let out a sigh.

"It'll get better Gabe. The hurt will lessen with time. You have a nice hot shower while I make us some sandwiches and a fresh pot of herbal tea. When it's ready I'll bring it back and we can talk a bit if you want and then you can get some much needed rest."

* * * * *

Juno pulled the bedclothes up under the old woman's chin and Gabe's grandmother smiled up at her.

"Thank you for your concern and support child. I don't know how you manage it, considering your own grief. You are a wonderful young lady Juno and you deserve better."

She let out a sigh and her eyes glistened in the soft light.

"It's the boy I worry about most. First his mother passes and now his father gone. He's so young and it just doesn't seem fair."

She brushed away a tear.

"Not fair for you either child, both of you, too young, far too young to lose your parents."

Juno shook her head and felt her own eyes begin to brim.

"No it's not fair, but it is part of life Mrs. Corvin and Gabriel and I are not the only orphans on Olympos. We have to grieve for our loss, which goes without saying, but we also have to be thankful for what time we had with our parents before we lost them and value and appreciate what they did for us while they were there to guide us."

She managed a small smile despite the tear sliding down one cheek.

"Don't you worry about Gabe, Mrs. Corvin. He is a fine young man with his whole life ahead of him and he is not alone, he has you and he has friends who care for him."

The old lady let out a soft sigh and closed her eyes.

"Yes, he does and I'm very thankful for that."

CHAPTER TWENTY-NINE

- *Impromptu Liaison* -

Juno waited until she was sure the plucky farmwoman was asleep before she left the room and headed down the hallway with a view to seeing if she couldn't find the makings for a good thick soup among the provisions available within the well-stocked galley shelves and in the on-board freezers.

* * * * *

Venus set the tray down in the hallway outside Gabriel's door, and then knocked softly. She bent down to retrieve the tray and then tilted her head slightly to listen for a response. When she didn't get one she repeated the process, and got the same result. Concerned, she lowered the tray until she could reach the door handle with one hand.

She pressed it down and the door sprung slightly open.

Venus could hear the shower running as she stepped inside and kicked the door closed behind her. She set the tray down onto the small dresser just inside the doorway.

"Gabe, it's me,"

She heard the shower turn off, but receiving no answer, she raised her voice a little and spoke again.

"Gabe, its Venus. I thought you'd be out of the shower. I can leave the food here and come back later if you like."

The door to the small bathroom forming part of the compartment opened a few inches and Gabriel's head framed by dripping hair and surrounded by a haze of steam, poked out at the top of the opening.

"No, I feel a lot better after the shower and I'm hungry. I'd like to take you up on that offer to talk too, if you're still up for it."

Venus was pleasantly surprised and pleased to find him somewhat enlivened spiritually and thought that the interest in food, Gabe's first since the incident with Hollis, was a good sign.

"Sure, I'd enjoy it."

A touch of a smile graced Gabriel's lips as he stuck his head out again briefly. She could see him bent forward slightly as he towelled his hair vigorously and aware that the steam had dissipated, using the door to shield everything from her view below his chest.

"Can you toss me the robe on the bed there please? I found it in the closet. These rooms seem to come supplied with everything you could ask for."

Venus's eyes rested on the expanse of his powerful chest which was covered with a mat of golden down and the clinging and shimmering prism-like droplets that remained after the shower. These little globules of moisture sparkled with soft reflected light under the single bulb in the compact bathroom.

Initially she'd assumed the growing warmth she was experiencing had to do with the release of steam into the room once the bathroom door had opened but she knew now that it had more to do with her view of Gabe than highly heated water.

The sensations wafting rhythmically through her body were not unlike those which had overwhelmed her back at old Harry's place while she had been nursing the muscular young Neanderthal and it was powerful enough to make her legs feel a little unsteady as she crossed the room and scooped the robe up off the bed before turning back toward the bathroom door which stood slightly ajar.

Gabe, towel wrapped around his waist, stuck his hand through the opening and accepted it from her with a smile of thanks. Venus knew she should turn and move away, but instead stood there for a few seconds watching him and relishing the view as her nostrils filled with the clean, but definitely very recognizably male smell of him as it emanated from the bathroom.

Gabe's attention was directed toward his reflection in the mirror as he drew a comb through his damp hair and Venus took advantage of his distraction, closing her eyes as she felt a little shiver of desire begin in her loins and slowly, deliciously, spread its way through the rest of her body in ever stronger, concentric ripples.

* * * * *

Having jointly agreed to split the responsibility of seeing that Sal would have support if needed during the remainder of the flight,

Jonah and Sebastian were taking turns sitting up front on the bridge of the big airship. They'd agreed to rotate the duty, each to stand watches of four hours on and four off. The further south they travelled, the better the weather below the airship had become. The air temperature registered on the gauge attached to the outside of the windscreen had risen considerably under the forbearance of the warm rays of the Solar and within a half hour the storm below them had blown itself out to reveal calm waters below. The conditions for flying were as near to perfect as they could get and the little Almie was making the most of the situation, spending the majority of his time sitting idly, but attentively in the big captain's chair situated directly behind the wheel. He had the steering mechanism itself strapped in place and only got up from time to time to periodically check gauges and confirm their course.

After they had been traveling for an hour or so Duanna wandered onto the bridge and moved up to stand beside Sal. Sebastian, who was on watch at the time was a little surprised to see the little Almie on her own and unaccompanied by her mistress.

Since meting them, he'd found the couple inseparable and naturally expected to see Venus arrive shortly to join her little grey friend. When that didn't happen, the monk wondered about it briefly but a few minutes later his attention shifted to the antics of the two Almies in front of him.

They were obviously communicating, turning to glance back and forth at each other and Duanna had picked up the ship's manual in her little hands and she and Sal were soon going over parts of the thick book, nodding from time to time as they pointed out different sections to each other.

* * * * *

Juno lifted the lid off the pot, ducked her head back until the steam evaporated and then reached in with a wooden spoon to stir the simmering broth.

Satisfied with the aroma, she replaced the lid, turned down the heat to its lowest level to simmer and set the spoon down on its rest. A few more minutes and it would be ready.

It had taken some time to produce and she had decided that she would not disturb Gabriel and his grandmother now that it was done.

She'd made a huge pot and they could help themselves when they awoke refreshed.

She dried her hands on the dishtowel resting on the counter beside the stove and then, humming softly, left the galley and started down the hall toward the bridge.

* * * * *

Up on the bridge Jonah, who had come forward to relieve Sebastian, stood beside the monk while they exchanged a few words and the monk brought him up to speed on their progress.

The two Almies sat in matching chairs in front of them, seemingly still deeply involved in discussions relating to the operations manual of the airship.

Dusk was passing and under clear skies the three moons were providing enough light to supply a clear view of the deep blue and lightly chopped seas now passing rapidly below the airship.

Pushed by a fresh tailwind and slicing easily through the warm outside air, they were making very good time.

* * * * *

Juno was reaching for the handle to open the door leading through the bulkhead from the hallway to the bridge, when it opened and Sebastian filled the doorframe.

Freezing her forward motion and tilting backward to avoid a collision with the wiry monk, Juno burst into laughter. Sebastian, quickly recovering from the surprise of her presence, immediately joined her.

Jonah, his attention drawn to the commotion stepped up behind Sebastian who then turned to him and grinned.

"Just about had a collision with our beautiful young gypsy"

Jonah smiled.

"Lucky you!"

Juno beamed at the two of them before she spoke.

"Just wanting to let you know that I have a big pot of soup on and it'll be ready in a few minutes. I wasn't sure whose turn it was on the bridge, or how many were up here."

Jonah nodded.

"Just me, I've just relieved Sebastian. It would be great if someone could bring me up a bowl when it's done. Maybe you could ask Venus to bring it, I haven't seen her for awhile and I'd like to talk to her."

A puzzled expression filled Juno's features and she couldn't resist peering passed the monk to view the inside of the small bridge.

"Really, that's strange; I haven't seen her either, not since I took Gabe's grandmother and got her settled into her bed for a little nap. I thought she was up here with you guys. Oh well, not to worry, I'll bring you up a bowl myself."

Jonah smiled and dropped into the seat behind the two Almies.

"Thanks Juno, I'd appreciate it."

Sebastian stepped though the doorframe and pulled the door closed behind him and as it closed Juno spun on her heels and the two of them started back down the long corridor, past the sleeping quarters, toward the lounge and galley area at the rear of the gondola.

* * * * *

As she went over the top, Venus let out a sharp cry of pure unadulterated pleasure and raked her nails down Gabriel's powerfully straining back and clenched his muscular buttocks with enough force to leave deep scratches.

Deep enough in several places, to begin filling with blood.

Gabe felt no pain, instead he crested at the feel of the intense sensation and his expulsion of deep husky groans of undiluted satisfaction instantly drowned out the now softening moans issuing forth from the gaping mouth of the perspiration covered Atlantian, whose body was still shaking and rigidly arched upward off the bed.

* * * * *

Outside Gabe's door, Sebastian and Juno both came to a halt and turned to look at each other, brows furrowed and quizzical expressions on their faces.

Sebastian spoke first.

What in Solar's World was that?"

They both turned to face the door beside them and stared at it, ears peeled.

Juno reached out and knocked.

"Gabe, you OK in there?"

* * * * *

As flushed as Venus was, she turned at least two shades darker and her mouth snapped shut.

Gabe, still struggling for breath, and bathed in the blissful afterglow sealed his lips too and sucked a deep breath in through his nose as his body went ridged.

Trying to regain control of his breathing and his mind racing, he felt the pressure of Venus's hands pressing upward against his heaving chest and he obediently rolled off her.

He lay there with a glazed expression on his face as the beautiful Atlantian moving in a blur and bathed in the soft light of the single flickering candle on the bedside table, scooped up her clothing from the floor and raced for the bathroom.

The door to that room had no more than closed behind her when there was a second knock at the one leading into the room from the hallway and then it opened a crack and Juno stuck her head in.

"Gabe we heard strange noises, are you all right?"

Two bold words flooded Gabe's mind.

"HOLY CRAP!"

CHAPTER THIRTY

- His Cup Runneth Over -

Before Juno could center her gaze on the bed, Gabriel grabbed the covers that had somehow ended up in a pile at its foot and hauled them up over his waist.

When he opened his mouth to speak he found it dry and there was no better way to explain the way the words squeaked out, than to call them a series of frog-like croaks.

"Yurss, I…I…mmmn …finnee."

He struggled to get some saliva flowing and finally managed it, although his words were still low and husky

"Just a nightmare I guess."

The door opened wider and Sebastian's dark and concerned face appeared over Juno's, both were backlit by the lights from the hallway.

Juno turned her head to trade looks with the Sebastian and then pushed the door open a little farther.

"He's really had a hard time of it. I'll stay with him for a bit until he settles down and can safely get back to sleep."

Sebastian had been a monk for a long time, but, he had been a young man before taking the cloth and the accompanying requisite vow of celibacy. In addition, and to be honest before Solar, he had to admit that since he had been absolved of all sin, both past and present, he'd strayed a little from that particular oath on a few occasions. It had occurred only in the line of duty of course, while bereft of his robe and in civilian clothing and while working undercover. The fact had caused him no particular concern; it was something one could reasonably justify under the circumstances and consider a form of fringe benefit that came with the job.

He also had an excellent memory and very good olfactory receptors and they were both telling him that the pungent odour wafting out though the open door was heavy with scents he readily recognized. His eyes took in the untouched sandwiches and the pot of tea sitting beside the unused cups on the tray.

A small smile formed on his lips. Before he spoke, he took extra care to ensure that not a trace of mirth touched his words.

"Yes, by all means child. I'll look after dishing out the soup and seeing that Jonah gets a bowl. You go ahead and spend as much time with Gabe as you think he needs."

* * * * *

By the time he reached the galley and got the door closed behind him Sebastian was laughing so hard he could hardly stand. He sat down at the small table, a huge grin on his face and shook his head slowly back and forth for a very long time.

He couldn't help but wonder if Gabriel was beginning to wish he'd followed the monk's earlier advice offered in old Harry's barn.

But he strongly doubted that was the case.

The young Neanderthal was in his prime, and for that matter, so was Venus and if the smell emanating from that compartment was any indicator, it had been worth it for both of them.

Still, it was going to be interesting to see how the current situation worked out, after all, unless he missed his guess, there were three of them in that compartment now.

* * * * *

Juno closed the door behind her and crossed over to the side of the bed.

Concern filled her beautiful dark features as she raised her right hand and placed it on Gabe's sweat-beaded forehead. Gabe was hesitant to breath and he certainly wasn't about to move.

Juno frowned and removed her hand.

"Holy Crap Gabe, you've got a fever and look at this bed, it's soaked with sweat!"

Gabe managed to nod and opened his mouth to speak, but before he could Juno's eyes welled up with tears and she bent down to kiss him gently.

"You, poor baby...I know how much it hurts, and I also know what would do us both a world of good."

Her lips pressed down against his again but this time they were demanding and her tongue forced its way deep into his mouth and began to explore. Then she frantically shrugged off her clothes, lifted the impressively tented covers, blew out the candle and climbed into the bed with him.

* * * * *

Venus stayed absolutely quiet in the small bathroom for the first half hour.

By that point she realized that no one would probably hear her on the other side of the door if she shouted at the top of her lungs, and she began to get dressed.

She'd decided some time ago that, under the circumstances, she would be foolish to begin a long term emotional relationship with Gabe, but that had not served to lessen the physical attraction she'd felt for him in the least, and she did not regret for an instant having shared his bed earlier.

It had been very much better than she could have hoped.

The activity going on in that same bed at the moment should have brought at least a touch of jealousy with it, but it didn't, and that realization pleased her greatly and brought about a small smile on her lips.

Her own experience had proved that there was more than enough of Gabe to go around; she certainly couldn't fault Juno for sampling just how satisfying it could be.

However, she strongly doubted that Juno would agree with that proposition and she therefore waited until the second heated session on the other side of the door got very hot and heavy before she turned off the bathroom light and quietly slipped out of the little room and made her way across to the doorway leading to the hall.

She couldn't resist turning to observe the action on the bed for a split second, then satisfied neither occupant was paying any attention whatsoever to anything but what they were personally indulging in, she gently pushed down the door handle and in one quick motion slipped out into the hallway and pulled it swiftly, but oh so gently, closed behind her.

* * * * *

Sebastian took a bowl of soup up to the bridge for Jonah and then returned to the galley to avail himself of a large serving of the hefty mixture.

Juno was a very good cook, and wondering exactly was taking place in Gabe's compartment kept him in good spirits as he ate.

When he finished his soup he cleaned up after himself and left the galley before making his way to his own rooms and then stripping and climbing into bed.

He had to relieve Jonah in the bridge in just over three hours and wanted to be rested when he took his next watch.

* * * * *

Venus returned to her compartment long enough for a quick shower and a change of clothes and then made her way down to the galley to have a bite to eat.

When she'd finished and taken enough time to let the wonder of her earlier tryst with Gabe fade enough to feel presentable before others, she left the galley and walked down the central hallway to the bridge bulkhead door and went inside.

She smiled at Jonah and he padded the seat beside him in invitation.

Venus dropped into it and they began to talk about the current situation and their future plans.

An hour later she, accompanied by her Almie, left the bridge and returned to her compartment to get some sleep.

* * * * *

Six hours later all the passengers on board made their way to the small confines of the bridge of the aircraft.

Sebastian had remained with Jonah after the last change of watch and he'd thoroughly enjoyed watching the others as they arrived.

Juno had been first, freshly showered, long dark hair still damp, her features demonstrating a healthy flush and grinning from ear to ear.

He couldn't resist commenting.

"Wow someone sure has a bounce in her step and rosy cheeks this morning - have an especially good sleep did you?"

Juno's dark features coloured briefly and the smile disappeared before she spoke.

"Yes I did, thank you for asking"

She turned her attention to the big windscreen.

"My, what a beautiful day!"

Sebastian's grin broadened, and he was tempted to expand his comments but decided to let her off the hook easily.

Juno moved up to one of the large side windows and turned her back on the others as she looked out and downward toward the gently rolling water. She didn't turn when the door opened and Venus entered the room.

Sebastian had to ensure he maintained a level playing field between the two young women and as he had done with Juno, he greeted the vibrant young Atlantian immediately.

"Boy, it must be the sea air; you look just as fresh and relaxed as Juno this morning."

Venus met his gaze and nodded.

"The flight had been so smooth since the storm that I was able to get the first good sleep I've had in some time. I feel absolutely wonderful this morning."

Both greetings seemed to Jonah as uncharacteristic for the monk who normally said little unless addressed. He looked over at Sebastian inquiringly but got no satisfaction from the monk who simply smiled and turned his attention to the windshield and the horizon ahead.

When Gabriel slipped onto the bridge, looking somewhat bedraggled but with a smile that looked permanently pasted on his face, Sebastian who could see him reflected in the expanse of the windshield, made no attempt to turn around.

"Well, it seems its either feast of famine eh Gabe?"

Gabriel felt the heat flush up from his neck and Sebastian grinned at the reflection in the window as he finished the sentence.

"The weather I mean, crazy storm and then nothing but Solar's light and much, much warmer temperatures."

Gabe frowned but didn't respond, simply nodding before crossing to an unoccupied side window to look out at the light reflecting off the calm surface of the water below the ship.

* * * * *

The arrival of the massive airship floating into the bay caused considerable concern and alarm among the city's inhabitants.

No one on the ground below them had ever, even in their wildest dreams, imagined anything like the huge dirigible.

Sal brought the craft into the port about one hundred feet off the calm, deep blue surface, moving very slowly, taking in the vista below them with deep concentration.

Sebastian and Jonah stood on either side of the little Almie.

The city of Almeca was large by any standard and the monk had been running a steady commentary since it had come into view and they began their approach, identifying various structures and points of interest as they closed on the metropolis.

As they entered the inner harbour, Sal asked the monk to provide suggestions with reference to where they could find a temporary mooring point for the gigantic airship.

Five long wharves extended from the shoreline and well out into the bay. Ships of every size were docked against the concrete strips. Sebastian pointed down at the closest of these and suggested it might provide what was needed.

"The vessels you see below are secured by ropes running to those big iron rings interspaced along the edge of the wharf. We could come in over one of the piers and drop the mooring hawsers down, bow and stern, then fasten them to the rings fore and aft of the ship. Probably the best we can do for now. As you can see, the bay is sheltered by hills on three sides reducing the likelihood of any chance of crosswinds. Tying up to the iron rings should hold the airship safely in place until we can arrange for something more permanent."

Sal bobbed his head and began to adjust his course to bring the ship in directly over the indicated wharf.

CHAPTER THIRTY-ONE

- *Safe Harbour* -

As the big airship drifted silently through a cloudless blue Solar-filled sky to a stop, those on the ground, within sight of, and directly beneath the airship, dropped whatever they were doing and froze in position, staring upward, pointing fingers and shouting to those around them in alarm and surprise.

Those on board observed this stunned initial response to their arrival, watching it grow, flowing out in concentric waves from the shadow cast by the craft. Soon, those further away from the docks began to crowd into the confines of the port area by the hundreds.

Sal, via Jonah, dispatched Sebastian and Gabriel to the upper levels of the ship to drop a pair of mooring hawsers from their drums fore and aft respectively.

Once they'd left the bridge, Sal released gas from the air chambers in short bursts and the massive airship dropped sedately downward until it floated approximately thirty feet above the wharf.

The crowd directly below the ship reacted in panic to the manoeuvre, pushing and shoving to get clear of the descending craft. There was general pandemonium until the crowd realized the airship had stopped sinking toward them and was now holding station.

Sal repeated the manoeuvre he'd used at the way station, keeping the crafts nose into the wind and the engines engaged, props turning slowly to allow them to hold the ship steady.

Jonah got his little buddy's message as the ship stabilized.

"We will have to keep a party on board to hold us in place more or less. We've got to find some way to maintain our position until we can manage to run a line from the bow hawser to a stationary object of the required height, perhaps to the crows nest of that big schooner tied up to the pier just ahead of us there, for now and we definitely need to find a more permanent and substantial mooring mast to hold her in place if we want to confidently leave the ship without someone on board to make the minor adjustments that will be required to keep her positioned as she is."

Jonah let out a sigh.

"Right, we'll take guidance from Sebastian; this is his home town after all, and he's the one we'll have to rely on to get things sorted out on the ground now that we've made it to Almeca."

He glanced out through the big windscreen and grinned

"Look at that, they're tying us down! I wonder how they knew what to do?"

Sal let out a derisive snort and verbalized his response.

"This is a port after all and although we are in the air and not in the water, I'm sure those below know a ship needs to be tied up when it comes into dock."

There were smiles and giggles from the women standing behind them and Jonah turned to look at his little friend and frowned.

"Anyone ever tell you that you're a pompous ass Sal?"

Talk about the conversation between the kettle and the black pot.

Sal refused to justify the comment with a response, instead he turned his attention to tying down the wheel and stepping back from it once he'd felt the hawsers, which were now securely affixed to iron rings, bow and stern, take up the slack.

The door in the bulkhead behind them opened and Sebastian and Gabriel stepped through to rejoin the others in the wheelhouse.

Jonah related Sal's suggestion of having a second bow mooring line tied off to the schooner to help keep the airship in position and then looked toward the monk.

"Well brother, we made it, now the ball's in your court I guess. How do you want to play it from here?"

* * * * *

After reaching consensus with the others, Sebastian unlatched and swung open the small man-door on the side of the gondola in the aft area of the ships bridge and let the coiled rope ladder drop through and down to the surface of the pier below.

Turning to the others, he paused before climbing down.

"Haul the ladder up as soon as Venus, Jonah and I get down, we don't want any brave soul coming up to join you while we're gone. We'll be back as soon as we can, but this could take awhile. I imagine things will get pretty crazy once we finish our preliminary meeting at the palace. If I were you I would take advantage of the shower facilities aboard and grab a bite to eat and then get some rest while you're waiting for us to return."

He led the way, followed by Jonah, Venus and Duanna, who quite obviously wasn't particularly enamoured by the idea of going down the ladder.

A hush fell over the crowd as Sebastian moved down out of the doorway and came into view.

The varying sensations of surprise, awe and unease that had initially rippled across the sea of faces faded at the appearance of the brother dressed in his readily recognizable attire. This was quickly replaced by a wave of wonder and curiosity, which was justifiably compounded by the presence of two members of the Atlantian race accompanied by a personal robot, whom all recognized but few had ever actually seen before.

Sebastian took advantage of the crowd's early stunned reaction quickly, knowing it would not last.

As his feet hit the wharf, he spotted a young sister dressed in scholastic robes standing among those nearby and beckoned to her.

She approached hesitantly, recognizing his Order, but uneasy about getting any closer to the strange craft hovering just above them.

When she was in earshot Sebastian identified himself and flipped the cover off the top of his ring to show the crest concealed below. The woman dropped to her knees and kissed the ring and then he urged her to her feet and spoke to her, keeping his voice low and enunciating carefully.

"Quickly my child, go to the palace and announce our arrival.

Arrange for a coach and a security screen to be sent here at once."

* * * * *

Having entered the port in the period of 'Vacancy of The Holy See" due to the death of Mitra VII; the small party was taken directly to the Almeca city offices of the Prime Minister of the state of Almeca which was located deep behind the thick stone walls of the sprawling palace of the Belief.

Despite the fact that the Conclave of the College of Mitra-Varuna was due to sequester within a matter of weeks for the election of the next Devi and her responsibility as Prime Minister for many preparations in that regard, Aabha greeted them personally and graciously received them into the palace. With only Brother Jacob in attendance in her office, Aabha listened with interest to the information provided by Sebastian and Jonah in regard to the situation facing the Atlantians as a result of Marduke's actions.

Venus, flanked by Duanna, sat quietly as the monk and her brother spoke and answered the few, but poignant, questions the Mitra-Varuna posed during their explanation of the purpose of their visit to the Holy See.

When they had finished Aabha asked Brother Jacob to take charge of the two Atlantians with a view to arranging for them to partake of refreshments and take their leisure while she had further discussions with Brother Sebastian in regard to other matters.

Several things happened in quick succession after that relatively brief but constructive meeting.

Within hours a large block of apartments, normally utilized by an order of ecclesiastical scholars was emptied of it occupants who were quickly moved to lesser quarters.

The self-contained block they vacated was then cleaned in haste and organized for the arrival of the Atlantian refugees who, upon completion of the preparations, would immediately be transporting en mass to the Holy See from Jericho.

Their upcoming arrival was cloaked in deepest secrecy. No one residing outside the walls of the Holy See was aware of their coming nor was any outsider made aware of the Decree of Sanctuary that placed them under the temporary care and protection of the Belief.

While these arrangements were being structured by others, Aabha and Sebastian moved on to other pressing concerns.

The moment the door closed behind Brother Jacob and his charges, Aabha sat more erectly and let her eyes meet Sebastian's

"I have other concerns I would like to discuss with you, but, of late, I have been having some difficulty getting answers from some members of your Order due to the Devi's passing. Will that be a barrier between us?"

Sebastian shook his head and drew an envelope from inside his robe. He handed it to her.

"No, this letter clearly allows me to disregard the restrictions of duty normally in place under the circumstances and directs that I take you into my confidence on all matters and offer myself to your personal service."

Surprised, curious, and very relieved, Aabha opened the unsealed envelope and withdrew the single sheet of paper inside. She read it quickly and set it down.

"Yes. Well, it clearly directs what path you are to follow in the instance of the Devi's passing. My aunt held you in high esteem and this will make it much easier for me to bring myself up to speed and, if I may say so, I could certainly use some moral support and wise council at the moment."

Sebastian smiled briefly.

"Your wish is my command Mitra-Varuna Aabha. I am at your personal service, at least until a new Devi is appointed, and if, Solar wills it so, perhaps after that as well."

Sebastian reached for the letter and carefully replaced it in its envelope before returning it to his robe.

"I'll just hang on to this in case someone happens to question my position in the days to come. I'm sure Brother Jacob for one is going to require me to produce it at some point in the near future."

Aabha raised an eyebrow and smiled.

"Yes, I fear you are correct in that assumption and he will not be alone in this regard I'm sure. Now, perhaps you would be good enough to bring me up to speed on the matter of this new Indus political party centered in Jericho."

Sebastian settled back into his comfortably upholstered chair, closed his eyes and began to report his findings on the fascist movement, its leader and what he knew of its aims. He spoke for almost an hour and Aabha took some notes but did not interrupt him.

When the monk had finished she took a deep breath and resting her lower elbows onto her desk, placed her fingertips together, steepling both sets of hands and resting her chin on the uppermost.

She took a few seconds to absorb what she had heard, and then she lifted a small bell from the corner of her desk and shook it softly.

The door to her office opened and a serving brother appeared. She ordered tea and light refreshments.

Once the brother left the room Aabha raised her eyes to meet Sebastian's.

"In a nutshell then, it is far worse than we first imagined. This megalomaniac is intent on not only taking over the state of Indus but probably as much of the rest of the world by way of political influence as he is able to manage, and the remainder by way of a military contest if that is what it will take. Supporting the whole plan is this rogue Atlantian you've identified as Marduke and who is in cahoots with Eisen and providing a host of advanced military hardware to assist him in his conquest for control of the planet. Were you able to get in to see this stored equipment within the warehouses while you were on the base?"

Sebastian shook his head.

"There was not time, but I did bring a couple of examples with me and if the others are as impressive, I would venture a guess that, although he is not ready to strike out yet, should the Rector decide to do so in a few months, he will quite likely be successful in any military conquest he might undertake."

Aabha's shoulders sagged slightly and she frowned.

"Yes I've already had several reports on the flying machine in the harbour. It frightened half the city when it pulled into the bay. Solar only knows what other weapons of mass destruction those warehouses harbour"

Sebastian's features hardened and he lowered his voice slightly.

"We, the others with me on the airship and the Atlantians you've met so far, already have some ideas as to how we can go about levelling the playing field and hopefully putting the Fascists out of business. That isn't going to be an easy walk in the park however."

Aabha straitened in her chair and managed a brief smile.

"Well, that is good to hear, but under the current circumstances of operating under a Vacancy of the Holy Sea, there is little we can do but plan until we have been graced by the appointment of a new Holy Mother who can exercise her authority in deciding how we, as the Belief, are to proceed against this threat."

There was a knock at the door and it opened.

Several brothers entered carrying a fresh pot of tea, two large mugs, two bowls, a small tray of sandwiches and a steaming container filled with thick seafood chowder.

CHAPTER THIRTY-TWO

- Safe Haven -

Adon and Gaia stood just inside the main doors of the hotel conference room.

The couple were taking the time to welcome each of the Atlantian team members individually; many whose features were drawn with worry and stress, and did their best to set their minds at ease before bidding them take advantage of the refreshments provided before seating themselves at the tables set up in the center of the room.

By the time the line of exiled Atlantians ended, only one of their number had been forbidden entry.

Demeter who had been stripped of her office and held in isolation and guarded by other members of the team on a twenty-four-hour basis from the time of their arrival in Jericho, remained upstairs in her room, her only company being that of her personal Almie.

The little grey robot had been carefully helmeted to prevent her from communicating with Marduke's Almie, Bellum.

Persephone, who had replaced her mother in the roll of financial advisor, had taken her early elevation to that post very seriously and was proving to be very capable.

Adon dispatched his Almie and three others to the hallways outside the chamber, stationing them to guard the four doors that provided access to the big room.

He then closed and locked all four of the double doors before joining Gaia at the head table.

* * * * *

Aabha ate sparingly, two of the small sandwiches to accompany her half bowl of chowder; Sebastian cleared the plate of the remaining sandwiches and availed himself of a second bowl of the delicious seafood concoction.

When they had finished, Sebastian stacked the dishes and moved them to a clear spot on the credenza situated against the wall under the single large window which overlooked the bay and Aabha poured them full mugs of the mint-scented and honey-enriched herbal tea.

She fastened a cozy around the large pot then got more comfortable in her chair before checking her note pad. She then raised her eyes to meet Sebastian's.

"You indicated this new Fascist party was carrying out medical experiments of some kind on both man and beast and that ex-Brother Hollis was being held prisoner and you were able to rescue him from the military facility you descried earlier, but he was later lost at sea. Were you able to determine the purposes of these experiments?"

Sebastian lifted his steaming mug to his lips and took a tentative sip.

"Apparently they're working toward accomplishing a couple of things. They are playing around with what was referred to as genetic engineering. It seems that in animals their aim is to interfere with the normal gene makeup of specific types of animals, either by substituting, removing or adding others. I have no idea how this works, nor do I imagine, do scientists in other parts of Olympos, but they are having some success with it apparently in at least one instance that I have learned of. They have created shift-changing Trolls who are maniacally aggressive and have loosed several of these with a view to causing panic among the population. They kidnapped Hollis Corvin and I imagine others in order to use the same type of system to secure genes from unique individuals who hold specialized abilities. Their plan here is to genetically engineer a perfect soldier, far superior to any other and with unquestioned loyalty and obedience and capable of a wide range of special abilities. They intend to go a step farther in their processes than they have with animals and use what they refer to as cloning to reproduce whatever numbers of these soldiers they wish. Being clones of the original genetically engineered unit, these warriors will apparently have loyalty to no thing or person other than the organization which produced it."

Aabha's brows raised and she set her mug down.

"Sounds farfetched to me, and even if it is possible, it would cost a fortune and take decades, would it not?"

"Well it's a way out of my league, and I know it is only in the initial stages with regard to the soldier idea but as I mentioned, they have already had some success with animals. Juno, the young gypsy who is part of our party, lost her mother and all her traveling companions to a Troll attack and what happened before her eyes wasn't what one would normally associate with a group of Trolls. Savage beyond belief would just begin to express the viciousness of their attack."

* * * * *

A general sense of relief was apparent through the room as Adon broke the news of the impending short-term solution to their immediate problem.

None of the gathered Atlantians questioned the wisdom of seeking sanctuary within the Palace walls of the Belief and under the protection of the Devi.

A gently rising clamber of relieved tension expressed itself by way of a shuffling of chairs and an outpouring of murmured verbal expression. It swept through the interior of the conference room and Adon paused to let the reaction play itself out before continuing.

"I am also pleased to be able to inform you of some additional information I've recently received. Although I am not at liberty to provide specifics at this time, I can tell you that I have every reason to believe a way has been found to retake Atlantis."

He raised his hands to forestall a repeat of the earlier disturbance.

"The Elders are currently discussing this new development and once we are safely settled and under the protection of the Belief you will be apprised as to when and how this can be accomplished. Now please return to your rooms and pack your belongings; we expect to begin transporting as a group within the next few hours."

* * * * *

On the night of the airship's arrival in the bay, the halftrack, under the supervision of Jonah and Gabriel, was unloaded shortly after darkness settled over the dockyard area and once the milling crowds of curious onlookers had degenerated to a small number of hangars on.

Once down the ramp and onto the dock, the vehicle was encased in canvas and loaded onto a huge transport vehicle. Six horses were then hitched to the heavy wagon and began to haul it over the broad cobblestoned roadway that wound it way up the hillside toward the palace stables.

Upon arrival it was securely locked away in an unused stall and a squad of the Devi's Personal Defence Unit were detailed to ensure twenty-four-hour security for the vehicle, on an ongoing basis.

* * * * *

It fell to Venus to organize and oversee the transport of the banished Atlantians from Jericho to Almeca.

In the end, the entire party, with the single exception of Demeter, transported in small groups spaced a few minutes apart to allow Venus time to welcome each upon arrival, and ensure that they had been settled into their new quarters before the next batch arrived.

It took the better part of two hours to accomplish the task and feel confident enough with the job to leave them in the care of several brothers and sisters who would see to their evening meal, while she attended a private dinner with Mitra-Varuna Aabha and the other members of the small team that had brought the airship into the bay.

The meal was to be in honour of their accomplishment and came in the form of a personal invitation from the Prime Minister of Almeca.

Brother Sebastian had delivered the gold embossed initiations earlier by his own hand and had taken the time to indicate to each of the recipients that the meal would be of a working nature and strongly suggested all attend.

* * * * *

Aabha glanced at the clock located on the wall on the other side of her desk.

"It is almost time to get ready for the diner. I have a few more things to discuss with you, but it will have to wait until later this evening."

Sebastian nodded his agreement and stood up.

"Yes, it has been quite a day and I could do with a nice long shower and a fresh robe."

Aabha smiled and then raised her right hands, palms up.

"Oh, I almost forgot. Your things have been moved, I've asked Brother Jacob to switch rooms with you."

A quizzical expression covered Sebastian's face.

He had been half turned away from her, headed toward the door and twisted his head to look back at her.

"Brother Jacob, but he has the rooms next to the Devi's apartments. As Leader of the Order he must, by duty, reside there to insure her personal protection. Those rooms are provided with a direct access to the Holy Mother's apartments."

Aabha's eyes met his and held them.

"True, but perhaps you are unaware of the fact that they also contain an adjoining door that connects with the apartments that I, holding the positions within the belief that I do, am supposed to avail myself. Due to a recent attempt on my life..."

Sebastian swung his entire body back around to face her squarely. Concern was etched deeply into his features.

"An attempt on your life, when? How, and by whom?"

Aabha raised both right hands and held them palms out.

"It's, complicated. As to the reasons why, those are some of the things we will need to discuss later tonight. Suffice to say that I have moved into those apartments since the attempt on my life. It seemed like the responsible thing to do in view of the situation and was primarily driven by Brother Jacob who threatened to resign from his position if I did not agree to make the change."

* * * * *

The transportation of the Atlantians to Almeca had gone smoothly and a few hours later, after eating and getting settled in, they met as a group in the large dining hall of their new quarters.

During the brief meeting that followed, a committee was created with a view to planning the retaking of Atlantis. It consisted of a central body of four Atlantian Elders and was to be jointly chaired by Adon and Gaia.

Additional members of the proposed committee were to include Jonah and Venus. As interested parties and at Jonah and Venus's joint request, Gabriel and Juno would also be asked to attend as advisors to the committee, and Brother Sebastian would be invited to the future meetings as a representative of the Belief.

Before the long day was through the parties had managed to meet for just over an hour. The result was the formation of a concrete proposal to complete the retaking of the moon.

It had been tabled with some confidence.

Prior to that meeting, elegant apartments within the main palace and on the same floor as those of the Devi and her advisors, were provided for Juno, Gabriel and his grandmother.

As directed by Aabha, Sebastian took up habitation in Brother Jacob's old apartment. The two members of the Brothers of the Golden Ring crossed paths during this process and Sebastian received a chilly reception from his superior during this brief encounter; however, no mention was made with regard to the actual change of rooms, making it obvious to Sebastian that Aabha had personally intervened with Jacob to smooth the transition and remove him from the loop of those having been responsible for making the decision.

* * * * *

An hour after dusk, couriers of the Belief dressed in full ceremonial white, emblazoned by the gold svastika with four dots, paraded out through the huge oak gates leading from the palace compound.

Each carried an official dispatch requesting a council of heads of state to secretly discuss the impending need of a military coalition for Crusade and scheduling a meeting for that purpose to be held thirty days hence at the Holy See.

Immediately thereafter, the leaders of both the Belief's land army and sea defence units had attended a meeting with the Prime minister and Aabha had sought their council with the result that a new military component had been created from members of both services to commence immediate training in the art of handling the airship on a war footing and recruitment was initiated with the aim of quadrupling the ranks of their standing armed forces within six months' time.

* * * * *

Knowing that the reaching of a definite plan with regard to the retaking of Atlantis would be welcome news to the remaining members of their race, Adon and Gaia quickly organized the second meeting of the day in the cafeteria available in the block that had been provided for them.

While avoiding specifics for security reasons, the attentive audience was assured that their residence in Almeca under the protection of the Belief would be of short duration.

Adon was unable to provide an exact time table but was confident in advising those in attendance that they could expect to return to Atlantis within a few weeks.

The sense of relief that swept thought the room at the sound of those words was palpable.

CHAPTER THIRTY-THREE

- *Growing Confidence* -

In consideration of the diversity of her guests, both in race and background and due to the short notice provided for the dinner, Aabha had requested an informal gathering in one of the smaller dining rooms available within the confines of the Deval Palace. As befitting her position, Aabha chose to take no part in the pre-meal socializing. She asked Brother Sebastian to greet her guests in the small antechamber off the room where the dinner was to be held a half hour before the meal itself was to be served, indicating that she would join them a few moments prior to entering the dining chamber itself.

This would allow the team to be provided with light refreshments with a view to providing them the opportunity to have a few moments to relax and acclimatize themselves within their new surroundings and get up to speed with each other in complete privacy. Sebastian had arranged for each to be conducted through the maze of palace hallways to the small but ornately decorated antechamber by a member of the Devi's personal Guard Unit.

Two large, floor to ceiling, cut-stone fireplaces, lit for the occasion, dominated the chamber and went a long way toward illuminating the otherwise dimly lit room. The softly reflected golden-red firelight served to accent richly-polished wood walls adorned by antique canvasses and ornate tapestries; several thick and intricately designed hand-woven carpets covered the majority of the floor and were framed by the shining marble floors beneath.

Gabriel, his Grandmother, and Juno, made up the first party to arrive and Sebastian, freshly showered and attired, greeted them with a broad smile as he thanked and dismissed their dark blue-robed guides.

The small group was obviously somewhat in awe of their opulent surroundings, and to help set them at ease, Sebastian immediately offered them a choice from the several vintage wines available on a sideboard before getting them settled into three of the comfortably upholstered armchairs which were centered between the two cheerfully burning hearths on a large coffee table in the middle of the room.

Sebastian served the glasses of their selected wine personally, having at Aabha's suggestion, chosen not to have any serving staff infringe upon the group's chance for solitude prior to eating. While he was serving the last of the drinks a second group of the Devi's Guard Unit safely delivered Venus, Jonah and their Almies to the antechamber.

Sebastian offered the two young Atlantians wine and when they had selected he poured for them as well as himself and they moved as a group to join the others; they seated themselves around the coffee table. The two little Almies moved to the wall holding the side table arrayed with the selections of wine and stood motionless facing into the room.

Sebastian raised his glass in toast.

"Mitra-Varuna Aabha, in her official capacity as Prime Minister, has asked me to take this opportunity to officially welcome you to the Holy See. Despite the fact that she is currently extremely busy with matters of state, she has arranged this informal dinner so that she may meet you all personally and get to know you. Because we have only recently arrived and have each been involved in separate endeavours since that time, she has arranged for us to meet together before the scheduled meal so we could have a chance to share amongst ourselves, our personal experiences in regard to what we have seen in Almeca so far. So here's to us. Together we have accomplished some pretty remarkable things and I for one think we've already proven ourselves to be a pretty unique team."

Sharing grins, they all stood, touched glasses, and drank.

Sebastian lowered his glass before raising it for a second toast "And I'd also like to lift a glass to one of our own who could not be here today; a man who selflessly gave his life to save ours.

He meant different things to each of us: son, father, partner and friend and in the end, became a savoir to all gathered here tonight. To Hollis: a brave and sensitive comrade."

* * * * *

Aabha, acting in her capacity as Prime Minister, supported by Daka who held the Diplomatic Chair and Jaboah who now held the Treasury Chair in addition to her other responsibilities, received Earhart Weiss, the Plenipotentiary of the State of Indus and his entourage of diplomats, in her official office.

The seasoned Ambassador appeared uncharacteristically ill at ease, no doubt in response to his sudden summoning to an unexpected meeting. Aabha, following protocol, rightly allowed Daka to take the lead and it was the emotionless and still remarkably beautiful fifty-two-year-old Mitra-Varuna who opened the conversation once steaming cups of tea had been provided to everyone in the room.

"Mr. Ambassador, it is with great surprise and disappointment that I call you here today. I will not waste time in a lengthy, preparatory exchange of accusations and denials in respect to the matters which have brought about this meeting. No such exchange is warranted under the circumstances, for none could justify the astounding betrayal of trust, malfeasance and treachery you have undertaken in your dealing with the Holy See."

Weiss raised his hands and opened his mouth to speak but Daka cut him off with an icy look.

"You do not deserve, nor will I allow any further deceitfulness on the part of the supposed representatives of the State of Indus who are now seated in this room. You have, in concert with an Officer of the Belief, illicitly received a fortune in funds, the rightful property of the Holy See, which has then been directed into the coffers of a fascist political movement, not currently the government of the state you lawfully represent. You have not only betrayed our trust but that of your own official government. What they will do with you, I neither know nor care, but for my part I order the immediate withdrawal of your entire legation from the State of Almeca, and I assure you that all the facts available to us with regard to your nefarious affairs will be provided to the rightful governing body of Indus."

Observed by everyone in the room, all colour drained from the Ambassadors face. Daka held the man's undivided attention as Aabha watched him intently. Daka, under Aabha's earlier instructions, paused briefly to let her words sink in before she continued.

"You should know that Mitra-Varuna Cala has been relieved of her post and that there will be no further funds going amiss. You should also be aware of the fact that the Holy See has been apprised of the likely existence of a number of illicit deep cover spies and agents who have been and still are no doubt active in your service. We will dig them out and deal with them I assure you."

Weiss visibly tensed and Aabha forced down an urge to smile as she settled back into her chair with some satisfaction.

As she'd suspected, there were others.

On cue Daka spoke again.

"You have seventy-two hours from the end of this meeting to remove your delegation, lock stock and barrel. Any member of your diplomatic staff found in Almeca after that period of time will be summarily arrested and charged with offences against the State of Almeca and of the Holy See. Our official relationship is now at an end."

* * * * *

Sebastian refilled the glasses as needed and the consumed wine and general ambience of the cozy room combined with an open and free exchange among them regarding recent happenings, quickly led to a shared spirit of relaxation and a rekindling of their common respect and affection for each other.

Gabriel who had been dreading sharing a room with Juno and Venus for obvious reasons, took the longest to loosen up, but despite what had occurred in his room aboard the airship he was pleasantly surprised to find that Venus had apparently found the whole incident enjoyable and more amusing than questionable.

Her eyes contained a merry twinkle whenever she let her gaze meet his.

Juno, who had obviously seen her sharing of his bed to be a positive step forward in their relationship, had in many small ways since, made it plain to him that she was eager for a rematch.

A little unsure of what was expected from him on both fronts. Gabriel, never very confident as to how he stood with an attractive female, was finding it difficult to look at either of the young women in quite the same way as he had before the separate but conjoined liaisons.

He certainly no longer held Venus in awe; well, that wasn't true - she had been amazing in bed and he still did hold her in awe, just not in the same kind of awe.

He also certainly couldn't any longer consider Juno as just a friend and a source of peer support. Not after the repeated heated sessions they'd shared over several hours that night.

That was for sure.

He knew he wasn't 'in love' with Venus, but he was aware the Atlantian didn't find that as a precursor of jointly fulfilling their physical desires, and he thought it was just possible that he might be 'in love' with Juno.

What he was absolutely sure of was that he was in deep lust with both of them.

He was seriously appalled to find it necessary to avoid looking at either of them for very long in order to prevent himself from drooling over them and making a complete ass of himself.

While it was only Venus who knew of the fact that they had both sampled the physical attributes of the handsome Neanderthal; individually, both Juno and Venus were aware of the effect they were having on him and enjoying it unabashedly.

Anyone with two eyes was also aware that both had become decidedly more 'feminine' around him since that night.

Sebastian who was privately enjoying the almost electrically-charged atmosphere between the three of them, happened to meet Gabe's grandmothers' eyes as he filled her wine glass and for a split second he caught a glint in them that gave him a distinct feeling he wasn't the only one who was aware of the change in circumstances between her grandson and the two young females.

He couldn't resist a broad knowing grin, which she readily returned with one of her own.

* * * * *

After the Ambassador and his delegation had left her office under escort, Aabha closed the door behind them and turned back to face the other Mitra-Varuna.

"I think that went well."

Jaboah humphed and then smiled.

"Yes, and you were right Aabha, they are not the end of it; we do have a rat's nest to clean out."

Aabha bobbed her head in agreement.

Daka, unruffled and still fortified by her impassive features, grunted and shook her head.

"Yes, the Ambassador's reaction to your little ploy certainly made that apparent. What concerns me now is that by so doing we may well have pushed them into a corner and forced them into taking a yet more determined action to permanently remove you, Aabha."

Jaboah arched her eyebrows and settled back into her chair.

"Daka has a point Aabha; we must see to it that we prevent any such attempt. The next seventy-two hours, while they are still here, will be crucial; but matters may become less threatening after that time, especially if we can expose and remove those who remain behind and are still loyal to them."

Aabha let out a sigh.

"Yes, well, I am not through with the Ambassador yet. I will be meeting with Brothers Jacob and Sebastian later this evening and I will bring the matter up with them, but for now I have a dinner to attend and I must get a move on or I will be late."

* * * * *

Sebastian rose to his feet the instant Aabha entered the small anti-chamber and the others began to stand as well.

Aabha raised her hands and smiled.

"No, please, remain seated and I will join you. Dinner will be served in a few minutes. I've experienced a busy day and have been looking forward to meeting you all and having a chance to offer you my thanks and unwind a little.

She crossed to the small side table and poured herself a glass of wine and by the time she'd turned back to face them, all but the brother had resumed their seats.

Sebastian pulled out a chair for her and held it until she was seated before he resumed sitting in the chair directly to her right.

The group politely waited for her to speak again and Aabha took a sip of her wine before she spoke.

"First and foremost, I want to let you know that I share with you the sense of loss at the passing of Brother Hollis Corvin. While I had little direct contact with him, I was aware of his outstanding dedication and support for the Belief before his retirement and can tell you that he was held in extremely high esteem by the late Devi."

She paused and took in the glistening eyes of both Gabriel and his grandmother before continuing.

"I would be both ungracious to him and irreverent to my Aunt, the Devi's memory, if I did not raise a glass to him now that I am among you."

She got to her feet and with no little ceremony, did exactly that.

She then thanked them for helping Brother Sebastian and bringing the airship safely to Almeca, and was then attentive as she asked the monk to convey to her the situation they had faced at the time and asked questions of all present with regard to what challenges they currently faced in their individual lives. She listened attentively, drawing in each member of the group, delving into their backgrounds, the current situation and ended by assuring them she was at their service for any assistance she could offer them. At that point dinner was announced and Aabha led them into the dining room. Light-hearted conversation passed between them until the meal had been placed before them, and while they ate. Aabha had asked Brother Sebastian to take notes on any matter that arose in which she might be of immediate assistance and he did so unobtrusively but with great deliberation.

By the time the meal was finished and after dinner liquors had been enjoyed by all, Aabha felt comfortable with them, and they with her.

CHAPTER THIRTY-FOUR

- *Surveillance* -

Aabha found herself comfortably revived despite the long day and she was both alert and eager when Brothers Sebastian and Jacob joined her in her office directly after the dinner was over.

She noted a slight chill in the air between the two brothers and addressing Jacob, took immediate steps to eradicate it.

"Gentleman, the Belief in general, and I specifically, currently face serious threats. As a faith, we face severe challenges and frankly we have no time for what the late Devi would refer to as 'a petty pissing contest', between my two most trusted guardians. Jacob, I have my reasons for asking you and Sebastian to change rooms. I do, and will always trust either of you with my life without hesitation but you are each specialists in your own disciplines and I will use you as I see fit and in a manner that I believe will best serve the Belief at this crucial time. Sebastian, you do not have now, nor will you ever have, the qualities that the position Jacob currently holds, demands. That does not mean that you do not continually demonstrate an unchallengeable excellence in your chosen field and in your service to the Belief. You are the very best at what you do, and all three of us know it. So put the foolishness aside and let's move on."

A pregnant pause followed and both Brothers flushed at the forceful and direct, if honey-sweetened, chastisement.

* * * * *

After dinner, Gabriel accompanied his grandmother back to their rooms.

As Juno was also quartered in that area of the palace, she walked with them, overtly taking advantage of the occasional opportunity to brush against Gabe with arm, breast or hip.

Each time she did Gabriel felt a brief and undeniably stimulating glow of warmth flow out from out from his loins and spread deliciously through the remainder of his body.

By the time they'd reached his grandmother's apartment door, Gabe, who had initially intended to see her comfortably established before leaving her for the night, had taken note of his partial arousal which had been brought about by the repeated contact with Juno's various and rather enticing body parts along the walk and as a result had changed his mind.

Instead of accompanying his grandmother inside as he'd originally intended, he bent to give her a kiss on the cheek and then promptly wished her a good night before he reached to close the door behind her.

Juno, who had both been hoping for, and expecting some kind of returned 'accidental' body contact from the muscular Neanderthal during the long walk back to their rooms, was a little miffed at not having received same. A thought passed through her mind.

Absence makes the heart grow fonder.

She came to a decision of her own.

She looked Gabe square in the eye as she arched her back slightly, causing the tight, low-cut bodice of her satin, formfitting top to pull tightly against the perfectly displayed mounds of her breasts, clearly outlining the partially aroused tips before pointedly turning away from him to reopen the door and address his grandmother.

"I'll just come in and get you properly settled for the night Mrs. Corvin."

She followed the older woman through the opening and pulled the door closed behind them without as much as a second glance at Gabriel.

Completely deflated, Gabe stood frozen to the spot for a few seconds, then shook his head slowly, turned and began a disenchanted shuffle across the hall to his own apartment.

He had been so sure about how the rest of the evening was going to be spent but he had obviously read the signals wrong, yet again.

Women were certainly a breed of their own.

As he opened his door, he found himself wondering if he would ever be able to understand what made any of them tick.

* * * * *

Venus and Jonah walked together across the courtyard to the block of apartments the Atlantians had been provided.

It was a warm clear evening with the buzz of flying insects and sounds of other garden creatures filling the air as they moved toward the building in the distance.

Venus shook her head in obviously disbelief as Jonah finished speaking.

"How can you simply dismiss their problems?"

Jonah, a little taken aback at the obvious depth of her displeasure with him, stopped in mid-stride, and turned to face her.

"What do you mean by that? I understand the basis for their concerns and appreciate the help the Mitra-Varuna is offering us. Solar knows we'll need it, but you can't really expect me to be seriously concerned with their minor problems knowing what I now do about the limited amount of time that Olympos, and therefore everyone living on this planet, have left. All their trepidation over their miniscule worries and their endeavors to solve them will be for naught after all. The planet won't be here in a few weeks and neither will they."

Venus crossed her arms over her breasts and her eyes began to brim with tears.

"I don't know how you can be so callous about it all, it's just so unfair."

Jonah shrugged.

"Crap Venus, I didn't say I was happy about it, I'm just being realistic."

Venus burst into tears and Jonah frowned and took her into his arms.

"I know sis, it's the shits; but there is nothing we can do about it."

Venus sniffed a few times and then leaned back out of his arms, wiped her hands across her cheeks and let out a long sigh.

"I don't know Jonah, but there must be something we can do. I'm not just going to stand by and watch my friends die, no way, not a chance."

* * * * *

Aabha spent fifteen minutes bringing the two brothers current on the situation involving the Indus diplomats and her suspicions relating to Brother Eustace.

When she had finished she turned her attention to Jacob.

"Jacob, I want you to take responsibility for keeping an eye on all members of the Indus delegation until they are aboard ship and headed for home. You will take responsibility for ensuring they all leave on time and in the meantime garner whatever intelligence you can about any others who may be in their employ or deeply embedded within the members of the Belief. Needless to say, you are to assign Brother Eustace to other duties for the foreseeable future, although I do not want you to take any overt action in relation to my suspicions. I want him to feel his secret is safe and that he is completely free from scrutiny."

Jacob's brow arched.

"I would feel better if we took some steps to ensure…"

Aabha cut him off abruptly but not unkindly.

"Before you comment Brother Jacob, please let me finish."

Jacob shifted his shoulders back and nodded. Aabha moved her eyes form his and fixed Sebastian firmly with her gaze.

"Brother Sebastian, I charge you with the heavy responsibility of providing me with personal protection over the next seventy-two hours and in addition want you to become Brother Eustace's shadow for all his waking hours until I advise you otherwise. I expect him to meet with the Ambassador in the near future and when he does I will need to know what transpires between them. I want proof that my suspicions about Eustace are well founded. Brother Jacob with provide you with the staff you require and it occurred to me that you might find good use for the young Neanderthal, Gabriel in accomplishing the later. I would not expect Eustace to meet with the Ambassador within the Palace confines but somewhere in the city, perhaps in the harbor area where they would both feel secure. In order to get the proof necessary to tighten the noose on Eustace, the young Neanderthal's newly granted ability might come in very handy indeed. He seems like a sincere and loyal young man and having him take part in the surveillance and investigation might give you a much greater chance for success while providing you with a firsthand chance to further evaluate him for possible service within the Belief."

Aabha turned her gaze back to Jacob.

"Does that answerer your concerns Brother Jacob?"

The older brother nodded and smiled slightly.

"Completely Mitra-Varuna Aabha and I now see the wisdom of your individual assignments for Brother Sebastian and myself. However, I would appreciate it if you would take advantage of the fact that the Devi's Personal Guard Unit is currently without a Devi to protect and make use of their staff to ensure your personal safety; you are after all the temporary head of state for Almeca."

Aabha nodded her acceptance of his suggestion.

"Yes, that seems sensible."

* * * * *

Jonah paused when they reached Venus's door and took hold of her upper arms gently.

"I'm sorry if I upset you, Sis. I do know how you are feeling. I share your frustrations and you know I will do whatever I can to help the others if it's possible."

Venus nodded and opened her door.

"I'll hold you to that big brother."

They exchanged smiles and wished each other goodnight, and then she entered her apartment and closed and locked the door behind her.

* * * * *

Venus, ear to the door, listened for the fading footsteps and the sound of Jonah entering his apartment which was next to hers. She waited until the sound of his door closing echoed in the long companionway, and then counted to ten before quietly unlocking her door and glancing out into the hallway.

Satisfied that it was empty, she slipped through and carefully closed the door behind her, then turned and started back toward the stairway at the far end of the corridor.

At the bottom of the stairs she made her way down to the centre of the lower hallway and crossed the small entranceway to the block, moving toward the door leading back into the courtyard she and Jonah had just crossed together.

The two brothers maintaining a protective watch just inside the doorway turned to face her as she approached and the one closest to her arched his eyebrows quizzically.

"Heading out again?"

Venus nodded.

"Yes, I think I'll get some air."

The powerfully built human reached for his staff and picked it up.

"Would you like some company?"

Sensing he might be misunderstood, he flushed and reworded his question.

"I have a responsibility to see you are all kept safe from harm. It's dark out there and although we are within the confines of the palace wall it might be a good idea if you were accompanied. I wouldn't intrude; just kind of make sure you were OK."

Venus managed a little smile and shook her head.

"No thank you, that won't be necessary. I'm a little concerned about Mrs. Corvin and I'm just going to go over and check on her. You can watch me safely cross if you like, but I may spend the night with her if she is feeling unwell."

The monk exchanged looks with his partner and then smiled back at her.

"As you wish, I will just step outside and watch you safely over though, if you don't mind."

Venus nodded.

"That's very kind of you."

* * * * *

After leaving the meeting, Sebastian immediately assigned a trusted pair of brothers to locate Eustace, keep him under surveillance, and report back to him at his new quarters.

He then went directly to his rooms and quickly changed out of his robe and into dark pants, a tight fitting black tee shirt and a lightweight dark blue canvas duster that reached to his ankles.

Dressed, he crossed the room to his closet, pushed the hanging clothing to one side and pressed a release at the back.

There was a soft click as a panel at the rear sprung free and he grasped the protruding edge to pull the panel fully open.

His eyes moved over the contents of the small compartment now revealed and he selected a short sword and scabbard from the array of weapons on offer and then unbuckled his belt and slipped it free of one belt loop before sliding the scabbard ring over his belt and refastening it.

After checking himself out in the mirror beside the closet and determining the weapon was not obvious under the coat, he went back to the closet, reached in, and closed the panel covering the hidden weapon stash.

CHAPTER THIRTY-FIVE

- The Ladies Wash Their Hair -

A soft knock sounded at the door as Sebastian was reaching up to grab a black close-fitting brimmed cap from the top shelf of the closet and popped it onto his head to complete his ensemble. Before heading for the door, he paused briefly at the mirror to view his image again. One glance was enough to satisfy him that as long as he didn't get too close to his quarry, his costume would suffice to obscure his identity.

Content, he stepped over to the door, opened it and then waved the brother standing in the hall inside and shut it behind him. He raised his eyebrows inviting the anxious monk to speak.

"We found him Brother Sebastian; he is having his evening meal in the cafeteria. He's just begun to eat, so Brother Milford stayed to watch him while I came back to report to you."

Sebastian nodded and reached out to grasp the young monk on the shoulder.

"Well done Brother Simon. I know this is not the kind of work your Order normally undertakes and I'm sure you find it somewhat harrowing."

They young monk shook his head fervently.

"Oh! No! Brother Sebastian. Not at all! Both Brother Milford and I are very excited to be chosen to assist a Brother of the Golden Ring. While we know serving and cleaning are very important tasks and we are very happy to do them, I must admit that acquiescing to your request has been most stimulating for each of us."

Sebastian wasn't quite sure what to say in response, but knew he had to hold back the smile that threatened to break out on his face and he did so with some difficulty.

"Yes, well that's good to know Brother Simon. Now if you could just return and assist Brother Milford, I will be there shortly to relieve you. Oh, and please be sure that you are unobtrusive in your task."

The young monk bobbed his head.

"Oh yes Brother Sebastian, have no fear in that regard. Although we are right under his nose: no one ever pays any attention whatsoever to the servers and cleaners."

* * * * *

Adon was seated at the small desk in the apartment and making some notes, but set his pen down and turned his head to smile up at Gaia as she rested her hands on his shoulders.

"It's getting late Adon, and it has been a very long day."

Adon nodded and swiveled his head in a slow circle in an attempt to disperse the kinks that had settle there.

"Yes it has. I was making up a list of who we should ask to form the panel that will be responsible for the selection of seed species for the new planet."

Gaia arched her brows.

"So soon, surely we have some time yet?

"Not a great deal. It is a matter of weeks now. The kafuffle over Marduke has upset the normal schedule and left it in disarray, but now that we believe we have a reasonable chance to retake Atlantis, our responsibilities to prepare for the new planet must now take precedence."

Gaia nodded solemnly and then frowned.

"Is it not standard procedure to form a committee of elders to make the choices?"

Adon nodded.

"Yes that would be the normal course of action, but under the circumstances, in that we have given the younger generation the knowledge of the pending destruction of Olympos, I'm not sure it would now be the proper way to proceed."

Gaia's features brightened.

"Ah, you are considering allowing the team's progeny to take part in the selection process?"

Adon smiled up at her.

"Yes I am, and what I'm suggesting is a step farther than simply letting them take part. I was considering the suggestion that they should in fact make up the committee under the direction of an elder of course, to act as chair. If we were to do that it could accomplish a couple of things. Firstly, it would involve them more directly in the planning for the new planet, thereby hopefully softening the impact of losing the old one, and secondly, we may find them better qualified to make the selection of pairs from the younger members of the species on Olympos. After all, they are of the same age group and might be in a position to provide some excellent input."

Gaia thought for a second before answering.

"So instead of having all the elders do the selection, you are considering creating a committee containing all our younger generation under the leadership of a single elder. Sounds like an excellent idea to me."

Adon smiled and reached up to rest his hands atop hers.

"I'm glad you agree with the concept."

Gaia smiled down at him and Adon continued.

"I was also hoping you might consider chairing such a committee."

* * * * *

Juno waited until Mrs. Corvin had talked herself out and was tucked in before she left the apartment and entered the hallway. She was about to cross to Gabriel's door and knock when Venus appeared from the stairwell at the end of the corridor and started toward her.

For the past twenty minutes Juno had been fantasizing about how the remainder of the night was going to play out, and to suggest that she was both surprised and disappointed to see Venus approaching down the hallway, was a gross understatement. She did her best to hide her feelings as a disgruntled Venus, a look of absolute distaste on her face, approached.

"Juno. What are you doing here?"

Juno indicated the doorway behind her with a nod of her head.

"Just getting Mrs. Corvin settled."

Venus recouped from her disappointment quickly and managed a weak smile.

Juno spoke without taking time to think.

"What are you doing here?"

There was a strained silence before Venus replied.

"The same as you I guess, just going to see if Mrs. Corvin was

OK."

The door on Juno's left opened and Gabriel stuck his head out. His mouth hung limp for a spilt second as he took the two of them in, then he found his voice.

"I heard voices. Hi guys. What brings you here?"

Juno eyes flickered from Gabe to Venus and back again.

"We were just checking in on your grandmother."

Gabe nodded and opened the doorway far enough to step though and was about to speak again when Sebastian walked out of the stairwell and started down the hallway toward them. Dressed as he was, it wasn't until he was a few feet away that they recognized him. When they did, they spoke in unison.

"Sebastian?"

The monk grinned broadly and did a slow pirouette before he replied.

"Didn't recognize me eh? What's going on, you having a union meeting or something?"

Venus responded.

"Juno and I were just leaving after checking on Mrs. Corvin and Gabe heard us talking and came out to see who was in the hall."

Sebastian grinned and turned to face Gabriel.

"It was you I came to see, Gabe, I was wondering if I could ask you for a favor."

Gabe nodded.

"Sure what do you need?"

"I could use someone to watch my back for a couple of hours, if you're up for it. Can I talk to you inside?"

* * * * *

Sebastian waited until Gabriel had changed into dark clothing then the two of them left the apartment with the monk leading the way down the stairs and across the square to a small building next to the main palace. He left Gabe in the shadows across from the doorway and then went to the end of the building and glanced through one of the small windows. Gabriel watched him raise his hand and a few moments later a monk in a brown robe came outside and spoke briefly with Sebastian then returned back inside the building.

Sebastian walked back to where Gabriel was waiting and stepped into the shadows next to him.

"He's still in there and he's in civilian clothes, which means he intends leaving the palace compound. My point men say he's finished eating and will probably be out anytime. You're sure you're OK with this?"

Gabriel grinned broadly.

"Looking forward to it brother"

* * * * *

Unbeknownst to each other both Venus and Juno had decided to have hot baths and wash their hair once they'd returned to their respective rooms.

Neither of them were particularity happy with the way the night had turned out, but it had been a hectic day and although going to bed alone was not a particularly inviting ending to the day for either of the two young women, there didn't appear to be a better option for either of them on the immediate horizon.

Both were fantasizing about Gabe while they bathed.

* * * * *

Sebastian nudged Gabe in the arm as the imposing figure, dressed in dark clothing and wearing a wide brimmed black hat, emerged from the small cafeteria, paused just outside the doorway to glance right and left, and then began to move off at brisk pace.

"That's him. We'll give him a little head start."

Gabriel nodded and watched the well-proportioned, rather intimidating figure, as he moved away, long strides making short work of the cobblestones in the general direction of the palace wall gates.

"Big guy, moves easily though, catlike almost."

Sebastian nodded.

"Yes, but don't let his size fool you, he can also move very quickly when he wants to. Okay let's go, I want to keep him in sight. Just stick close to me and we'll make use of the shadows as we tail him. He feels secure within the palace walls and has no reason to assume he's being watched, but don't ever let yourself forget he's a pro in this business. He seems to be in a hurry. Hopefully his mind is on other things at the moment but they say he's got eyes in the back of his head so keep a low profile. Once we get out through the gates the foot traffic will pick up considerably and we should have an easier time of it from then on."

Sebastian kept Eustace in sight but continued to use the many pools of shadow provided by the buildings within the compound to cover their progress, necessitating short bursts of speed on the part of the watchers from time to time to ensure they didn't lose him completely.

Gabriel heard him give a gentle sigh of relief as the compound gates came into view and the dark figure ahead of them passed through and moved out of sight and into the street beyond.

Seconds later he followed Sebastian through the massive opening and watched as the monk quickly searched the wide cobbled roadway in both directions before turning to the right and slipping easily into the flow of ambling pedestrians.

A few moments later the monk let out a snort of laughter and Gabriel turned to look at him. The monk slipped between a cart and oncoming foot traffic with Gabe at his side and once he was clear he shrugged.

"Mitra-Varuna Aabha said he would probably head for the dock area and it looks like she was right. He's moving with purpose; I think she might just be right about the meeting spot as well. All we have to do is pace him now without being seen."

Easily hidden among the heavy flow, they had no difficulty keeping the man in sight and after about twenty minutes of pressing their way through the crowded streets, Sebastian reached out and placed a hand on Gabriel's arm, gently pressing him deeper into the shadow provided by a small alcove leading to a shop that had closed for business for the day.

They were deep into the dockyard area, very close to the waters of the bay and standing directly across the street from the decrepit excuse for an inn into whose tavern entrance Eustace had just disappeared.

The monk reached into his pocket, took out a timepiece and glanced at it.

"I'm just guessing of course, but it's ten minutes before the hour and I'll wager that Eustace is early and that the meeting was set for then. We'll just watch for a bit and see if anyone interesting turns up."

CHAPTER THIRTY-SIX

- *Plot Confirmed* -

Gabriel and Sebastian waited in silence for six minutes, watching the traffic flow past and in and out of the tavern door.

Sebastian was about to suggest they change position when he heard the sound of carriage wheels echoing on the cobblestones, a strange occurrence indeed, in this seedy area of the city.

It approached from his left and he pressed deeper into the shadows as it came abreast, and then swept past.

The coat of arms on the carriage door was briefly illuminated in the flickering flame of a guttering streetlight and he easily made it out.

They were those of the State of Indus.

His eyes followed the vehicle as it moved down the roadway and turned the corner to disappear from sight.

"That's it Gabe. There is no other earthly reason for an Ambassadorial carriage belonging to Indus to be down here. Okay, here's what we'll do. Eustace will have found a table somewhere in back against the wall off by itself, but where he can watch the front door. We'll head around back by way of the alley and come in that way."

He stepped out into the street and Gabriel dropped into step behind him. They stayed on the far side of the road until they were well past the Inn then crossed the cobblestones and made their way back to the laneway that led in behind the squalid building.

The smell flooding their nasal passages as they entered the lane was overpoweringly putrid and Gabriel raised one hand to cover his nose as he felt his stomach begin to turn. He forced the bile back down as he dropped in behind the monk and they began to move more deeply into the confines of the rank, ill-lit passageway.

Sebastian could just make out a single burning lamp over a doorway at the far end of the building in question and eager to reach it he picked up the pace while taking care to step warily through the foul-smelling litter which was heaped up in ever-increasing piles around them.

When Sebastian reached the doorway he tried the handle and found it unlocked. He tuned it quickly and pushed the door open then stepped through and waited for Gabe to join him before pulling it closed behind them.

As it swung to, cutting off the weak glow afforded by the outside lamp, they found themselves in complete darkness.

Adrenalin kicked in for Gabe the instant the door clicked shut and he felt his pulse quicken.

He was about to speak when he felt Sebastian's restraining hand on his arm.

The monk whispered softly.

"It's some kind of storage room I think. Just hang tough for a second, let's let our eyes adjust to the darkness and see what we can hear and then I'll strike a match if necessary."

Gabriel liked the idea of striking a match but was not overly enamored with the thought of remaining in the dark, even if it was for only seconds.

He sucked in a deep breath and strained to hear what he could.

The sounds of muted conversation and clatter of shifting china and cutlery coupled with the smell of cooking meat, which was now thankfully managing to overpower the stench from the laneway, seemed to satisfy Sebastian and Gabe let out his held breath as a match flared between them in the darkness.

The flickering light revealed a small chamber filled with stacked crates on both sides and a dingy walkway that led to a doorway in the far wall.

Before Gabriel had a chance to take it all in the match flickered out dropping the room back into darkness and Sebastian's lowered voice flowed back to him.

"We're close to the kitchen. With any luck that door probably leads to a hallway that runs past the kitchen and into the tavern. Follow me, don't look directly at anyone we come across and let me do any talking."

Sebastian began to move forward and in his eagerness to keep up Gabriel bumped into the monk as he was opening the door.

Soft illumination from the narrow, dimly lit corridor it opened onto revealed a short hallway.

Midway along on the left side a double swinging door that was partially ajar, gave out the, now much louder, kitchen noises they'd heard earlier and with a nod to Gabriel, the monk strode purposefully forward to the end of the hallway passing a washroom reeking of urine before they stepped out into the raucous atmosphere of the tavern proper.

Sebastian quickly took in his surrounding and without breaking stride, headed for an empty table, which was by itself behind a pillar, and in a dimly lit area against the wall to their left.

They settled into chairs and Gabriel allowed himself a deep sigh of relief as Sebastian, grinned across at him.

"See, nothing to it. I can't see him from here, which means he didn't see us come in. Now if you will be so kind as to do your thing, I'll watch your back."

Gabriel nodded and rested his elbows on the top of the table then cupped his chin in his hands. Sebastian watched with eager anticipation as the young Neanderthal, just as he had when they had earlier practiced the transition, closed his eyes and began to concentrate.

Suddenly Sebastian found himself alone at the table and he glanced around the room quickly to assure himself that no one had noticed the change.

The empty chair across from him shifted backward before coming to a rest and the monk grinned.

* * * * *

Gabriel was concerned about how long he would be able to remain invisible and unused to being that way, and anxious to get the job done as quickly as he could. As a result, he did not take into account that the people going about their normal business around him within the room could not see him.

As a result, a serving wench carrying a large wooden tray of steaming dishes walked straight into the young Neanderthals' back as he was making his way to the far side of the room.

The buxom girl let out a shriek of surprise and the tray flew out of her hands and slammed into the floor with a horrendous crash of broken china, mangled food and scattered cutlery.

Gabriel, struggling to maintain his balance and hold his concentration after being struck, dodged to one side and then froze for a few seconds as he worked at getting the rhythm of his breathing back into check.

He looked back over at the table where Sebastian was sitting and noted the monk start to rise up out of his chair and then settle back down into it again.

Gabriel took a deep breath and turned slowly, looking around to make sure he wasn't about to be run into again and then satisfied he was safe, at least for the moment and now far more focused on what was going on around him, continued to make his way across the smoke filled room.

He spotted the table against the far wall where Eustace was sitting with his back to the wall and noted that the big monk had looked away from the man sitting across from him to investigate the crashing tray.

The massive monk was looking directly at Gabe and the young Neanderthal, fearing he had been seen, felt his heart begin to race with trepidation. It took him a few seconds to force himself to ignore the piercing eyes centered on him and accept the fact that the monk was looking straight through him and not at him.

As Sebastian had anticipated, the two men were sitting at a table against the wall and at some distance from the other tables around them, two of which were unoccupied.

Gabe moved to the closest of these and without shifting the chair carefully dropped into it and turned his attention to the conversation that had now recommenced between Eustace and his table companion.

The man across from the monk was speaking.

"…and I have no idea how much she knows but I do know that she is a danger to both of us and needs to be removed."

Eustace let his gaze shift from the barmaid who was now down on her knees cleaning up the mess and arched his brows.

"Well, that has already been tried and it failed dismally as we both know, and even if it could be done, what will it change. You say that she's already cut off the funds and kicked your entire diplomatic core out on its ear."

The other man's sullen features darkened considerably.

"Well for one, you might avoid being arrested if they have not linked you with me as yet. Once she has been removed we might well find her replacement to be more supportive of our position in the world."

Eustace rolled his shoulders and nodded.

"Yes, there are those possibilities to consider, however slim they may be"

"You'll do it then? You'll kill her?"

Eustace nodded.

"Yes, and very soon or it will be too late to bother."

* * * * *

Sebastian gave a start and knocked over his goblet when Gabriel reformed in the chair across the table from him.

"Solar's Wrath; I was even expecting it, and you still scared the crap out of me!"

He stood the goblet back up, ignoring the puddle left on the table and, face twisted in a concerned frown, studied Gabriel's features carefully.

"Are you all right? You're pale as a ghost and look like you've been on a three-day bender and finished up being pulled backwards through a knothole."

Gabe nodded and took a few deep breaths.

"Ya, I'll be OK! Just a little drained. Bed is going to look very good tonight that's for certain I'm sure glad we've been doing all the practicing though; I don't think I could have lasted that long if we hadn't."

The monk nodded, but didn't take his eyes off the young Neanderthal.

"I hate to push you but are you able to tell me what you heard?"

Gabriel, excited and more than a little pleased with his accomplishment, began speaking quickly and a little too loud. Sebastian rested a hand on his partner's forearm and squeezed gently.

"Take your time and keep your voice down."

Gabe closed his mouth and looked around carefully then leaned in toward Sebastian and began to repeat what he'd heard.

By the time he'd finished all the color had drained out of the monk's face. He removed his hand from Gabe's arm and his eyes narrowed as they shifted toward the center of the room.

"Well that certainly clinches it, Eustace is in it up to his ears. What's worse is that what had started out as an intelligence gathering errand had now turned into something much more!"

A quizzical expression filled Gabriel's features.

"It has?"

Without looking back at Gabe, Sebastian nodded. When he answered his voice came out in a hoarse whisper.

"Oh yes, they both want her dead and will now individually strive toward that end. We cannot afford to let either of them continue to draw breath - not for an hour. The risk is far too great, for all of us. If we lose Aabha, we will all pay. Solar only knows where her replacement might lean within the political spectrum. If we were to, for whatever reason, lose the support of the Belief for our future endeavors, we will have no future worth counting."

* * * * *

It took Sebastian and Gabe ten minutes to locate the waiting carriage which they found parked in a side street two blocks away from the Inn. The driver sat on his box smoking and tapping one foot, obviously impatient with the wait and eager to be leaving the area.

They stood in a doorway just behind and to one side of the coach.

Sebastian took in the scene in front of them. There was little foot traffic on the street in this decrepit area which consisted of mostly of down at heel commercial premises. These were all closed for the day.

An occasional group or single pedestrian passed by, usually quite obviously inebriated but there was often no one in sight for several minutes at a time.

He turned to whisper to Gabriel.

"OK, do you think you can put on a show as a drunk?"

Gabe nodded.

"Ya, I guess, why what do you have in mind?"

The monk nodded toward the coach.

"The carriage is waiting for the Ambassador. I want to get inside so I can surprise him when he climbs aboard. Do you think you could provide me with a distraction that will give me time to get inside without the driver knowing? Play a drunk maybe and wander out there past the horses, then grab one and spook it enough to shake the carriage. Keep it up long enough for me to get the door open and climb up without the driver noticing and then just wander off again and find yourself a spot where you can watch the action but not be seen. I'll do the rest."

CHAPTER THIRTY-SEVEN

- *Threat Removed* -

Sebastian dropped into the center of the seat with his back to the driver and settled himself into a comfortable position before the carriage stopped rocking.

His eyes quickly adjusted to the dark interior of the coach and as he carefully withdrew the sword from its scabbard and laid it across his knees he studied the seat across from him and familiarized himself with the location and operation of the handle for the doorway on his right, and then settled back to wait.

Gabriel was hunched against a cold, slimy wall of the laneway running off the side street where the carriage sat, rubbing vigorously with his right hand at the spot on his left wrist where the tip of the driver's whip had bitten into the flesh shortly after he'd grabbed two of the startled horses,

The resulting lurching of the coach had sufficed to accomplish two things.

He'd watched the monk make it aboard and it had thrown off the coachman's aim just enough to prevent a more serious laceration. The original pain of it had been sharp, but what remained after fifteen minutes was no worse than a distinct stinging sensation. Gabe had already checked and the instrument had barely broken the skin. There appeared to be very little blood oozing from the wound which he had now wrapped with a strip of cloth torn from his shirttail.

The sound of footfalls on the cobblestones caught his attention and he swiveled his head in their direction in time to see the figure approaching the coach at a healthy pace.

The young Neanderthal leaned back a little farther into the alley entrance and then froze as he watched the darkly dressed figure who he immediately recognized as one of the men at the table in the inn move up the side of the driver's box and say something to the coachman before opening the door and climbing into the back of the carriage.

As soon as the door had closed, the driver, obviously pleased to be leaving this part of town, cracked the whip over the horse's heads and the carriage rolled away from the curb.

* * * * *

Snapping out of her comfortable doze, Juno lurched bolt upright in the steaming tub.

Gabe has been injured!

* * * * *

The Ambassador had no more than settled into the seat across from Sebastian when the blade flashed forward.

Absolute terror flooded the man's features and he opened his mouth to shout.

Before the words could form Sebastian drove the blade through the Ambassador's heart and four inches deep into the cushion behind him, then rapidly pulled it out before wiping the bloodied shaft clean on the man's cloak.

The monk then returned his sword to its sheath and crossed himself as he whispered.

"May Solar have mercy on your wretched soul, my son!"

The coach door facing the center of the roadway popped open and Sebastian stepped down from the moving carriage and dropped silently into the street.

* * * * *

The horses swept past Gabriel followed by the bulk of the coach and his jaw dropped open when he saw Sebastian standing in the center of the street.

The monk casually fastened his coat into place as he crossed over to where Gabe was standing.

He flashed the young Neanderthal a broad grin and spoke with an air of pleasurable expectancy.

"Well that's going to cause quite a stir when the coach pulls in under the portico in front of the consulate of Indus. I would imagine it might just stimulate the rest of the delegation to leave Almeca by the first transport available to them."

Gabriel turned to watch the carriage round the far corner and nodded.

"Ya, I'm sure it will! What's next?"

Sebastian's smile faded.

"Brother Eustace I'm afraid, and dealing with him is going to be a far more dangerous and challenging task than was the removal of the late Ambassador."

* * * * *

At the sound of the knock on the door, Aabha, who was sitting at her desk, looked up from the documents she had been reading.

"Come"

* * * * *

Sebastian and Gabriel made much better time on the return trip to the palace compound than they had in making their way to the Inn.

A shared sense of urgency filled the pair and both were breathing heavily by the time they passed in through the gates.

They quickly made their way inside the main building and through what were, due to the late hour, lightly traveled and dimly lit hallways leading to Aabha's office.

When they'd reached the door Sebastian knocked and didn't wait for a response before entering.

There was a single gas lamp burning in the room. It was sufficient to illuminate the desk itself but left shadows in the corners of the room, which, to their combined unease, was currently unoccupied.

Sebastian's eyes moved around the walls in a slow pass, looking for anything out of place but found nothing.

"She's been here recently or the light wouldn't be burning and if she hadn't planned to return she would have put it out."

They exchanged glances and Gabriel shrugged.

"Do we wait for her to return or try to find her?"

The monk paused for a second and then turned to face him squarely.

"There could be a hundred explanations for her having to leave for some reason, but I want to find her as quickly as possible and ensure she's safe before I deal with Brother Eustace. We'd better split up. You stay here and wait for her in case she comes back. If she does tell her I asked that she remain with you here in the office until my return. I'll arrange for a couple members of the guard detail to come here and back you up. Once I've got them on the way I'll head out and see if I can locate her elsewhere. If she does turn up, send one of the guards to let me know and I'll come straight back here. If I find her, I'll bring her back to the office with me. Our search for Eustace will just have to wait until we are sure Mitra-Varuna Aabha is safe."

Gabriel nodded and the monk opened his coat and undid his belt then slipped off the short sword and sheath.

"Here you may need this."

The young Neanderthal took the offered weapon in his hand and looked up from it to meet the monk's eyes.

"What about you, what if you run into Eustace."

Sebastian smiled and shrugged.

"I can make a weapon out of almost anything if need be. Don't worry, I'll be fine."

"But you intimated earlier he was, well probably, more than a match for you."

Sebastian nodded his agreement.

"Yes, he is a formidable opponent in any one on one situation for sure, but it isn't likely that I will run into him; he'll be keeping a low profile for the moment."

* * * * *

Juno slipped a towel over her wet hair and pulled a robe around her damp body then crossed to the door and opened it quietly before peering out into the hallway.

Finding it empty she stepped out and closed the door behind her before hurrying down the passageway until she reached the door of Gabriel's apartment. She knocked lightly and when she got no response tried the knob.

It turned in her hand and she pushed it open and stepped through.

"Gabe, it's me Juno, you here?"

She glanced around the main room quickly and then pulled the doorway closed.

* * * * *

Two of the members of Devi's Personal Guard Unit burst into Aabha's office.

In the flickering illumination provided by the single gas light hanging over the desk they were simply huge forms in dark clothing and Gabriel's reaction was predictable; he immediacy unsheathed the short sword and extended it toward them.

Both Neanderthal monks raised their hands, palms outward and the closest to him spoke.

"Easy my son, Brother Sebastian sent us."

Gabe lowered the sword slightly and froze.

The two bulky Neanderthals, hands still held where he could see them, stepped forward into the light and were instantly identifiable to Gabe by their plain dark blue robes tied at the waist with braided white ropes from which swung plain wooden svastikas.

* * * * *

A wave of relief swept through Sebastian as he rounded the corner of the hallway and very nearly bowled over Mitra-Varuna Aabha and her two accompanying guardians, both robed members of the Devi's Personal Protection Unit.

Dressed as he was, Sebastian was not immediately recognizable to them in the dim illumination offered by the widely spaced and flickering gaslights that ran the length of the narrow passageway.

Aabha let out a shocked snort, dropped the documents she had been carrying and began to back-pedal as she fought to maintain her balance.

The guards recovered quickly and one reached out a hand to steady Aabha as the other stepped between the Mitra-Varuna and Sebastian.

Both had immediately drawn wicked short swords from within the confines of their robes.

Sebastian took off his hat and raised his hands as he quickly identified himself, then bent to pick the scattered papers up off the floor as he spoke.

"Solar be praised, I thought he had you."

* * * * *

Juno made her way across the room and checked to ensure the bathroom was unoccupied and then dejectedly returned to combination bedroom and sitting room.

Various articles of the clothing Gabriel had been wearing the last time she'd seen him were laying on the bed and floor of the large room. She bent to pick up the shirt that had been dropped on the floor at the end of the bed, with the intention of placing it with the others bits of clothing on top of the bed, paused before putting it down, instead raising it to her nose.

It smelled of him and despite the sense of foreboding and concern she harbored, she felt a little shiver of warmth surge through her as she took his scent in.

She held the garment against her nose for a few seconds and then let it drop down onto the bed.

What should she do? There was no sense in trying to find him, she had no idea where he and Sebastian had been going or what they were doing.

Looking for him would get her nowhere. In view of the relatively unfamiliar surroundings of the Palace compound she would only end up wandering aimlessly and probably get herself lost. Besides, wrapped in a thin robe and towel, she was hardly dressed to go wandering about.

She sat down on the edge of the bed to think. In her vision, she had been aware that he had been hurt but she had no idea what type of injury it had been, although, as she relived it in her mind, she sensed that if he had been seriously injured of killed, she would know.

The only thing that made any sense under the circumstances was to wait for him to return. It was late; surely he would be returning to his rooms soon.

CHAPTER THIRTY-EIGHT

- Deeds Transferred -

Sebastian gave an audible sigh of relief as he reached Aabha's office door, opened it and held it for her to enter. Aabha stepped through the opening and then turned to ask the four guards to take up positions outside her office door.

When it had closed behind them she set the documents she'd been carrying down on the top of her desk, went around behind it and sat down before waving the monk and Gabriel into chairs across from her.

Once they were seated she lifted her eyes to meet Sebastian's.

"I take it your little information gathering sojourn bore fruit then?"

Sebastian nodded, and Aabha turned her attention to one of the folders she had been carrying.

"Before you bring me up to date I'd like to speak briefly with Gabriel, whom I notice seems to be utterly exhausted and also appears to be suffering from an injury, no doubt gleaned as a result of your little tryst. It will take me only a few moments to cover what needs to be discussed and then he can to seek medical attention and get some, quite obviously, much needed rest. Then, Brother Sebastian, you can share with me what information the two of you were able to garner."

Sebastian looked over at Gabe and noticed the bloody, temporally bandaged wrist for the first time.

"You're hurt? How'd that happed Gabe?"

Gabriel lifted the wrist in question and started at it briefly, almost as if he too was also noticing it for the first time.

"This, oh it's nothing serious, the coachman used his whip to get me off the horses. It just needs to be cleaned up and properly bandaged, nothing to worry about."

Aabha opened the top folder on the desk in front of her and withdrew two documents, then handed them to the young Neanderthal.

"These are transfers of deed titles for your father's and grandmother's properties in Indus. In view of your services to the Belief and the resulting inability for you and Mrs. Corvin to return to Indus, I felt it only just that the church, offer to purchase them from you. Please take these with you and if you and Mrs. Corvin find the price offered acceptable, sign where indicated and return them to me at your first opportunity. If you each find the funds offered for purchase satisfactory the monies indicated will then be deposited in your names in the Belief's bank where you may then withdraw them as you see fit."

Both surprised and grateful, Gabriel took the documents from her extended hands.

"Thank you Mitra-Varuna Aabha. I don't know what to say. I have been very worried about my grandmother losing her farm. This will allow her to settle safely elsewhere and on her own terms. It will also provide me with the inheritance my father would have wished for me. I know how busy you are and I cannot thank you enough for taking the time to worry about us at a time like this."

Aabha smiled.

"No my son, on the day that I cannot find the time to thank and reward the people who give of themselves for me and my faith, it will time for me to give up this robe of office I wear. Your family has given a great deal, much more than should have been asked of them and it was unquestionably owed a large debt of gratitude. In signing these documents, I have done nothing more than, in a small way, paid that debt in the name of the Belief."

* * * * *

Gabriel was feeling very tired as he made his way back to his apartment from Aabha's office. He seemed to be aching in every joint and by the time he was opening his door he felt somewhat unsteady on his feet.

He was sure that when he'd left earlier had he'd turned of all the lights and he was somewhat surprised to find a single gaslight burning in the small sitting room portion of his rooms.

It was turned low and as such served to illuminate only a small area near a big overstuffed armchair in the corner and suddenly alert and suspicious, he paused with his back to the door and let his gaze move over the expanse of the room, to make certain that he was alone.

He saw nothing untoward, but his straining ears then picked up the sound of light rhythmic breathing and his heart leapt into his throat as he balled his hands into fists.

All thoughts of fatigue momentarily disappeared as he listened carefully trying to pinpoint the source of the sound.

He realized that he had been holding his breath and he released it slowly and began to relax a little as his exhausted brain, now awakened by the surge of adrenalin that had filled him upon entering the room, expressed the opinion that if there was someone in the room as he now suspected, it probably wasn't an attacker who could have easily taken him by complete surprise the moment he came in the door.

His clenched hands relaxed a little as he concentrated his gaze on the gloom on the far side of the room where his bed was located. That's where the sound was coming from and after straining his eyes against the darkness for several seconds, he was just able to make out a reclined form.

Small of stature, dressed in what appeared to be light colored clothing and some kind of similarly hued headgear against the dark brown spread covering the bed.

Whoever it was, they certainly didn't look threatening.

He began to move forward.

The sound of rhythmic breathing stopped and he paused still halfway across the room.

"Gabe is that you? I must have dozed off. I was so worried. What time is it?"

"Juno? What are you doing here? Is something wrong? I don't know, but it's late."

Gabe turned and crossed to the gaslight by the chair and turned it up, then spun to face her as she rolled off the bed, stood up, yawned, stretched and started across toward him.

"You've been injured."

Gabriel raised his brows and put his hands on his hips.

"Just a little cut, looks worse than it is, but how did you know?"

He took in the towel wrapped around her hair and the fact that she appeared to be wearing only a robe but despite his surprise at her attire, said nothing.

Juno glanced down at the robe, pulled it tighter together at the front, retied the belt and laughed.

"I must look a real treat. I was half dozing in the tub when I sensed you'd been hurt so I just wrapped my wet hair, grabbed a robe and came over to find out what had happened. Then when I got here and you were gone I remembered you were going to help Sebastian and I didn't know where you were so I decided to just wait here until you got back."

* * * * *

Sebastian finished his rendition of the exchange between Brother Eustace and the Ambassador, indicating that the latter was no longer of any concern without specifics and then waited for Aabha's reaction.

"It's just as I'd thought then, and we don't know where Eustace is I don't suppose?"

Sebastian frowned apologetically and shook his head.

"Well he will have come back to the palace I'm sure. He has no reason to believe that we are on to him. I had a couple of brothers staking out the gate so they will have picked him up when he came back through and one of them will be coming here to tell me of his movements as soon as Eustace settles to roost someplace. He has likely returned to his rooms to change as he was dressed in civilian clothes when he left for the meeting."

"Very good, so how to you intend to deal with him?"

"Well, I don't want to beard the lion in his den, so to speak. As do all members of the Order, he will have defenses in place there to protect himself when he is sleeping. Ideally I would like to slip something into his food and could probably arrange for that to happen at his morning meal. It would be both ironic and fitting for him to die of poisoned food."

Aabha allowed herself a little smile.

"Yes I suppose it would."

Sebastian let out a soft sigh and raised his hands.

"Only problem with that is we have no idea what he has in mind. We know what he intends to do, but not how or when he intends to do it. He might choose to act tonight and if he does, setting him up for the morning will be too late."

Aabha arched an eyebrow and began to muse.

"Yes, you have a point. Well it is late and if we find that he has returned to his rooms and remained there, we will probably be safe to have his apartment watched and wait until morning to act, but I certainly won't get much sleep for wondering if we have misjudged his intent."

Sebastian shook his head slowly.

"No, nor will I. It would make for a very long night."

There was a soft knock on the door and one of the members of the guard unit stuck his head inside.

"There is a young brother here, a cafeteria worker I believe. He's asking to speak with Brother Sebastian. He says it's important"

Sebastian rose from his seat and started for the door.

"That will be my man now."

* * * * *

Juno sat on the edge of the bed, her head bent over as she vigorously rubbed the strands of her still damp hair with the towel. Gabriel, who stood looking down at her from a couple of feet away from the edge of the bed, shifted slightly to his left for a better view of what the front of the robe, which was gaping considerably as a result of her industrious attempts to dry her long tresses, had revealed.

His attention was riveted on the view and any thought of tiredness and a need for immediate rest had been unceremoniously dismissed from his mind.

He was completely enchanted by the sight, his voice deep and compelling as he extended his hands toward the towel and spoke.

"Here, please, let me do that for you."

Juno lifted her head and could hardly have missed the outline of his arousal straining forcefully against the front of his pants. She gave him the towel and as he took it from her she laughed.

"Oh, wow, I guess I must not look that bad after all!"

Gabe let his gaze meet hers and grinned.

"Ah what the hell, a little damp hair is no big deal. I'll dry if for you after."

He tossed the towel to the floor, and settled down onto his knees in front of her, reached for the tie for her robe and undid it.

Juno leaned back slightly as he pushed the robe open and she pushed it off her shoulders.

* * * * *

Sebastian returned to Aabha's office and closed the door behind him before he spoke.

"To further fortify Eustace's sense that he is not under suspicion, I had Brother Jacob send a messenger to him informing him of an assignment for duty as part of your protective screen for tomorrow. Hopefully that may help him decide against taking any action against you this evening. He got back to his apartment about an hour ago and hasn't come out. Apparently all the lights have been extinguished, so it would appear he's turned in for the night."

Aabha stifled a yawn and rolled her shoulders in an attempt to reduce the stiffness in them.

"Well if he's just half as tired as I am, I wouldn't blame him. So we'll call it a night then shall we?"

Sebastian smiled.

"Yes, but I would like you to do me one favor before we do that."

* * * * *

Juno and Gabriel, a glistening sheen of perspiration coating their naked bodies, sat facing each other cross-legged in the center of the rumpled bed. They were exchanging foolish grins of delight as they struggled to regain control of their breathing.

Gabe felt great. It appeared he'd discovered something just as effective and a heck of a lot better than sleep to help him recover from the exhaustion that followed one of his disappearing sessions.

When Gabe could speak he smiled down at her.

"I think they might have laws in Almeca against what we just did."

Juno laughed heartily and raised herself up to kiss him firmly on the lips.

"You're probably right. Let's keep it our little secret. Now let me have a look at that hand of yours."

He didn't shift his eyes from her as he held out his hand. She gently removed the temporary bandage and then lowered her gaze to study the injury.

"It's an ugly looking thing. It doesn't need stitching but it's going to leave a scar. It could have been worse."

She rolled to the side and sprung off the bed and onto her feet.

"C'mon into the bathroom and I'll clean it up and we'll see if we can find a proper dressing for it."

Gabe's attention shifted and locked onto the intriguing movements of the individual muscles beneath the skin of her high, tight rump as she headed away from him tiptoeing through his haphazardly discarded clothing.

Completely engrossed in the delicious play of those two superbly rounded cheeks, he found himself longing to lovingly kiss both. Subsequently it took him a few seconds to process what she'd said. Once it had registered in his lust-addled brain, he hopped off the bed and eagerly followed her.

CHAPTER THITY-NINE

- *Threat Removed* -

Aabha prepared to retire under the watchful eyes of Ester and two other members of the Sisterhood of Penance.

When she was in bed she nodded to Ester who then led the others to the doorway and opened it. The two younger sisters turned and headed down the hallway to return to their own dormitory and their own beds.

Ester, who under the circumstances, had stubbornly pointed out that propriety demanded she be allowed to spend the night with Aabha if there were to be males in the room while she slept, then waved those standing in the dimly lit hallway inside the rooms.

Four dark-blue robed members of the Devi's Personal Protection Unit, who had been waiting on the other side of the door entered and moved to positions against the walls around the bed where the Mitra-Varuna lay, slipping into the shadows offered by the single gas light now burning at the far end of the room and placing their backs to the walls.

Each carried their staff of office and in addition wore a sword hung from the white rope about their waists.

As he watched them, Aabha who was convinced she wouldn't be able to sleep a wink with the several sets of eyes looking on, let out a deep sigh of resignation and Ester who was settling into a large overstuffed armchair next to the bed withdrew a short dagger from beneath her robe and placed it on the small night table between her and Aabha and tut-tutted firmly.

"There is no need for childish petulance Mitra-Varuna. Surely you are mature enough to see the need for protection. You need not concern yourself, I will remain vigilant through the night. Have no fear with regard to the presence of the need for overnight guests in your bedchamber."

Despite her frustration at the situation, Aabha had to smile to herself at the woman's comment and did her best to settle herself comfortably below her covers.

She couldn't help but wonder who Brother Eustace would find more formidable should he decide to menace her while she slept: the four members of the guard unit, or an armed and determined Sister Ester."

* * * * *

Juno paused at the bathroom door and turned to look at him, noting both where his eyes were resting and the fact that he was beginning to grow again.

She fought a smile as she shook her head in pretend distaste and moved past him to reach down and pick up the robe she had been wearing earlier. She dangled it in her right hand.

"Do I have to put this on so you can relax long enough for me to take care of that cut?"

Gabriel followed the direction of her eyes and laughed before reaching out with his hand, to slap down the rising protuberance.

"No! Please! I promise I'll just look and admire, not touch."

She nodded, albeit without any great sign of real conviction in relation to the truth of his response, and let the robe drop back to the floor before moving back to rejoin him at the bathroom door.

He looked, but true to his word, he did not touch.

"You still haven't told me how you knew I'd been hurt."

She frowned and turned to face him as she entered the small bathroom and turned up the light.

"I'm not really sure, to tell you the truth. It has to do with the foretelling thing, but it's gone a step beyond what it was from when I first got here. I only used to get impressions of things when I was with a person, but I was alone in the tub when this realization hit me. I really don't fully understand how the whole foretelling thing works. You weren't with me and yet I knew you had been injured."

Gabriel gave her a quizzical look and she continued.

"It was a little frightening to tell you the truth. It seems that in addition to seeing into someone's future on some stuff when I am with them, in this instance I could actually sense when you got hurt as and when it happened. I've been thinking about it as I waited and I figure this extra ability probably only kicks in when whatever happens relates to someone to whom I have a deep emotional attachment."

She met his eyes with hers, saw his lack of understanding and shrugged.

"This is the first time I've experienced it, but I do seem to be becoming more attuned to anything that affects you strongly in an emotionally sense even when we are apart. It has been like that since that first time, we, you know, did it."

* * * * *

Brother Jacob, Sebastian and six other members of the Order of the Golden Ring, all of those, with the exception of Brother Eustace, who were currently residing within the walls of the Devi's palace, stood in the center of the sleeping chamber of the apartment.

Jacob had issued all present with flintlock single shot pistols from the Palace armoury, and was speaking in soft tones.

"I don't want any heroics. I know that all of you are used to working by yourselves but in this instance we require a team effort. We are probably only going to have one chance at getting him. Once he knows we're after him he will disappear, as would each of us, like smoke from a chimney during a windstorm. I want this to be over as quickly as possible and I want teamwork. You are all familiar with the weapons, but keep in mind that we are within the confines of theses rooms and there are eight of us in here. When you get a clean shot, take it, but each of you consider where the bullet will go if it happens to pass through its intended target."

He waited until he got nods of understanding from all round then he turned his gaze to Sebastian.

"Brother Sebastian has structured the plan for us, so I will turn it over to him now."

Sebastian cleared his throat before speaking.

"I have done everything I could think of to set Brother Eustace at ease and have taken steps to ensure that if he doesn't act tonight he will not manage to take up his duties in the morning. However, we can not afford to chance some action on his behalf before that time. You are all aware, albeit with varying levels as to the extent, of the fact that the palace is honeycombed with secret passageways located within the thick walls of the structure. You may not, however, be aware that one of those passageways passes this room and the panel holding that large portrait beside the fireplace allows access from it into this apartment. I have arranged for Mitra-Varuna Aabha to take up other lodgings for the evening and if Eustace chooses to act tonight, I believe he will come here by way of that secret doorway and we must be ready for him if he does."

* * * * *

When she'd finished cleaning and bandaging the new injury Juno unwound the old bandage on his calf.

Sebastian had removed the stitches the day before and she was pleased to find that the wicked tear in Gabe's flesh had scabbed over and begun to heal nicely.

"Wow! You heal quickly, don't you?"

She wound a new bandage into place to cover it and Gabriel, who had hopped up to sit on the counter while she worked, peered down at her hands as she worked and he smiled.

"Yes, all things considered. I haven't exactly been babying it."

Juno arched her eyes and leered up into his.

"No you haven't. I can personally attest to having benefited from some recent and rather wild gymnastic exercises, involving this very calf."

She let the fingertips of her right hand lightly and slowly caress their way upward from the newly wrapped injury.

The sensation caused by the feel of it, coupled with the sight of her kneeling naked on the floor of the small bathroom in front of him had the effect she desired.

Things began to grow again and Juno burst out laughing as he let out a deep groan and reached for her.

* * * * *

At the sound of the muffled gunshot, Sister Ester stiffened, reached for the knife on the night table and rose to her feet.

Simultaneously four dark figures moved out from the walls around her and weapons ready, took up positions around the bed.

Surprisingly, Aabha, having finely settled into a deep sleep, barely stirred at the sound.

All eyes were glued to the connecting door that led to the adjoining apartment on the far side of the room.

Moments later the door opened and Brother Jacob stepped through into Sebastian's rooms from Aabha's adjacent flat and nodded his head.

Tensed muscles visibly relaxed in those around Aabha's sleeping form and Sister Ester, still clutching her wicked looking little blade, let out a deep sigh of relief before slumping back down into the chair.

* * * * *

It was almost daylight when Juno urged Gabriel to dress and go out into the hallway to ensure she could safely return to her room in her robe without being observed.

Inwardly he didn't think it made a lot of difference but Juno was having none of it and he was in a very agreeable mood and didn't wish to cause her upset, so he accepted the request and performed his assigned duty with some diligence.

He kissed her on the forehead as she hurried past him and watched her until she'd disappeared safely and unnoticed into her own rooms. Then he stretched and yawned before going back inside and totally relaxed and very pleased with the world in general, climbed gratefully into his rumpled bed, hauling the damp covers up to his chin.

Despite a growling stomach, exhaustion took precedence and he had every intention of giving breakfast a miss.

* * * * *

Sebastian, torch in hand, led the way through the narrow passage, closely followed by two hunched and straining dark-robed brothers who were carrying the counterpane-wrapped remains of Brother Eustace between them.

It had gone as planned with no surprises and Sebastian, no longer running on pure adrenaline, now that the main job was done, was beginning to suffer from the exhaustion resulting from what had been a very long and trying day. It was settling forcefully into his bones as he moved.

Only the tidying up was left, thank Solar.

It only remained for them to return the body to Eustace's rooms by way of the secret passageway, clean it up, and place it in his bed.

He would himself find the body in the morning and the passing would be determined to be a result of natural causes, heart failure came to mind, and a fitting burial would be quickly arranged.

He sighed at the thought of another hour or so of work to get things wrapped up neatly, but the relief at knowing that the danger to Mitra-Varuna Aabha was past, at least from this specific source, made the whole endeavour worthwhile and he willed himself to draw upon a second wind to enable him to see it through to its conclusion.

* * * * *

Venus and Jonah, their Almies in tow, had decided to join their parents for breakfast, well, more precisely; Jonah had succumbed to Venus's strongly defended suggestion that they do so.

Often the younger generation took meals with each other and left the elders to eat at separate tables and so it was with delighted surprise that Adon smiled upon his children as they joined their parents at a table for four in the cafeteria of the building housing the Atlantian party.

Gaia, somehow always more perceptive that Adon when it came to the activities of their children, had taken note of both Jonah's obvious lack of enthusiasm and the determined expression on Venus's features, as they had approached and she sensed Adon was in for a lively meal.

She didn't have long to wait to confirm her assessment of the situation.

Venus opened the conversation as she was in the process of sitting.

"Dad, we of the younger generation are to be the ones deciding on which breeding stock from the current species will be selected for settlement on the new planet that replaces Olympos, right?"

Gaia, who had just raised her mug to take a drink of tea, froze and set it back down onto the table and then turned to meet Adon's gaze.

CHAPTER FORTY

- Reflection -

Adon said nothing; simply met Gaia's eyes as he waited for her to speak.

"I told Venus of your plans last night dearest, when I dropped in to wish her goodnight."

Adon looked from his life partner back to his daughter and nodded.

"Well, I haven't had an opportunity to discuss it with the elders, but your mother and I felt it would be the proper thing to do under the circumstances. Why do you ask?"

Jonah let a deep sigh and closed his eyes.

They abruptly popped open a second later, the instant Venus's foot connected sharply with her brother's shin under the table.

Her eyes were flashing angrily when they met his.

"You promised you'd help the others if it was possible Jonah. I expect you to keep that promise."

An eerie silence engulfed their small table which was surrounded by soft chatter coming from those waiting to be served around them.

Venus's eyes never left Jonah's.

Adon and Gaia, both becoming a little uncomfortable, began to fidget and Jonah quickly accepted defeat. He let out a snort and straightened up in his chair.

"OK, Sis, a promise is a promise."

He looked from Venus to his parents and back to her.

"It's just that with all the other serious stuff going on, it seems to me that this kind of thing should be going onto the back burner, that's all."

Venus nodded her head and a portion, but definitely not all of the fire went out of her eyes.

"I'm good with that. Of course we have other more serious things to consider and deal with in the short term, but that shouldn't stop us from preparing for what is coming down the road."

Gaia, who had a good idea about why her daughter was pushing the issue beamed over at Venus.

"I don't say this to be unkind Venus, but I believe you may have finally taken a giant step forward in your progress within the river of life. You seem to have found your chosen path and I see the first signs that you have begun to consider the wellbeing of others over your own. I'm proud of you and so is your father, I'm sure."

Adon wasn't quite sure exactly what Gaia was intimating, but he trusted his life partner's intuition enough to go with her statement. He beamed across at his daughter, nodded and instantly felt Gaia's hand rest on his knee under the table, in a pleased response to his support.

* * * * *

The huge airship, bow supported by its newly constructed mast, floated majestically in bright light above the calm, deep blue water of the busy Port of Pag.

Mooring ropes ran from the rear, the thick ends of the hawsers fastened securely to iron rings affixed along the five fingers of one of the handful of stone docks which extended out a quarter of a mile into the bay.

Just inland of the dockyard area, what had originally been a large warehouse was being renovated by hundreds of workers. The roof had already been removed and the outer walls had begun to rise as the structure was prepared for use as a permanent hangar for the massive craft.

A month after its arduous trip across the bay the airship appeared no worse for wear. There were visible changes however; the insignia of the inverted crosses were gone, having been replaced by large golden svastikas encompassing the four dots to represent the pillars of the Belief.

* * * * *

The College of Mitra-Varuna had been sequestered for three days. The huge walled square situated directly in front of and below the Devi's official apartments had been filled with patiently waiting members of the Belief from the first day; all eyes riveted on the small smokestack centered in the huge slate roof.

Two votes had already been taken but the dark brown smoke arising from the stack after both occasions had clearly indicated a failure of the Conclave to reach a decision.

Evening was drawing near and the warm temperatures brought on by the long Solar-filled day had begun to moderate somewhat.

In spite of the long hours of waiting the throng filling the paved courtyard had not dwindled by a man.

Despite the numbers, there was little conversation as those standing below on the cobblestones now waited expectantly for the next expulsion of smoke.

When it came, it was white and the resulting cheers of unqualified pleasure and relief were deafening.

Minutes later the large French doors leading out of the Deval apartments and onto the small stone railed balcony above the crowd opened wide and Aabha, to be known forthwith as Her Holiness Vita III, backed by two Mitra-Varuna and dressed in the full regalia of her new office, stepped out and began to offer blessings to those in the square below.

* * * * *

A day after the Holy Mother had been elected, The Rector, Kobe Eisen led the National Socialist Peoples Party to an overwhelming victory over the other parties in the state of Indus's election. It was the largest majority ever achieved by any political party in the history of Olympos.

He accepted the unprecedented cheers of congratulation from his newly bonded subjects like an emperor, perched on a broad balcony four stories above the massive quadrangle in front of the parliamentary buildings which were situated in the centre of the capital city of Jericho.

He was simply but elegantly dressed in an unadorned but meticulously cut sky-blue military uniform exhibiting no badge of rank other than simple golden collar dogs depicting the inverted cross in black on a white and red background. Backed by other members of the party faithful, many in much grander uniforms in relation to ornamental accessories of rank and position, he beamed down at the crowd.

Despite the manner in which the others were dressed, no one could have doubted as to who was the man of the hour.

This military attire could well have been recognized as the harbinger of what was to come, had anyone bothered to wonder; but no one did.

It was a staged performance; two powerful spot lamps illuminated the leader who stood well in front of the others.

Floodlit party banners bracketed the balcony as, in the lightly falling rain, a steady progression of torch-bearing Redshirts paraded by on the glistening paving stones below the balcony.

The Rector, his features now frozen in an officious, self important mask, alternated between saluting the marchers and those crowded and cheering followers filling the square beyond.

Shouts of "Hail Eisen" echoed within the confines of the square in a repetitive cadence; rising and falling in intensity throughout the entire production of the party's public victory celebration.

* * * * *

After a leisurely bath, Jonah slipped into the robe Sal held out to him and accepted the glass of wine the little Almie had poured, then walked out though the open French doors to stand on the balcony of his suite.

He leaned against the railing and looked out over the deep waters of the bay, which were brightly lit by the three moons, as he raised his glass to his lips to take a sip.

Over the past few weeks Jonah had found himself occasionally reflecting on how much his fellow team members had grown both as a group and individually. An even deeper and more poignant realization had expressed itself suddenly to him the day before during their final planning session.

Initially, it had been the recognition of his own maturing that had struck him.

Just over a month ago he had been living what he'd then thought was the good life, meeting his official commitments with only a half-hearted energy level and spending his free time partying with a vengeance. Now, suddenly having been selected by the others of the group as leader for the small team that would attempt the retaking of Atlantis, he had been placed in a position of considerable responsibility

To all intents and purposes, he held the future in his hands. Not an insignificant responsibility.

Despite his previously demonstrated light-hearted and generally feigned dedication toward any accepted or assigned responsibility, Jonah had grasped this new challenge with a sincere humbleness and a heartfelt determination to fulfill its need for a mature and accountable leader and with a previously uncharacteristic enthusiasm he accepted the personal changes that commitment would entail.

At that earlier meeting, unnoticed by the others who were deeply engrossed in the discussions, he'd looked around the small table and let his eyes rest briefly on each of them in turn. He'd realized then that they too had developed, expanded and matured since their arrival in Almeca.

His attention had settled on his sister first.

He had known Venus since her birth and had watched her ripen and evolve as she'd progressed unsteadily through the river of life.

It had been a slow process, small changes over long periods.

Today his sister was not the person she had been even a month ago.

In many ways he found the changes apparent in her to be sad and regrettable; any tinge of the child in her had been abruptly swept away.

He missed that youthful enthusiasm for life that had been so much a part of her, now replaced with a mellow, much more mature personality, a far less demanding presence. This new Venus was a person of deep concern for others, her inner thoughts wrought with serious concentration and an ongoing internal re-evaluation of what her place in the world should be.

No longer a petulant child; she had evolved into a deeply caring woman who gave every impression of carrying the weight of Olympos on her slender shoulders.

It had been an impressive change to date and yet he doubted her metamorphosis was complete. He believed she would continue to morph and those adjustments that had already taken place within her simply bespoke of what additional transformations might yet be on the horizon for his sister.

His eyes shifted from Venus to Gabriel who was sitting next to her.

The changes in Gabe were more, subtle than those of Venus, and it wasn't until he'd scrutinized the young Neanderthal carefully that Jonah began to pick them out.

The light-hearted and eternally smiling persona that everyone had come to expect in Gabe had hardened somewhat. His fresh, boyish face had begun to show signs of the recent changes in his life. There were new and clearly outlined furrows in his brow and between his eyes, and there was just a hint of the beginning of marionette folds on either side of his mouth, which was, of late, often drawn downward at the edges, where before it had been elevated in that perpetual, impish smile.

Over the past few weeks, the air of frivolity, which had often appeared to cover a lack of self-assurance on the part of the young Neanderthal and had initially been an endearing part of his make-up, had been replaced by a growing level of poise and self-confidence.

Gabe now spoke less, but when he did open his mouth, it was with more authority and conviction. He no longer carried himself as a gangly unsure youth, a demonstration of that, somewhat uncoordinated, lankiness of early manhood.

That had given way to a more confident and assured stride and posture; both Gabe's stance and movements had become those of a secure young man. That metamorphosis, coupled with his maturing, muscular and toned body, and ruggedly handsome features now invariably attracted both the interested gaze of females, as well as the considered respect of other males.

Jonah's gaze shifted again and rested on the monk seated beside Gabe.

When Jonah first met Brother Sebastian he had taken him for what he appeared: a devout member of a religious order, a simple man, leading a simple life. Jonah was sure the man had changed very little since that time, but his own perception of the monk certainly had.

The man was like an onion, each and every layer peeled back only served to reveal yet another façade below.

Since their arrival at the Holy See, Sebastian had played his part when in their small group, but Jonah would have had to be blind not to notice the respect and deference shown to the monk by those of the Belief, of whatever rank, up to and including that of the newly elected Devi.

Everyone in the palace was well aware that Sebastian had spent a great deal of one-on-one time with the Holy Mother since her ascendency to the pinnacle of power and that she valued his council highly.

Jonah was not exactly sure what part Sebastian played within the Belief; but he had become convinced that the monk was definitely not just a simple man of the cloth.

CHAPTER FORTY-ONE

- It Is Time -

As dusk descended over the bay Jonah, who had been dragged away from his mental reminiscing to enjoy the beauty it offered, raised his glass and drained it, then turned and went back inside his rooms, leaving Sal to close the doors to the balcony behind him, before the little Almie slipped out to fulfill his task.

When Sal had departed, Jonah set his glass down, shrugged out of his robe and began to dress and as he slipped into his clothes he returned to his earlier musings of that last meeting when he'd found himself re-evaluating the qualities of the rest of his team. He picked up on the thread where he had left off, at the point when he had shifted his eyes from Sebastian to the final member present, the little gypsy seated next to the monk.

At that time, as had always been the case, Juno's poise and beauty had kidnapped his thought process for a split second before he could step past them and concentrate on her many other attributes.

Of all the members of what they now, after their experience on the airship and among themselves, loosely referred to as 'The Team'; Juno was the newest and Jonah had only known her for a short time.

Yet, in his estimation, it was perhaps she who had changed more than any of the others in his eyes.

The first time he'd seen her, when he and Sal had gone to the rescue of the gypsy caravan under threat of attack, Jonah had given little thought to anything other than her stunning physical beauty and her obvious spunk, both of which he had appreciated at the time.

Only a shell of that self-confident young woman had remained when he'd seen her next, after the appalling attack by the Trolls and the death of her mother.

Under the stress of the days since however, that initial impression had returned with a vengeance and had been bolstered by an obvious high level of intelligence, a newfound and well rounded maturity and inner strength of character.

Since their arrival in Almeca Juno had managed to put much of the horror behind her and she had spent most of her waking hours buried deep within the caverns of the Holy See library, where, with the assistance of 'The Sisters of Knowledge', she had read every tome, recent or ancient, that delved into the unusual and unique ability of the rarely experienced phenomenon of a gypsy Human's ability to foresee.

Almost immediately her visions had become more numerous and had grown in clarity daily to the point were even Venus, who had originally been a doubter, had become convinced of their value and accuracy.

Juno had instantly become a very valued member of the group. That was not to say that Juno had in any way lost her unique and endearing beauty. Arriving at the Holy See with little more than the clothing on her back, the vivacious gypsy had immediately taken advantage of the offering of assistance in solving her immediate needs by the seamstresses of the Sisterhood who had readily adopted her.

Admittedly, there had been some raised eyebrows when she'd made her selections of materials, colours and designs for her new wardrobe, but it was when she'd begun to wear the finished products within the walls of the Palace that her very presence had caused upheaval, the like of which had not been seen in generations.

Juno's tendency to wear brightly coloured low-cut tops and formfitting breeches was, at the outset, openly frowned upon by many of the female members of the Belief and very definitely tended to draw a good deal of attention from their male counterparts in spite of fact that many of those had taken oaths of celibacy.

Despite these initial reactions, Juno's sharp mind, bubbling, outgoing personality and an intense work ethic coupled with an air of innocence that seemed to surround her in a warm halo of light, quickly dispelled any suggestion of intentional wickedness and over time had tended to soften the initial shock for those around her.

As a result, few official complaints reached the ears of the Devi and when they did she repeatedly accepted them with a soft smile, usually followed by a comment akin to:

"That child is like a breath of fresh air wherever she goes."

* * * * *

It was just short of midnight when the little band, arriving in ones and twos, began to make their way toward the small, dimly lit cobbled forecourt of the palace stables.

Normally bustling with activity during day, the stable yard was eerily quiet at this hour, only the sound of serenading crickets filling the warm night air.

Jonah, as the appointed leader of the expedition, accompanied by Sal, was the first to move out of the shadows and into the empty enclosure.

He paused briefly just inside the gateway. His nostrils filled with the sharp aroma of fresh horse dung as he let his eyes sweep over the area in front of the long, low stone building.

He began to walk slowly along the high stone fence until he arrived at its juncture with the building. As he reached it his eyes picked out the dark bulk of the halftrack sitting in the shadows out in the centre of the cobblestones and some distance from the surrounding buildings.

In order to minimize the disturbance for the horses, Sal had driven the vehicle out of the stables and into the centre of the yard at dusk. Like the airship, the machine no longer wore the insignia of the Rector's party.

Approaching the vehicle, Jonah could clearly see the replacement golden svastika and four dots of the Belief outlined in the flickering light given off by the widely spaced gas fired torches in the distance, arranged along the top of the stable.

As he waited quietly for the others, his thoughts drifted over the plan one more time. Over the past two days, they had been through it again and again, polishing, tweaking and committing it all to memory. It was as good as it could be under the circumstances and he was comfortable with it.

A shadowy movement out of the corner of Jonah's eye brought him out of his thoughts and a grim smile formed on his lips as he picked up the movement of other silhouetted figures.

In moments they had silently gathered around him.

He waited until all had arrived then began to speak in soft clipped tones.

"Before we go, I want to give everyone a last chance to reconsider."

He paused looking from one to the other before continuing.

"You all know the risks. Sal can't give us a guarantee that the halftrack will make it through the shield."

The little Almie lowered his head slightly to stare at the cobblestone surface of the courtyard. Jonah let the words sink in then went ahead.

"If the vehicle does not pass through, it and everyone on board will be destroyed instantly. Venus and I have a responsibility to try, but you do not. If anyone wants to back out now, there will be no recrimination. Each of you has every right to do so."

Juno interrupted him.

"We've been through this ad nauseam, besides, I've seen the future. If we stay together, we will make it through safely."

Venus stepped forward and hugged Juno tightly and the others quickly moved to join them.

They separated and moved toward the halftrack.

It was time.

<u>Other books by Patrick Laughy</u>

Murder Mysteries

The Little Black Book

Alumni

Historical Fiction

The 4th Reich series

Books 1-7

Fantasy

Atlantis-Ship of the Gods-a trilogy